"What are you af

asked in a low, ge

Stephanie couldn't answer. She couldn't say "you" because that would be admitting there was something there between them, something so strong that she still hadn't moved when she should be running like hell.

"I don't want to get involved with anyone," she finally said.

"Why?"

"You're here just for a short time," she said, seeking a more logical reason than fear. "It makes no sense to start something. It's not... practical."

His fingers moved to the back of her neck again. "And you're big on practicality?"

Go. Go. Go...

She swallowed hard, then summoning all the self-control she had left, she moved away from him and stood on trembling legs. "I try to be," she said in what she feared was not a very convincing tone.

"I don't give up easily," he said.

Dear Reader,

When I first envisioned my previous book, *The Soldier's Promise* (Harlequin Superromance April 2014), and created the fictional Colorado town of Covenant Falls, I thought it would be a stand-alone book, a story about a wounded soldier returning home and a military dog with PTSD and how they healed each other.

But I fell in love with the town and its citizens who believe baked goodies cure all ills, who have an infinite curiosity about newcomers and who band together in times of trouble. From Maude, who runs the diner, to Doc Bradley, the irascible town doctor, they did not want to go quietly into the night.

Most of all, I fell in love with Stephanie, the town's veterinarian with the big but very cautious heart. It would take a very special guy to break the barriers she'd constructed against the opposite sex, and Clint Morgan, an army helicopter pilot with a mild traumatic brain injury, was just the man to do it as he tried to rebuild his life.

And no story in Covenant Falls would be complete without a cast of animals. Braveheart is back and plays no small part in matchmaking.

Enjoy!

Patricia Potter

USA TODAY Bestselling Author

PATRICIA POTTER

Tempted by the Soldier

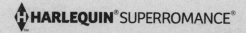
HARLEQUIN® SUPERROMANCE®

Recycling programs
for this product may
not exist in your area.

ISBN-13: 978-0-373-60897-3

Tempted by the Soldier

Copyright © 2015 by Patricia Potter

Printed in U.S.A.

Patricia Potter is a bestselling and award-wining author of more than sixty books. Her Western romances and romantic suspense novels have received numerous awards, including an *RT Book Reviews* Storyteller of the Year Award, a Career Achievement Award for Western Historical Romance and a Best Hero of the Year Award. She is a seven-time RITA® Award finalist for RWA and a three-time Maggie Award winner. She is a past president of Romance Writers of America. Patricia is also a passionate animal lover, which is reflected in many of her books, but never more so than in her Covenant Falls series. She believes curiosity is the most important trait of any writer, and she's often led far astray when researching a subject.

Books by Patricia Potter

HARLEQUIN SUPERROMANCE
The Soldier's Promise

HARLEQUIN BLAZE
The Lawman

HARLEQUIN HISTORICAL
Swampfire
Between the Thunder
Samara
Seize the Fire
Chase the Thunder
Dragonfire
The Silver Link
The Abduction

Visit the Author Profile page
at Harlequin.com for more titles

Dedicated to the volunteers in our society,
from the volunteer firefighters,
to the search-and-rescue teams,
to people who deliver meals to the homebound.

CHAPTER ONE

Pueblo, Colorado

FASTER. FASTER. HE ran the gears, his foot heavy as he edged up to ninety miles an hour. The road ahead was straight and empty. Plains stretched in every direction. He relished the power of the used Corvette that had cost him nearly every penny he had and hundreds of hours of work.

The road was perfect for his purpose. Rarely, if ever used, it connected one Texas ghost town to another. A fellow chopper pilot, who was also a car enthusiast, had told him about it. A forty-mile strip of pavement from nowhere to nowhere.

He had finished restoring the car two weeks earlier. In ten days, he would be back in Afghanistan. This was his last chance to put the Corvette through its paces.

The sun danced and shimmered on the pavement ahead. His foot lightened on the gas pedal as the road took a turn and mounted an incline. An old battered truck appeared from nowhere, turning into... He slammed on the brakes...

Clint Morgan, former army warrant officer and

military helicopter pilot, jerked awake as the bus stopped. It took him several seconds to realize where he was. Some place going to no place.

"Hey, mister," the bus driver said. "Your stop."

Clint reluctantly stepped through the open doors into the first day of the rest of his life.

He was the last passenger to leave the bus, an indication of his total lack of enthusiasm for his new reality. He glanced around. He had been told someone named Josh Manning, also a vet, would meet him at the bus in Pueblo. But Clint saw no former-military-looking guy.

Damn but he hated being dependent on a stranger, even a fellow vet. It was bad enough that occasional blackouts and blinding headaches kept him from driving, but the helplessness he felt now was searing. What in the hell was he doing standing here in the middle of nowhere on a blistering September day?

The other bus passengers quickly dispersed. He was alone with a large duffel at his side. As he contemplated his alternatives, which were few, a van roared onto the street and squeezed into a parking spot. A woman emerged and strode quickly toward him.

"Clinton Morgan?" she asked.

"Clint," he corrected. This woman did not look like a Josh.

"Sorry to be late," she said. "I hope you haven't been here long." She thrust out her hand. "I'm Stephanie."

He took her hand, and her grip was as strong as his. She was nearly as tall as his own six feet. No makeup, but then she didn't seem to need any. Her eyes were a dark blue, and her skin was tanned, the kind that came from working outdoors. Her hair was a mass of unruly rich copper curls, some of which escaped the braid that reached below her shoulders. Clad in jeans and a checkered cotton shirt splotched with dirt, her body was more lean than curved. Athletic.

"I volunteered to pick you up since I was inoculating some cattle not far away," she continued. "I had a bit of a problem and ran late. Thus, my less-than-suitable chauffeur attire. I *had* planned to change and wash. I'm afraid I smell like cow and sweat."

She said it all in a hurry and without apology, although her tone was friendly. Husky. Sexy as hell.

Things were looking up, even if the odor of cow *was* strong. He was intrigued. She was good-looking now, but add a bit of lipstick and a dress, and she would be striking.

"But a very pretty chauffeur," he said with a grin that usually had a positive effect on the opposite sex.

The friendliness seeped from her eyes, replaced with something like wariness.

"Is the duffel all your luggage?" she asked, ignoring the compliment. Her question had a definite edge to it.

He felt duly kicked in the rear. "That and my laptop," he said. "You learn to travel light in the army."

She started for the duffel, but he beat her to it and hefted it over his shoulder.

Without another word, she led the way to the dusty red van with the words "Langford Animal Practice" on the door. "I hope you don't mind dog hair," she said in a businesslike tone. "My dog, Sherry, usually rides with me."

"Fine with me. It's not as if I'm going to the opera," he quipped. "And I like dogs." He went to the passenger's side. The door was unlocked and he climbed inside.

"Darn good thing," he heard her mutter in a barely audible voice.

Before he could respond, she started the van and roared out of the parking lot, obviously ignoring the thirty-miles-per-hour speed-limit sign. He glanced at her, but she concentrated on the road ahead. He admired a good driver, and she was that. He looked at the speedometer. The van had a hundred and fifty thousand plus miles on it, and she was going over the speed limit. Both said something about her.

He felt an immediate kinship. Interest sparked in him, the first since the accident that doomed his military career. He definitely wanted to know more about her. Particularly whether she was already taken. Not that he was interested in any long-term involvement. He sure as hell didn't have anything to offer a woman. Struggling for conversation—strange as it usually came easier—he asked, "Are you the Langford in Langford Animal Practice?"

She shrugged. "I'm not Langford, but I do own the vet practice or at least the small part that's paid off. I bought it from Tom Langford and never changed the name on the van. Never really saw a good reason to do it. I'm Stephanie Phillips."

"Dr. Phillips?"

"No one calls me that. It's just Stephanie." Her tone seemed to cut off any other questions.

He took a deep breath and shifted restlessly. He ached to take her place at the wheel. Just as everything in him ached to reach for the controls of a chopper. Ached to be in the house he shared with other chopper pilots on the base or even a tent in Afghanistan. Sitting in a passenger seat, dependent on a driver—even an interesting woman—was his idea of hell.

He stared out at the plains spread out in front of him. Arid desert.

The blurb he had read online called this area of Colorado high desert. To him, it resembled parts of Iraq and Afghanistan. So did the heat.

"Is it always this warm?" he asked.

"This is a bit unusual. It's usually in the low nineties in July and then starts going down. This year, it's hanging around. It's a bit cooler in Covenant Falls. We're higher, altitudewise, from here, and the town is nestled next to the mountains." Her tone was cool. It had lost something since he'd said she was pretty.

He shifted uncomfortably in the seat and stared ahead. He had been doing that a lot since leaving the hospital. The journey to Pueblo from Denver had been agonizingly long, or maybe it had just seemed that way. He had been a passenger on a plane, in a car and on a long-distance bus. Brutal. He yearned for his seat in a chopper, in controlling a complex machine that both protected and destroyed. He had been doing both for most of his adult life. Flying *was* his life. His identity. At gut level, being a pilot was who he was. Who he had been since he was seventeen.

Now he might never fly again. Or even drive a car. Worse, he didn't have a goal for the first time in his life. A driving force. A purpose.

Stop it!

He was a fighter. Always had been. Since he was eight years old and his stepmother decided she didn't want him in *her* house any longer, he'd looked ahead, determined to plot his own path.

"You'll like the cabin," Stephanie said, interrupting his thoughts. "Josh did a great job in rehabbing it."

"I'm not sure how long I'm staying."

She turned to him and gave him a wry smile. "Neither did Josh when he came. Covenant Falls can get to you."

"Have you lived there long?"

"Five years, but even if I'd lived there twenty years, I would still be a newcomer. You should know that everyone is rather curious about new residents, and gossip spreads faster than a sky full of locusts."

Her cell phone rang. The thunderous tone was the theme music from the movie *The Magnificent Seven*.

She glanced down at it, then steered to the side of the road and stopped the car. Quick questions. Something to do with a cow. When she hung up, she turned to him. "A short detour," she said.

"Something wrong?"

"An ailing heifer. She's not far from here. Shouldn't take more than an hour. Okay?"

"Fine," he said. He didn't really have much choice. He was hitching a ride, after all. He was at the driver's mercy. But he had to ask: "*The Magnificent Seven*? That's an interesting ringtone."

She shrugged.

"Dr. Phillips to the rescue?"

"Stephanie," she reminded him.

"I beg your pardon," he replied with a quick grin.

She frowned. "That's not why I have it. I just like the tune. It's hard to ignore. Very effective in cutting off conversations."

Wry humor. It intrigued him. "You like cutting off conversations?"

"Inane ones, yes."

Well, she had put him in his place. Neatly. Maybe Covenant Falls wouldn't be as dull as he'd thought it would be. That prick of interest was expanding.

He tried another tactic. "What's wrong with the cow?" he asked.

She shrugged. "A rancher says one of his heifers

isn't eating, which could mean a number of troubles. All bad. Like I said, the ranch isn't far from here."

It was an obvious though unspoken question.

Clint settled back. "I have nothing pressing in mind."

"Good." She turned back to the road. "I'll call Josh and tell him we'll be late. He's going to meet us at the cabin to give you the keys and probably tell you the best way to piss off the town. He did a great job when he first came to Covenant Falls."

Clint grinned. "Are you saying diplomacy is not one of his virtues?"

"You could say that, but he's learning. Too bad." There was amusement in her voice again. He was discovering she didn't go out of her way to be diplomatic, either. He liked that. No bullshit. No false sympathy or concern.

He tried to remember exactly what Dr. Payne had said about the cabin and its owner.

The psychologist hadn't been very forthcoming about the cabin or his new landlord, although he'd been good at prying into Clint's life. Dr. Payne's first visit had been to introduce himself and say he was available. The second had been two weeks before Clint's discharge. He'd asked about his future plans, and the fact was, Clint had none.

He closed his eyes and thought of their meeting.

"No family?" the shrink had asked, and Clint suspected the man knew he'd had no visitors.

"No," he said, but his records proved otherwise.

"No support system?"

"I don't need one. It's just a headache now and then."

Dr. Payne stared at him. Waited. "Well, maybe you can do a favor for me, then. A friend of mine, a former patient here, is looking for someone to look after his cabin. He just married and moved in with his wife. He rehabbed the cabin after it was vandalized, and he doesn't want it to happen again. It's in a small town with a lot of veterans. You can walk to nearly every business in town, and there's both a lake and mountains."

"What's the rent?"

"Just the utilities. And keeping it in good shape."

"Where is it?"

"A little town named Covenant Falls in Colorado. It'll give you time to decide what you want to do…"

Clint suspected there was more to it than that, but hell, he had nowhere else to go and Payne knew it. He couldn't pilot or drive because of recurring blackouts. His career was over, even if the injury to his brain healed. There were too many young guys coming up behind him. And family? That was opening another can of worms. Despite some doubts, he'd accepted…

"We're here." Stephanie turned into a long driveway, drove past a sprawling ranch house and parked in front of the barn. She made a quick phone call, apparently to Josh, explaining there would be a slight delay in reaching the cabin. Then she turned to him. "You can stay inside the van if you want."

No way. He was damned tired of being passive. He shook his head.

She eyed him speculatively. "Your clothes are a little fancy for a ranch."

He looked at his chinos and dark blue polo shirt. They were new because he'd lost weight in the hospital. He kind of liked them. He also liked the comfortable loafers. A welcome relief from heavy combat boots. But fancy? Not in his wildest imagination.

Clint stepped out of the van and waited as Stephanie grabbed a medical bag, then they both strode over to a weathered-looking man who walked up to meet them.

"You got new help, Stephanie?" The rancher's gaze measured Clint.

"Nope," Stephanie said. "A passenger headed for Covenant Falls. Clint Morgan. A friend of Josh." She turned to Clint. "This is Hardy Pearson. He breeds the best cattle in this part of Colorado."

Hardy held out his hand. "The most troublesome, anyway. Good to meet you, son," he said. Then he turned to Stephanie, his eyes worried.

"She's in the barn. My best heifer. Hasn't been eating. I've seen this twice before. Pretty sure it's a twisted stomach."

"How long since she ate?"

"She didn't look good yesterday, and I brought her

into the barn. I put hay out and she wouldn't have any part of it. Can't tell you how unusual that is."

"Did she calve recently?"

"Three months ago."

The questions and answers came quick. Clint observed the trust between the rancher and Stephanie. She was all efficiency as she threw him one question after another. He followed as Hardy led the way into a big barn where a large cow was tethered by a rope halter to a post. The animal stood on a pile of hay. Stephanie retrieved a stethoscope from the medical bag and examined the heifer's stomach.

She glanced up at Hardy, "You were right. It's a twisted stomach. The ping is definitely there. There's a lot of gas."

Hardy sighed. "What do you recommend?"

She hesitated. "I think we should roll her stomach. It might not work, and it could be dangerous for the heifer, but the alternatives are worse."

"An operation would be just as dangerous, wouldn't it?

She nodded. "And expensive."

"Let's roll 'er."

"You got anyone else who can help?" she asked.

He shook his head. "My son's at a cattle auction. And my wife's been ailing."

Two sets of eyes focused on Clint. He sensed that wasn't a good thing.

"Sorry to hear that," Stephanie said to Hardy even

as she studied Clint. After a few seconds, she asked, "You game to help?"

"Help how?" he asked cautiously.

"Roll over that heifer. Putting it simply, she's got three stomachs and one of them is in the wrong place. If it isn't fixed, she'll die."

He hesitated, then shrugged. "What do I do?"

"We use some ropes to get her down. Then you help Hardy hold her down while I palpate her and move the wayward stomach into its rightful place. Then I suture it. Okay?"

He met her challenging gaze, then studied the cow. It was a damned big animal. Hell, he didn't have anything to lose. He nodded. "I'm a city boy, but I'll give it a go."

She hesitated, tilting her head to the right. "Is there any medical reason you shouldn't?"

"Not that I know of."

"Hardy will help, but this really takes three bodies." She looked at the old man. "Have a pair of muck boots he can use?"

The rancher nodded and hurried inside the house, returning with a pair of worn, heavy rubber boots. "Here, son, try these. Don't want to get those new shoes messed up."

Clint regarded the boots warily. Well, he'd worn worse. He removed his shoes and replaced them with the boots. What in the hell had he gotten himself into?

Stephanie crouched and ran her hands over the

heifer's belly. "We'll do this together, girl," she whispered. "You'll feel better. Trust me."

Her voice was surprisingly soft and gentle, and her hands stroked the cow's stomach soothingly. Clint found himself envying the animal.

Stephanie and Hardy unwound a rope. She ran it under the cow and Hardy passed the end to Clint. Stephanie pulled it tight under the cow while Hardy stood at its side.

"We want to flip the heifer on its back," she said.

Clint wasn't sure about that. But when she said "flip," he flipped the rope and felt a certain satisfaction when the heifer landed on her back.

Clint dodged two back hoofs.

"Tie them together and hold them," Stephanie said. She palpated the stomach, then nodded to Hardy. "Place a knee on the abdomen. Not there, to the right. A little more to the right. Good."

It took all of Clint's strength to tie and hold on to the rear legs of a very unhappy and very big cow as Stephanie scrubbed an area of the stomach with what smelled like disinfectant. She gave the heifer a shot. "Antibiotic," she explained. "And a local anesthesia. We should wait a few minutes until it starts to work. Can you two keep her in this position?"

Hardy nodded. Clint wasn't so sure. The heifer wasn't happy. She wanted up. He couldn't blame her. It was an indelicate position. He dodged flailing legs. Barely. A damaged chopper was easier to hold steady than this cow.

After what seemed hours, Stephanie pulled on fresh medical gloves and took a deep breath. He remembered what she said about the procedure being dangerous.

She nodded at him. "Keep her steady."

Hell of a lot easier said than done. She made a small, quick incision. Clint gagged as a nauseating odor escaped from the cow's stomach, practically suffocating him. It was as bad a smell as any he'd experienced in Afghanistan. He held the cow's legs tighter. He might not be able to do a lot of things, but, by damn, he could hold on to a cow. Hardy, a man twice his age and more, was doing just fine with his knee on the cow's abdomen.

Stephanie palpated the heifer's stomach, then sutured the wound before standing. She nodded to Hardy and turned to Clint. "You can let her go."

As he did, the cow scrambled up, and before Clint could move out of the way, it stepped hard on the instep of his left foot. He fell, sprawling in the hay as his foot exploded in pain. "Damn!" The cow relieved herself on Clint's leg, mooed indignantly and ambled away as if nothing had happened.

Hardy looked on in horror. "I'm real sorry, son. I've never known Isobel to kick. She's a pretty docile heifer."

"Can't say I wouldn't have kicked, too, if I was tackled, held down and had someone messing with my stomach," Clint said. "Isobel, huh? I'll have to be sure to avoid females named Isobel in the future."

Stephanie looked stunned. "Dang," she said. "Josh is going to kill me when he finds out what happened to you."

Despite the pain, Clint started laughing. Two chopper crashes, several bullet wounds and a car crash, and he was ultimately felled by a cow. A heifer at that. No little irony here.

Unfortunately, it followed the current trajectory of his life.

CHAPTER TWO

STEPHANIE WAS APPALLED at the sight of her charge clutching his foot in the hay. His obviously new clothes were stained with cow urine, the last indignity the cow bestowed on him. The fact he was laughing made her inwardly groan. *Laughing.*

It was deep and rumbling, and that was the last thing she'd expected or wanted. He had to be the world's best sport, and that annoyed her to no end.

Josh was not going to be happy with her. To be honest, she wasn't happy with herself. Fine. She had to admit she'd felt a certain satisfaction in enlisting him to help. She and Hardy probably could have managed alone, although there was no question that her passenger *had* helped.

She sighed. Warning bells had sounded when she first saw him, standing alone on the street, a duffel next to him. Tall and lean with short dark hair, he had a definite presence.

Those bells really pealed when he'd grinned and said she was pretty. She was familiar with charm, too familiar, and this man had it written all over him. It had been in his smile, as well as the compliment, in the warmth of his voice even though she had been late picking him up, smelling like cow and dressed like a ranch hand. That charm scared her as little else did.

That was of no consequence now. Guilt weighed heavily on her, and she didn't often feel that particular emotion. He had come here directly from a military hospital. He experienced blackouts, which was why he had needed a ride. Her friend Josh was reticent about what had happened to him, but then he was about everything. Maybe that's what she had expected when she'd volunteered a ride: someone like Josh.

This man was nothing like Josh.

She knelt beside Clint and helped him remove his boot. Having experienced the same injury several times, she knew how painful it could be. His body tensed, and his lips pressed tightly together. He released a long breath when his foot was free, but no other sound escaped. He looked directly at Hardy and quipped, "If Isobel is usually docile, I would hate to see one of your cows that isn't."

Hardy chuckled. "You're all right, boy," he said.

Clint removed his sock and studied his injured foot. It was red and already swelling, but the skin hadn't been broken. He touched the skin, feeling around, as he'd had some medical training.

"I'm really sorry," she said, truly contrite now. She stripped the soiled gloves from her hands and pulled on clean ones from the bag, then she knelt next to him and examined his foot. "We'll stop by the doctor when we reach Covenant Falls..." Her voice faltered. She was close to him, too close. His eyes were a rich, dark brown. Almost black. Challenging. Too challenging.

"No need," he said. "I'll be fine."

She shook her head. "I want X-rays," she insisted, trying to keep her voice steady. "I might lose two good friends if I don't take care of you, and so far I haven't done very well."

"I've had a lot worse injuries," he said. "Maybe not as humiliating. I have met the enemy, and it is Isobel."

Stephanie couldn't help but grin.

"You *do* smile," he said.

"Occasionally," she replied. "Can you stand? I've been stepped on several times. It's an occupational hazard. I know how much it hurts."

"But obviously not fatal."

Dang, but he was getting to her. *No. No. No.*

She held out her hand. He took it, and heat ran through her like an electrical charge. He rose easily, even gracefully, although he gritted his teeth as he put weight on the injured foot. He took a step and nearly buckled, his face draining of color.

His clothes were filthy. Hay tangled in his hair and dirt smudged his face. He smelled like the wrong end of a cow.

Yet, he looked far more attractive now than he had

standing in new clothes at the bus stop. The rueful half smile was all too beguiling.

Didn't make any difference. She'd worked too hard to get to where she was today. She was a terrible judge of men. Twice, she'd allowed outward appearances to blind her. A third would prove her the fool she'd felt at the end of both of her marriages. Now she ran like hell when her body tingled with even a little initial attraction.

She couldn't run right now. She had agreed to pick up Clint Morgan and now she felt responsible for what had just happened. Hell's bells, she *was* responsible. Josh was not going to be pleased, and he and his wife were among the few people whose opinion she valued.

She inwardly shuddered as she thought about telling him. Josh planned to be waiting at the cabin. Now the meeting would be at a doctor's office.

Hardy had watched with concern. "You're welcome to come inside and clean up a bit," he said.

Clint inspected his clothes, and his eyes lit up with mischief.

"I'm good," he said. "Dr. Phillips and I will be a matched pair."

She groaned. She looked almost as bad as her charge. "We'll stop at the doctor's office just to make sure nothing is broken."

"Nothing is," Clint assured her.

"I would rather have a doctor tell me that," she replied stiffly. "I'm responsible..."

His gaze hardened. "You are *not* responsible. Hardy is not responsible. I'm responsible for being so damned clumsy. I volunteered, remember. I'm not a hothouse flower."

Anger, mixed with frustration, laced his voice. She nodded, backing off. She well knew the frustration of feeling helpless.

"Okay. Can you get into the van?"

He nodded, then shook Hardy's hand. "I hope you don't have more problems with Isobel."

Hardy grinned. "I'm afraid she needs a few lessons in gratitude. I, however, don't. You need anything, you have a friend here." He turned to Stephanie. "You should hire him. You could do a whole lot worse. And send me your bill for Isobel. Include any charges from Doc Bradley."

She stared at him for a moment. Hardy was usually cantankerous and argued about every bill. "Will do." She eyed Clint. "Need some help?"

"A shoulder, maybe," he said, and she detected amusement in his eyes.

She was trapped. She suddenly wondered whether he sensed her reluctance and had used his foot as an excuse to touch her. But she *had* offered, and she owed him. She put her arm around him and together they hobbled to the van. "Maybe I *should* change," he said, peering at the wet stains on his pants and wrinkling his nose at the accompanying foul odor. "I have clean pants in the duffel."

Hardy had already headed for the ranch house.

Had Clint waited until Hardy had returned to the house before making that decision? Maybe she was just too suspicious. "You can change in the back of the van," she said. "I have a couple of calls to make." She hesitated, then asked suspiciously, "Do you need any help?"

"Maybe to get into the van. Not to change," he said with that oddly attractive upward turn of the left side of his lips. The half smile was crooked and endearing. Vulnerable. And as tempting as forbidden fruit.

She was in trouble. She needed to keep her distance from Clint Morgan. As soon as she helped him into the van, she closed the door without another word. She walked over to the fence, called Doc and told him she would be there in thirty minutes, then she called Josh for the second time.

"We're a bit more delayed," she said. "There's been a little accident and I'm taking Mr. Morgan to Doc Bradley's."

A long silence at the other end, then, "What kind of 'little' accident?"

"A heifer stepped on his foot."

Another silence.

"And…" Josh prompted, inviting a fuller explanation that she was loath to give over the phone.

"I'm pretty sure nothing is broken. Just want to be sure. He also…umm…kinda needs a bath."

"What did you do, Stephanie?"

"You know Hardy Pearson. One of his cows was

in trouble. A twisted stomach. Mr. Morgan offered to help. Isobel stepped on him."

"Who in the hell is IsobeI?"

"The heifer. She's one of Hardy's prize breeding stock."

Still another long silence. It was Josh's quiet way to indicate he was not happy. "I'll meet you at Doc Bradley's," he said finally and hung up.

Her passenger must have had enough time to change. Then she spotted the new-looking loafers near the fence. She picked them up and headed to the back of the van. She knocked. No way was she going to barge in.

The door opened. Clint Morgan hadn't changed his soiled shirt, but now wore a new pair of khakis. His feet were covered only by socks, and his thick dark hair was rumpled, as if he'd just combed it with his fingers. His eyes were the color of rich dark coffee, and they appeared far more alive than before the heifer affair. Instead of reflecting pain, they practically danced with mischief.

An unwelcome warmth spread through her. She willed it away. She didn't trust it. She didn't trust him. Hell's bells. She didn't trust herself.

He stepped down on his good leg, then put an arm around her shoulder for the short hobble to the front of the van. Once again, she felt trapped. He was too close. Along with the lingering cow smell, she got a whiff of a tangy aftershave scent and, oddly enough, it was a sensuous mixture that probably only a vet would appreciate. His arm was warm. The air was also warm and getting warmer, and not just from the sun.

They made it to the passenger side, and he stepped inside, using the door handle for support. She handed his shoes to him and hurried around to the other side of the van. As she settled into the driver's seat, she was too aware of him, much more so than during the trip to Hardy's. She was afraid she liked him now. Liked the way he had laughed after Isobel kicked him and his quick quips with Hardy. She was fascinated by his subtle and not so subtle challenges.

Wow, she needed to get herself in hand. "I called the town's doctor—Doc Bradley—and he'll be waiting for us. Josh will be there."

To take Clint Morgan off my hands.

His grin was just too potent. Whenever she saw handsome, smiling men nowadays, she searched for the treachery she was sure lurked within. Think Ted Bundy. Or her former husbands.

Clint Morgan *was* good-looking with a beguiling smile. Dark, slightly curly hair, dark eyes, strong cheekbones, a cleft in his chin and a slight wry turn to his lips. In short, Clinton Morgan raised every single one of her red flags. But she tried to reserve judgment. All she really knew about him was that he couldn't drive because of his blackouts, and he was ex-military. Josh had been characteristically uncommunicative. Well, it was none of her business, nor the business of Covenant Falls.

She needed to keep it that way.

Clint sat back in the seat, shoved his good foot into a shoe and watched Stephanie drive. She drove with the same concentration she showed when treating the cow. He thought back to that moment she'd smiled. Openly. Not guarded as she had been since they met.

He'd thought her pretty before, but when she smiled, she was stunning. And when her blue eyes had darkened with concern while she examined his foot, he'd felt a tingling interest he hadn't experienced in a long time.

Down, boy. He knew nothing about her. He had a pile of troubles at the moment. Plus, he wouldn't be staying long. Just long enough to chart out a future.

But in that moment immediately after the cow had stepped on him and she'd knelt next to him, their eyes had clashed, challenging each other. It had made him feel alive for the first time since the car accident. Call it sexual attraction, awareness, or whatever, something was there, at least for him.

"I don't need a doctor," he said. "I've seen enough injuries to know this doesn't even count as a pinprick."

"Then you didn't need my shoulder?"

She had him there. His foot hurt like hell, but he probably *could* have walked on his own. He just hadn't been able to resist the offer. "It helped," he said, somewhat lamely.

A small smile started on her lips, then faded. "We *are* going. So far my track record in seeing you safely to Covenant Falls is near zero."

Was she being adamant because of this Josh? She'd made it clear she valued the opinion of his benefactor more than his. It was rather a blow to his pride, but then except for that one extraordinary moment on the ground, she'd been stilted since they'd met. It was as if she knew something about him, something she didn't particularly like. The reason he'd left the army? That he failed his buddies for a dumb stunt?

At least he hadn't had a blackout during the afternoon. He didn't know what triggered them. The doctor suggested tension, anxiety, but they occurred at other times, as well. The only warning was a god-awful headache.

"I really am sorry," she said, breaking into his thoughts. "I shouldn't have asked you to help. You haven't much experience with animals, have you?"

He shrugged. "It felt good to be doing something useful, even holding two legs of a reluctant cow." He stayed silent for a moment, then said, "Tell me about Josh Manning. All I know is he's a vet, not to be confused with your kind of vet."

"He's a good guy. He's one of about three people whose opinion I respect."

Clint raised an eyebrow. "That's not very many."

"I've been here only five years," she said with a trace of a grin. It was the first time she'd lowered her guard with him. He knew about that. He had his own walls and recognized them in others.

"Just what does he want? Why is he doing this?"

"Josh inherited the cabin from a fallen friend, a fellow soldier, and rehabbed it. It was a mess when he arrived. Time and partying kids had pretty well destroyed it. He worked like hell to fix it, and he doesn't want it to fall into disrepair again."

"Couldn't he rent it?"

"Covenant Falls isn't exactly on the tourism map," Stephanie said. "Josh and his wife hope to change that, but in the meantime, he wants someone to use it, and who better than a vet."

"And the town?" Clint asked. "I looked it up. It's pretty small."

"It is. And quite elderly on the whole. A little over three thousand people spread over a large space. Most have lived there all their lives."

"Where are you from?"

Her lips tightened. "Pennsylvania. Once upon a time."

"What brought you here?"

"What brought *you* to the army?"

A deflection. Interesting. But then everything about her was interesting. Contradictory. There was a standoffishness, a message that said "hands off," yet she had been very easy with the rancher. And his being stomped on by a heifer had apparently broken through some kind of barrier. She wasn't a bundle of warmth, but she was communicative. Progress.

He shrugged. "I wanted to fly. The army was the fastest and cheapest way to do that."

"Risky, though."

"Not if you know what you're doing."

"What did you fly?"

"Choppers. Black Hawks mostly."

"How long?"

"Seventeen years."

He waited for the next question. Why had he left? It didn't come, which either meant she wasn't interested or she already knew. He tried to tamp his growing interest in her. He couldn't even get from point A to point B without help. It was galling. He leaned back in the seat and closed his eyes. His foot throbbed, but it was a minor annoyance. It was the emptiness ahead that was agonizing.

WHY HAD SHE asked so many questions? It only invited more conversation and questions of his own.

Still, curiosity tickled her. She glanced at him. His eyes were closed. Resting? Dang it, but he was…

Remember your first reaction. That smile. The compliment. Remember Mark's smile.

Still, it was her fault he was injured. She'd needed him, true, but she and Hardy *could* have handled the cow alone. It would have taken longer, been riskier. She hadn't truly given Clint a choice, though, knowing full well she had challenged him. She'd known he would take it, having judged in the first few minutes of their meeting that he couldn't ignore a challenge. However, she hadn't expected him to get stomped on and, when he had been, to laugh.

Her passenger stirred as she slowed and she wondered whether he had been feigning sleep. Either way, it was fine with her. As soon as she delivered him, even if not totally intact, to Josh, the happier she would be. He was…disturbing. She pushed aside any notion of being attracted to him. She was just… worried about that foot. She had made conversation to keep his mind from it. Didn't mean anything.

As she pulled in front of the doctor's office, she noticed Josh's Jeep. He had probably decided to see for himself how much damage had been done. It never ceased to amaze her how he had gone from being the angry loner to one of the town's best liked citizens. Her friend, Eve, was much better at magic than she'd ever been.

Clint straightened up and blinked at her. He glanced around at Main Street, and the two-story building flanked by businesses. A sign proclaimed it the "Covenant Falls Medical Clinic." Josh Manning leaned against a wall.

She cut the engine. "That's Josh. He can help you inside."

"I would rather *you* did," he said. "I'm becoming accustomed to your shoulder."

She had to smile. His quirky, self-deprecating

sense of humor was appealing. "I expect Josh will be more help than I was."

He gave her a long steady look. No smile. Just a glance that seemed to see right through her. Then he nodded. "I appreciate the ride, ma'am."

She knew that "ma'am" was a common address to women by soldiers. It also distanced them. Huh. He hadn't been resting at all. He opened the passenger door as she stepped out of the van. Josh approached them, introduced himself to Clint and offered his arm. Josh nodded to her, and she mouthed "Sorry." They headed inside and she fought the urge to go with them. She overcame it and hurried to her office down the street. Guilt and confusion swamped her. She should have stayed with him.

She went inside the reception area, and her golden retriever, Sherry, frantically wagged her tail in welcome. Stephanie leaned down and gave her dog a big hug. "Missed you," she said.

"She hasn't moved from the window since you left," Beth, her vet tech, said. "What is the new guy like?"

"Pleasant enough." And because she knew everyone in town would shortly know what happened at the ranch, she told Beth about Clint and the cow.

"By one of Hardy's? I hope he didn't hurt him."

"She. A heifer, but a rather large one. But it's just a minor wound, I think. Josh is with him now at Doc's office."

"Oh my," Beth said. "Is he anything like Josh?"

"No, not at all. Were there any calls?"

Beth got the message and didn't ask any more questions. "Some appointments for tomorrow, Wednesday. Annual shots and physicals. Thurday and Friday are pretty booked up, too. Mr. Crane called about this weekend's search-and-rescue training program."

"Thanks." She looked at her watch. Nearly six. "Why don't you go home? I have a few things to do here."

Beth nodded, then obviously couldn't restrain herself from asking one more question. "The new guy... is he married?"

"I'm pretty sure he isn't."

"Good-looking?"

"Some might think so."

"Maybe I should take him a casserole."

Stephanie sighed. Beth was nineteen and pretty. She was smart and liked both people and animals, and they liked her, which were great qualities for a vet tech. But Beth had made no secret that her life goal was marriage and a houseful of kids.

She, on the other hand, was never, ever going to marry again. She was a terrible judge of character, at least in the husband department, and now she treasured her independence. Never again would she lose control of her own life.

"I would give him a few days," she said, refraining from saying Beth was too young for their newest resident. Or maybe not. What did she know about the man's tastes?

She waited until Beth left, then checked on two dogs that were boarding at the clinic. She completed some paperwork and ordered more medicine. She couldn't concentrate. She shouldn't have just left Clint with the doctor, no matter how…disconcerted he made her.

The tune from *The Music Man* popped into her head.

Something about trouble coming to River City.

Or maybe Covenant Falls.

CHAPTER THREE

"NOTHING'S BROKEN," CLINT insisted to the elderly doctor.

"You a doctor?" the man asked.

"No, but…"

"I'll get my supper a whole lot quicker if you just answer my questions. Leave it to Stephanie to come in after hours," he groused.

"You know you're her biggest fan," Josh Manning said. "She certainly helps your bottom line."

Doc Bradley muttered something Clint couldn't hear, but he didn't think it was gratitude. An older woman in scrubs decorated with tiny smiling elephants wheeled him into a treatment room where the doctor examined Clint's foot. "I want an X-ray," he said when he finished. "Janie, my nurse, will take you."

Ten minutes later, the doctor came into the dark, tiny X-ray room and studied the film. Then he wheeled Clint into a third room. It was small, made smaller by the bookcase full of books and a large file cabinet. Several diplomas decorated the wall, along with a painting of a waterfall.

Doc Bradley pulled a chair next to Clint. "No break, but it's badly bruised and going to be even more painful tomorrow. Probably worse the next day. Are you taking any medications?"

Clint handed him the pills he always kept near him. The doctor looked at the bottle, then asked, "Do you have your medical records with you?"

"They're in my duffel and that's in Stephanie's truck, but basically I was injured in a car accident. Mild traumatic brain injury, they told me. I have blackouts, usually preceded by headaches."

"Bad ones, I take it."

Clint nodded.

"As strong and frequent now as they were just after the injury?"

"Afraid so."

"Any other injuries?

"Nothing of any importance."

"Why don't you let me decide that," Doc Bradley said.

"Two bullet wounds. Neither hit anything major. Some broken bones after a chopper crash. My knees took a beating at the same time I had the brain injury."

The doctor nodded and took a paper from the desk. "If you want me to be your doctor—and since I'm the only one in town you don't have much choice—you can sign that paper giving me permission to obtain your records from your former doctor."

Clint liked him. No nonsense. Not much bedside manner. He approved. "I do, at least, as long as I'm going to be here. Not sure how long that will be." He scrawled his signature.

"That's what Josh told me when he first came here, and I think he's here for good."

Clint shrugged. It was the second time he'd heard that, but then, he wasn't Josh Manning.

"In any event, I'm giving you an anti-inflammatory and some pain medication. Not as strong as the pills you have now. Stay off the foot as much as possible and use ice packs on it. I have a spare pair of crutches. You can bring them back when they're not needed. I'm available at any time. Just ask Stephanie." There was a humor in his voice that belied real annoyance.

He wheeled Clint back into his office where Josh Manning waited. "I have free samples of both medications and I'll be back with the crutches," he said and disappeared into the examining room.

Manning, who had been sitting on a chair in the reception area, stood.

"It's just a bruise," Clint said. "No big deal."

"Bad enough," Manning said. "I'm damned sorry about that. You probably want to run for the hills right now. I wanted to do that when I landed in Covenant Falls, even without being stomped by a cow."

Clint shrugged. "Don't blame Stephanie. I offered to help. I chalk it down to a new experience. A close encounter of the bovine kind."

Manning grinned. "I was going to ask you to have supper with my family tonight, but now you probably just want to get to the cabin. There's plenty of food there, although my invitation is still good. I have to warn you, though, it could be chaotic."

"Chaotic? That sounds about right today."

"Well there's five dogs, one very curious and bright boy who will ask a million questions, and my wife, the mayor, who will try to convince you that Covenant Falls is heaven on earth."

"And is it?"

"Depends on your viewpoint," Manning said. "I'm sort of leaning in that direction after a rocky start."

Stephanie appeared then with a dog, a golden retriever, at her side. She also carried his duffel and his other shoe.

"Sherry?" Clint asked, and the dog's entire rear wriggled with delight at the sound of her name.

Stephanie's eyes widened. Perhaps she was surprised he had remembered her dog's name. In truth, he recalled every word of conversation since she had met him at the bus stop. He stuck out his hand and Sherry sniffed it, then held out a paw.

Clint took the paw and shook it. He'd always liked dogs, but at private schools it was a definite no-no, and in the service, he'd never felt it fair to have one.

Stephanie tilted her head as Sherry stayed close to him. Had she expected the dog to dislike him?

He'd obviously made a poor impression on her, and that puzzled him.

"I brought your duffel," she said. "Josh had planned to meet you and show you the cabin, and so I thought...he could drive you there."

So, she was dumping him. "I appreciate the ride. It certainly ranks among the most interesting I've ever had."

She gave him one of those rare smiles, but it disappeared almost immediately. "Interesting, huh? I'll call you the next time I have to roll a cow."

"Do that," he challenged.

She turned him to Josh. "I leave him in your hands."

The doctor returned, holding a pair of crutches and two pill bottles and a business card. "Call me if you need anything."

"Thanks, Doc," Stephanie said. "Send me the bill. Hardy said he would pay it."

She started for the door, Sherry at her side, then glanced over her shoulder, smiling. "Thanks for being a good sport. I really am sorry." Before he could answer, she was out the door.

Josh frowned, then picked up both the duffel and shoe. "Can you manage with the crutches?"

"Sure."

"What about that dinner?"

Suddenly, Clint was exhausted. His body ached. His mind was fuzzy. He hadn't slept much in the past two days, and he knew lack of sleep often brought on the headaches. "Can I take a rain check?"

"Sure. I'll drive you to the cabin. My wife insisted on stocking it with food, including some chili that just needs heating. There's also a roasted chicken, cold cuts and some sliced veggies. Eve was appalled at my eating habits when I first moved there."

"Sounds good. Better than good. Please thank her for me."

"I added a six pack of beer. Are you okay to drink it or…?"

"If I'm not taking medicine for headaches, I'm fine. And I don't take it unless I feel one coming on. One or two beers is okay."

Josh nodded. "My Jeep is just outside."

The ride to the cabin was short. Clint watched carefully as the Jeep continued down what appeared to be the main street.

"That's Maude's on the corner," Josh said. "Best steaks in town. Hell, best steaks in this half of Colorado, and Maude will adopt you if you give her a chance. The city hall is on the left. The police department is there, as well. This street runs into a park that backs the lake. There's also a combination recreation center and library in the park. The cabin is on the far side of the lake. There's some good fishing there." He paused, then added. "You can walk to all of it when your foot is better. In the meantime, I'm a call away."

Clint wasn't sure how to respond. He hated being

dependent, but right now any place was better than the military hospital where he'd felt a fraud.

Most patients had been wounded in battle; he was there because of a stupid whim. "I want to pay rent for however long I stay," he said.

Josh was silent as he turned down a road that bordered the lake, then pulled into a driveway shaded by pines. He parked, and Clint struggled to his feet with the crutches and hobbled toward his temporary residence. He had envisioned something small and rough, but this cabin was far more than that. Larger. More…picturesque. A wide screened porch stretched across the front.

A throbbing began in his head. All he wanted was to get inside and lie down. He followed Josh inside the screened-in porch and his new landlord unlocked the door.

He made his way inside. Whoa. Unlike the simple cabin he'd envisioned, he walked into a spacious room anchored by a huge rock fireplace. A large leather sofa and two matching chairs were placed around it, and a small dining room table with four chairs was located next to a set of windows.

"There's two bedrooms and a bathroom down the hall," Josh said. "The kitchen is on the left." He led the way down the hall to a bedroom and placed the duffel on a double bed that was already made.

He looked at Clint with concern. "Are you okay?"

"I will be," Clint said, the throbbing increasing.

"Do you have a cell phone?"

"Yes."

"Mind giving me the number?"

Clint did and Josh handed him a card. "Here's mine. Call me if you need anything."

The headache was on its way to pounding. He needed a pill. And fast.

"Any rules?" he asked.

"Nope. I have a suggestion, though. Your doctor in Texas said you have blackouts. Since you're alone here, why don't you give me a call every morning, any time. I know when I moved here, I didn't want anything to do with anyone. Only wanted to crawl under a rock. So you just tell me to back off anytime you feel crowded. Okay?"

Clint nodded. "Why don't you just rent this place?"

"It's not mine," he said. "Maybe on paper it is, but it was willed to me by a friend who died in Afghanistan. This is what he would have wanted, a refuge for vets. It was that for me. And that's probably the last time I'll talk about it."

"I want to pay something."

"I won't take money, but you can build a dock down on the lake. I planned to do it but ran out of time."

The headache was getting worse. "I can do that."

Josh gave him a searching look. "Can I do anything before I leave?"

"No, thanks."

"Call me or Doc Bradley if you need anything.

Don't forget about the food in the fridge." After Josh left, Clint used the crutches to get to the kitchen. He poured himself a glass of water and swallowed a pill. He hadn't eaten anything since breakfast, but he didn't think he could eat anything now. Using only one crutch so he could carry the glass of water, he made his way to the bedroom and sat down on the bed. He fought the headache by reviewing the day. The ups and downs. The downs were definitely the bus ride and being kicked by a cow. The up was Stephanie, although she obviously didn't consider *him* an "up."

Was that part of the attraction? He was rarely rebuffed by women, and he definitely had been this afternoon. She had bristled almost immediately at the bus stop. Her gentleness with the cow and easy friendliness with the rancher contrasted with her brusque manner with him. Puzzling, especially since he'd liked her instantly. Maybe it was her slow, reluctant smile. Or the fire he suspected lay under the icy exterior.

Just as well she didn't return the interest. He sure as hell wasn't ready for a heavy-duty involvement. He had damn few assets. A vanished career, a brain that didn't work right, a near-empty bank account and now a bruised foot...

He closed his eyes. He was dead-tired physically. He'd had damned little sleep since he'd left the hospital yesterday. But then again, he'd gone days without sleep as a chopper pilot...

The sun danced and shimmered on the pavement ahead. His foot lightened on the pedal as the road took a turn and mounted an incline. An old battered truck appeared from nowhere, turning into... He slammed on the brakes...

He woke suddenly. The end of the nightmare was always the same. It was the last thing he remembered before waking up days later in the hospital. One moment that changed his life. That haunted him.

For several seconds, Clint couldn't remember where he was. He was in a strange room in a strange house in a strange town. The glowing numbers on the clock next to the bed told him it was three thirty in the morning. He had slept longer than usual.

He reached around in the dark and turned on the bedside lamp. He still wore yesterday's clothes. The shirt still smelled of cow. The pounding headache was a memory, but a dullness remained.

Had yesterday really happened? The weird afternoon. The pretty veterinarian who intrigued him. Was it real? Or another of the crazy dreams that plagued him since the accident. The pain in his right foot told him it was, indeed, real.

It still throbbed, but he was damned thirsty and the water glass next to the clock was empty. He was also ravenous. He placed his good foot on the floor, then the injured one. He could put some weight on it now, but he had learned recently that caution was a good thing.

Clint grabbed the crutch and hobbled out of the

bedroom and down the hall, turning on lights as he went. He entered the kitchen and looked in the fridge.

It was full as promised: a whole roasted chicken on a plate, a casserole dish probably filled with the chili, packages of cheese and ham, a quart of milk and veggies. A loaf of bread sat on the counter.

He opted for a ham and cheese sandwich, which was easier to handle than a whole chicken. With one hand, he made a fat sandwich and took it to a chair in the living room, then returned for a glass of milk.

He surveyed the cabin. He hadn't noticed everything yesterday afternoon. He'd been too worried that the headache would spiral into a blackout. But he felt better now, and he looked around with interest. The walls were newly painted—a soft sand shade—and the wood floor was partly covered with a colorful Indian rug. Light from the moon filtered through the windows.

Clint hobbled to a window and peered out. There was enough light to see a backyard with a large stone barbecue pit, and behind that the lot steepened into woods.

Loneliness hit him like a sledgehammer. He'd lost his friends, his community, even his identity. He was used to being in a crowd, the life of any party. At the base, he'd shared a house with three other pilots, and in Afghanistan, he'd shared a large tent. He was used to noise, people coming and going, laughter, clowning, sharing harrowing stories, which made them less painful.

After learning he probably wouldn't fly again, certainly not in the near future, he had assessed possibilities. He was good at mechanics. He had accrued credits at the University of Maryland in computer engineering, although he was about twenty hours short of a degree. People generally liked him. He had learned to compensate for the loneliness and rejection he'd felt as a boy by being gregarious. He wasn't sure whether it was learned or natural, but he was usually comfortable with others, and they with him.

Dr. Stephanie Phillips was an exception. He pictured her in his mind: her deep blue eyes and copper hair tied back, the high cheekbones and full mouth. And grace. Despite her height, or maybe because of it, she moved with the grace of an athlete. She was a natural beauty who seemed totally unaware of it. Or even contemptuous of it.

He thought about looking her up on his laptop to see what he might find, then realized it wasn't with him. He rarely forgot it, but he'd been distracted and left it tucked next to his seat in the van.

A good excuse to call her tomorrow.

CHAPTER FOUR

STEPHANIE WAS FEEDING her two canine boarders when the phone in her office rang. She glanced at her watch. Seven thirty. She looked down at the ID display.

She didn't answer "Unavailable" or "Name unknown" or "Anonymous," all tactics her ex-husband had used.

But it was none of those. Instead, the ID reported "C. Morgan." She muttered an oath, disliking the treasonable reaction of her body, the sudden warmth that crept up her spine. She could ignore him, but doing so would give him power. She knew all about that kind of thing.

Stephanie had worked too hard to let anyone knowingly or unknowingly dictate what she would or would not do.

She picked up the phone. "Mr. Morgan."

"Clint," he insisted. "Surely, my adventure with Isobel elevates me above the 'Mr.' status."

She couldn't resist his self-deprecating charm, dang it. "Clint, then."

"Next time, too," he teased. "No more Mr. Morgan. I don't answer to that." Then his tone changed. "I hope I didn't wake you, but I left my laptop in your truck, and right now, it's my world. I figured a veterinarian would be up early."

He'd figured right. In fact, she'd been up at six after a restless night. She couldn't get him out of her mind. She'd gone over the afternoon a dozen times trying to find something out of kilter, something wrong, some sign of a major character flaw.

Maybe he was a stalker. She hadn't given him her number.

But she certainly owed him a few minutes of time this morning. Beth would arrive at 8:30 a.m. Her first appointment was at nine. It would take her maybe fifteen minutes to deliver the laptop.

"Where is the laptop?" she asked.

"I left it down the side of the seat," he said.

She had little choice. She owed him. She had practically thrown him out of her van yesterday.

"I'll be there in ten minutes." She hung up before he could answer.

She looked at her clothes. Jeans and a blue shirt. Good enough.

She thought about lipstick, but discarded the idea. She hadn't had time to refresh it yesterday before picking him up and if she wore some today, he might think it was for him.

Why on God's earth was she even thinking about him? She finished feeding the boarders and found her keys. Her dogs, Sherry and her brother, Stryker, looked at her anxiously.

"Okay," she said. "You both can go."

Their entire bodies wagged with delight as they followed her out the back door, then through the fence gate to the driveway where she parked the van. The dogs jumped inside, Sherry taking the passenger seat and Stryker edging behind the seat. She found the laptop lodged tightly between the seats. No wonder she hadn't noticed it.

For a moment, she wondered whether he left it there on purpose, but why would he? He certainly had reasons to be distracted. Injured vet. New town. New home. Bruised foot. She pictured him again in her head. He was maybe in his midthirties, possibly a year or two younger than she. She had no idea— Josh had been as reticent about Clint Morgan as he had been about himself.

She didn't need to know more. She wasn't interested. She had Sherry, a trained search-and-rescue dog, and Stryker, a rescue dog in training. She had a horse stabled at Eve and Josh's ranch and loved riding on Sunday mornings and whenever else she had time. She had a satisfying practice that paid the bills.

Living quarters? She lived in the apartment above the practice. It was spacious, practical and cheap, and she didn't need more. It was good to have someone in residence while boarding other people's pets. Her fenced backyard served as an adventure land for dogs with an agility track, balls and pull toys.

Life on the whole was good. More than good. She had no intention of changing it.

Why did she think this newcomer *could* change it? He was nothing more than a passing stranger. She had learned hard lessons, and she damned well wasn't going to forget them. Still, she had slept terribly last night. Clint's warm dark eyes constantly interrupted it.

She drove slowly, so slowly it took her more than the ten minutes she'd promised. It seemed strange to drive to the cabin that Josh Manning had made his own. She remembered the first time she had met Amos, Josh's ex-military dog with a bad case of PTSD. It was seeing Josh with the dog that convinced her most of the rest of town was wrong about him…

She grabbed the laptop and stepped out of the truck. Sherry and Stryker waited until she gave them permission to jump out.

Clint sat on a swing in the screen porch, a cup in his hand. A crutch leaned on the wall behind him. He started to get up.

All he needed was to be knocked down by her dogs, compounding her sins against him. Still, Stryker and Sherry were well mannered. They were protection, a distraction against…against what?

"Come on, guys." They followed her to the porch. Clint Morgan was standing when she reached the steps.

"I wish you wouldn't stand," she said. "I suspect Doc told you to stay off that foot."

"Did you stay off your feet?" he asked. "You said it had happened to you several times."

"No," she admitted. "But I had patients to care for."

A shadow crossed his face, then vanished so quickly she wondered whether she'd imagined it.

His gaze left her face and went to the dogs. Sherry pushed her way to him and held out her paw. He took it, then turned to Stryker. "Who is this?"

"Sherry's brother, Stryker."

Clint sat back in the swing and offered his hand to Stryker, who sniffed it suspiciously, then wagged his tail slowly.

"There's coffee in the pot inside," Clint said as Stryker moved back to her side.

"I can't stay. I have patients."

"Can you refill my cup, then? It's not easy to carry..."

She would swear she saw a twinkle in his eye, but how could she say no? So much for running in with the laptop and leaving. Then she noticed it was still in her hands. "Where do you want this?"

"The table in the living room is near a plug, and I'm sure the batteries need charging."

She opened the door, turned back when the dogs started to follow. "Stay," she told the two dogs who promptly sat next to her nemesis.

"And would you put some bread in the toaster?"

Now she knew. Payback for the cow.

But she did as he asked. The sooner she did, the quicker she could leave. Cow or not, there was a limit. She hurried inside before he thought of another errand. She placed the laptop on the table, found an outlet and plugged it in. She strode into the kitchen. A major inroad had been made in the open loaf of bread. An open package of cheese lay next to it, along with two dirty dishes and two empty glasses.

She tucked two pieces of bread in a toaster and washed dishes while she waited for them to toast. The kitchen was well stocked with appliances. Josh had probably left behind all the stuff he'd bought for the cabin when he moved in with Eve. She wondered what Eve would think of the newcomer. Most likely, she wouldn't share her own misgivings. Eve liked everyone, and everyone liked Eve.

The toast popped up. She buttered the two pieces, filled a cup with coffee and took both outside.

"Thank you," he said. "While you're here, could you also bring the jar of jam in the fridge?" This time he made no attempt to disguise his amusement.

She gritted her teeth and returned to the kitchen, found the jam. She grabbed a knife to go with it, and returned to the porch. He gave her a bland look as he scratched Stryker's ears who, in turn, groaned in delight.

Traitor.

"I appreciate you bringing the dogs," he said. "A friendly tail is welcome."

She didn't know whether it was a rebuke or whether she imagined it. "You've had dogs?" He seemed so natural with her two.

"Nope. Always wanted one, but I was never any place long enough."

"Not even as a kid?"

The shadow returned to his face. "No," he said without elaborating.

She hated that his answers were so...uninformative. That part of him was like Josh although the delivery was softer.

She was curious despite herself. "Are you from the west? I can't place your accent."

"No, but I did some survival training here. I like the mountains."

He obviously wasn't going to say anything more. "I have to go," she said. "Four-legged patients."

He nodded. "Thanks for bringing the laptop. And breakfast."

Stephanie decided to leave before he wanted anything else. "Sherry, Stryker, come." She opened the porch door.

Sherry glanced back at Clint as if reluctant to leave, then trotted toward the van. The dogs jumped inside and Stephanie drove off without looking back.

CLINT WATCHED THE VAN disappear between the tall pines that lined the dirt drive. The lake was just barely visible. To the left were the mountains. It was cool this morning, and the scent of pine freshened the air. It was, in a word, peaceful.

Stephanie had certainly spiced it. Something about her challenged him, and he hadn't realized how badly he needed a challenge. He'd drifted since the morning he'd awakened from a coma and discovered he might never fly again. He hadn't been willing to explore a future without it. He'd refused to make plans.

Dr. Payne had pried and prodded, suggesting he contact his father. The shrink knew from Clint's record that Frank Morgan was alive. But he wasn't alive to Clint and never would be. He hadn't talked to him since he was eighteen. A far as he knew, his father had never tried to contact him, either.

He wanted nothing to do with him now.

But now it was time to stop feeling sorry for himself. What was done was done, and he needed to decide his next step. He'd had a plan before the accident: obtain a degree in computer engineering and eventually work in helicopter computer systems. He was damned good at operation and repair. Better than most of the chopper mechanics. Now he didn't know whether he could work around choppers without flying.

Maybe he would switch to computer programming. In any event, the enrollment for online sessions at the University of Maryland was over. He would have to wait for the next quarter.

He hobbled back inside and opened his laptop to

check emails. There were a number from pilots in his unit in Afghanistan. No losses, thank God, but some close calls. A woman had joined their unit as a pilot. She wasn't the first, but it was still a novelty. The weather was fierce as usual, hot as hell during the day and freezing cold at night. They envied him.

The last was a lie, and he knew it. Most of his buddies, especially those without families, would prefer being in that godforsaken country to being back home. Like him, they would miss the adrenaline rushes that beat any other feeling, the exhilaration of a successful mission, the camaraderie between missions. He didn't allow himself to think about the bad stuff.

He closed his email and plugged "Stephanie Phillips, Covenant Falls, veterinarian" into a search engine.

Not much. No website. No background information. Several newspaper articles, though, most of them involving search-and-rescue missions. One mentioned she was also a volunteer firefighter. He found a candid photo of an exhausted-looking Stephanie and Sherry apparently being thanked by a mother holding a child. Search-and-Rescue Team Find Five-Year-Old, the caption reported.

It was another side of his chauffeur from yesterday. An intriguing lady, indeed.

That was it for information. Someone really had to work at privacy not to have more.

He closed the computer. He was damned restless, but his foot precluded the long hike he would have liked. He went into the second bedroom, which contained a single bed and two bookcases filled with books. He rifled through them. An interesting mixture. Biographies. Novels. History. His host obviously had eclectic taste.

He found a suspense novel, moved slowly to the kitchen for a glass of water and took both to the porch.

He settled in the swing and opened the book, but couldn't concentrate on the words. Too many other images crowded into his mind: his last combat mission, the rush of adrenaline as he pulled Rangers out of a killing zone, the military doctor's verdict, or lack of one. He hated feeling powerless. He'd lived with it too long as a boy.

He needed that control back. He couldn't sit here and read a book on someone else's dime.

He removed his cell phone from his pocket and punched in Josh's number.

CHAPTER FIVE

CLINT WAS READY when Josh drove up in his Jeep.

He'd shaved and changed into a clean pair of jeans and a pullover knit shirt. His swollen foot still hurt like hell, but he didn't want to use crutches. He had put on his only pair of sandals.

Clint was already bored with his own company. He'd always been active, driven to excel in sports and physical training. He'd always wanted to be the best. At first, it had been to earn his father's approval, then it had been to get into the service, then to be the best in his unit. He had always asked for the most dangerous missions. A death wish, one of his fellow pilots said. But it wasn't that. He simply needed to challenge himself. Dr. Payne had probed at that contention. Why? He hadn't had an answer.

Why had he accelerated the Corvette that day?

Josh jumped out of the Jeep, limping slightly. Clint hadn't noticed that yesterday. He'd been too tired, too focused on the veterinarian and, he admitted, on himself. A dog trotted after Josh, keeping in step with the man.

Josh walked up to the porch and opened the door. "This is Amos." He pointed to the dog. "Say hello."

Amos offered his right front paw just as Sherry had. What was it about polite canines in Covenant Falls? Was it contagious? Nonetheless, he took the paw gingerly.

"You're a friend now," Josh said. "Unless, of course, you attack me."

"Then what?"

"He wouldn't be happy. You do not want to run into an unhappy Amos."

"He's a handsome dog."

Josh plopped down on a chair, and the dog sat next to him. "He's ex-military." He changed the topic. "How's your foot?"

"Did you have to remind me?" Clint grinned. "It's an experience I would rather forget."

"Good luck," Josh said. "This town is a gossip mill. I imagine that rancher has probably told the story far and wide."

Clint shrugged. "I won't be here long."

Josh raised an eyebrow. "Would you like to go for a beer?"

"Sure."

"Good. I'll introduce you to the town's best bar. The Rusty Nail. It also has the best burgers."

"Sounds good. And Amos?"

"Amos is allowed inside. He's considered a hero around here."

"Why?"

Josh shrugged. "He saved my life a couple of times overseas, and here in town he saved the mayor's son. Twice."

"How?" Clint asked.

"He took a rattler bite meant for Nick, then later found Nick after he was kidnapped. It's a long story, probably better told by my wife and Nick." He stood. "Let's go."

Clint hesitated. "Don't you have something else to do? I don't want to interfere." He didn't want to be someone's cause, but he damned well wanted that beer. He also wanted to know a hell of a lot more about Stephanie.

"You're not. Nate, my partner, has everything under control."

"What do you do?"

"We're starting a construction business. We're doing some remodeling, and we're talking to the bank about buying and rehabbing a run-down motel here. Our goal is to bring new business and residents into Covenant Falls. The town desperately needs jobs."

"What did you do in the army?"

"Ranger. Staff sergeant. Learned a lot about building things, as well as exploding them."

Clint stood, balanced on the bad foot, then ignored the pain as he followed Josh to the Jeep. Amos jumped into the backseat, and Clint climbed into the passenger seat in front.

"Miss it?" he asked. He knew he didn't have to say what.

"Parts of it," Josh admitted.

"You were a lifer?"

Josh started the Jeep. "I thought I would be. This leg sorta ruined that."

"And now?"

"Things are good. You'll know why when you meet Eve and Nick."

"Nick?"

"Eve's son. Really bright kid. Full of curiosity. Pretty good baseball player, too."

"Stephanie said you had several dogs."

"Five, to be exact. I went from being a loner to a husband with a stepson, five dogs, two horses and a cat. Talk about adjustment. I still think I'll wake up and it will all be a dream."

"You seem happy."

"I am. But not without a hell of a lot of mistakes, miscues and doubts. Sometimes, I need to escape, and thank God Eve understands that. You ever been married?"

"For a very short time. Turned out absence didn't make the heart grow fonder. Got home from a deployment and found she had moved in with someone else, and there had been several other someones."

"Rough. I saw a lot of that in the service."

Clint nodded. "After the initial feeling of betrayal, I was relieved. We'd married too fast, and for all the wrong reasons. I thought I wanted a home to return to, but I really didn't know what a home was. She thought she was marrying someone who would party all night, every night. It was not an unrealistic expectation since that's what we did in the two months before we married." Why in the hell was he telling a stranger so much? But he had immediately liked Josh Manning, had felt a kinship with him. "But that wasn't what *I* wanted in a home. Hell, I didn't know what I wanted."

He looked ahead and saw a sprawling building with a sign that read The Rusty Nail in big letters. The gravel parking lot was about a quarter full.

Josh parked, and they both limped inside. Sawdust covered the floor and a long bar lined one side of the room. The rest of the bar was filled with mismatched tables and chairs with maybe a third of the seats occupied. A bandstand stood out in one corner.

A pretty young girl hurried over to them as they sat. "Hi, Josh. Haven't seen you in a while. What can I get you two?"

Clint glanced at him. "You order. You know what's good."

"Two of whatever crazy beer your dad is experimenting with today, two cheeseburgers and fries."

"Gotcha." She dashed off.

Clint eyed his companion. Josh still had the look of a Ranger about him. His gaze never stopped roaming the room.

"Is the veterinarian taken?" Clint blurted.

Josh looked amused. "Taken? You mean in marriage or engagement? Nope. She scares the hell out of most of the eligible men around here. I take it you aren't one of them."

"Oh, she scares me, too." Clint chuckled.

"Good. I like her a lot, and she's Eve's best friend. I wouldn't like to see her hurt."

"I won't be here long enough."

"I've heard that before," Josh said. "Mainly from me. When I came here, all I wanted was to be left alone, and now look at me. A wife, a son, two horses and five dogs."

Clint grinned. "Well, I doubt lightning strikes twice, but while I'm here, I want to be useful. You mentioned building a dock. I would like to do it."

"Good." He paused, then said, "Any idea of what you want to do in the future?"

Clint shrugged. "I'm thinking of going back to college in January. Get my computer science degree."

"You're good at that, then? Computers, I mean?" Josh was looking at him speculatively.

Clint wasn't sure he liked it. He would rather talk about Stephanie. "I'm okay."

"Eve's pet project is teaching our older citizens how to use computers. She just bought new ones for the community center. We've been looking..."

"Whoa there," Clint said. "I'm happy to build a dock. I can do that. But teaching a bunch of older people about computers, I just don't think I would be any good at that. I can't make that kind of a commitment."

"I'm not talking about a commitment. A couple of hours a week whenever you have time."

"Why don't you do it?"

"I have all I can handle right now, and I'm not good with people. You appear to be. I've never seen Stephanie flustered before."

"You haven't, huh?" Clint mused.

Two men approached their table. Josh introduced them as Jeff Smith and Mace Edwards, two vets from the Iraq War. "Heard you were coming," the one introduced as Mace Edwards said. "Wanted to say welcome. You need anything, just want to get a beer, talk, call us." He offered a napkin with phone numbers on it.

He placed his hand on Josh's shoulder. "Hear you might have some big work soon. If you need any workers, we can sure use the jobs."

Josh nodded. "Hope it will be soon. Join us for a beer."

"Don't mind if we do," Mace said.

Clint mostly listened to the three men talk. It felt good. He never discussed his service or the war with civilians, but he could open up with other vets. They understood the unbreakable bond that united members of a unit, and nearly every man and woman who had been in war. Many, maybe even most, were closer to each other than they were to their families.

No one else could understand.

But now he was with people who understood. After sharing beers, the two men left, and Clint glanced at Josh. "You're really making it here, huh?" he asked.

"It's not always easy. I still have sweating spells at night. And nightmares. I worried about that with Eve. That I might hurt her or the boy. But she knows how to wake me when I have them. And I'm crazy about Nick. The dogs, now, that's another matter." But he grinned as he said it, and Clint got the definite impression he really didn't mind the dogs one bit.

"You miss being over there?" Clint asked.

Josh didn't say anything for several minutes. "The army was my family for a long time. I miss my team, but most of them died in my last mission." The trails in his face deepened. A lot of pain was etched there.

Clint hadn't known. Dr. Payne had said very little about Josh. "I'm sorry." Then he asked the question that had been needling him. "Why me? Why did you select me for the cabin? You must know I wasn't injured in battle. It was a dumb car accident."

Josh shrugged. "Injured in the field or not, we all have scars. Nightmares. Horrors we can't talk about except to someone who has been there, and still they continue to burn in our heads. And then," he added in a voice so low Clint could barely hear it, "there are those we left…" His voice trailed off.

Clint could relate. He'd lost several close friends

in chopper crashes. One was in his chopper when enemy fire hit it. He could usually lock those memories in a mental box, but sometimes they escaped, swamping him.

He nodded, cleared his throat. "It's a great cabin," he said, changing the subject. He regretted asking his question. It was none of his business and it brought back too many memories of his own.

"It was my salvation, that and Eve."

Their order arrived, and the conversation stopped. The cheeseburgers were fat and greasy and, well, terrific, or maybe it had just been a long, long time since he'd had a good one. The draft beer was icy cold and served in frosty glasses. The world was looking better.

"We'll go by the grocery store on the way back, and you can pick up whatever you need. The invitation for dinner is also good for tomorrow night," Josh said. "I think Eve plans to ask Stephanie to join us."

"Sounds good." More than good. He hadn't felt much anticipation for anything since the accident, but he did now.

Josh looked at his watch. "We should probably go."

As if on cue, their server appeared. "Dad said there's no bill this time," she said. She turned to Clint. "Welcome to Covenant Falls."

STEPHANIE AND EVE met for their weekly luncheon.

"What do you think of him?" Eve asked.

Stephanie shrugged. "He dresses like an Easterner."

"You used to dress like an Easterner."

Stephanie tried to think of something bad to say. She couldn't, and that was really annoying. *He* was annoying because he wasn't annoying. Stephanie took another bite of her patty melt, one of her few food weaknesses. "What does Josh think?"

"You know Josh doesn't say much, especially if he doesn't know someone well."

"He had to say something."

"He went over to see him today, took Amos with him. I haven't talked to him since. Nick is beside himself with excitement. A real live helicopter pilot. I kinda feel sorry for Clint Morgan."

"Believe me, he can take care of himself," Stephanie said.

"Do I detect a note of disapproval?"

"No. Yes. Maybe."

"Are you the Stephanie I've known for five years?"

"That incoherent?"

"Yeah," Eve said. "I can't wait to meet someone who affects you this way. Josh is inviting him over for supper tomorrow night. You're invited, too."

"Why?"

"To protect him from the motley crew," Eve said.

"I think he can handle himself," Stephanie retorted.

Eve raised an eyebrow.

"Josh told you about the cow?"

"He did. He said Mr. Morgan called it a close encounter with the bovine kind. He's still chuckling about that." She let a few moments go by, then added, "I heard from others, as well."

"Damn. What did you hear?"

"A bull attacked and crippled him."

"Good lord!"

"Obviously, that is not correct or Josh would be more upset than he was last night."

"He didn't say anything to you?"

"You know Josh. He doesn't say much. He considers a person's privacy as inviolate."

"I don't." Stephanie said. "We were rolling a heifer. Clint helped hold the hind legs. When he released them, the cow stepped on him. It's happened to me a number of times. He has a bruise, nothing more."

Eve's eyes bored into her. She hadn't meant to sound defensive, but she knew instantly she did.

Eve's smile told her that much. "What about supper?"

Her friend was daring her. To refuse would only serve to raise Eve's antenna higher. "Sure," she said, hiding her misgivings. "Can I bring something?"

"Yourself is just fine. Josh is grilling steaks. I'm just popping potatoes in the oven and making a salad."

"Sounds good."

"Try not to have an emergency."

That was exactly what Stephanie was planning: an emergency.

"Why me? Why not invite, say, my tech? She can't wait to meet him."

"Because he's already met you," Eve explained patiently.

"Why have anyone in addition to you and Josh? I would think the fewer the better. You know how Josh was."

"If you don't want to come, you really don't have to," Eve said. "I just think he probably needs as many friends as possible here."

She was being played, and she knew it. Eve had been her champion from the moment Stephanie had appeared in Covenant Falls. Not everyone had wanted a woman vet. Some of the ranchers refused to use her and sent to Pueblo for a vet of the masculine variety. The West, particularly the rural West, was set in its ways.

Eve had browbeaten reluctant clients into going to Stephanie, as well as recommended her to everyone within a fifty-mile radius. Fine. She could do this dinner for Eve. One evening. Clint Morgan would be gone soon. Covenant Falls would be too quiet for him. He needed a large city with buses and taxis and people to charm.

"Okay. Unless there *is* an emergency." She took a deep breath. Maybe yesterday was an aberration. "But I might be late. It's super busy since I won't be here this weekend for my Saturday hours. I'm participating in a search-and-rescue certification."

"Whenever you can get there," Eve said.

The devil danced in her friend's eyes. Blast it. They had bonded over their aversion to marriage, although each had very different reasons for that aversion. She feared that since Eve had succumbed to the call of love, her friend had her sights on Stephanie. *Hell, no.*

"Have to go," Eve said. "We're still looking for a police chief, and I have an interview this afternoon."

"Promising?"

"Unfortunately, no. But Tony took the job temporarily and has already stayed longer than he wants." Eve paid her bill and stood. "See you tomorrow night."

Stephanie rose with her. She had a heavy appointment schedule this afternoon, plus a meeting later with three people interested in search and rescue. She doubted they would be as enthusiastic after learning the particulars, but if she enlisted one, she would be happy. Training both handler and dog could take as long as two years, never mind the fact they were volunteers and incurred a lot of expense along the way. It was a calling, often without rewards when the result was bad. But those moments of success were worth every minute of time and every dollar spent.

At the very least it would take her mind off the town's newest resident and what would be a very awkward dinner tomorrow night. For her, anyway. She suspected Clint Morgan would enjoy every moment of her discomfort.

Now Eve owed her.

AFTER JOSH DROVE him home, Clint sat on the porch, staring at the lake. He needed something. A purpose. A goal. Hell, a life. Rehabbing the cabin had helped his host. Maybe it would do the same for him.

A dock couldn't be too difficult.

He walked painfully down to the lake and looked at the other docks along the lake. Two were rather elaborate with boathouses. The others just stretched out into the water. Several had fishing boats tied to them. Another had a canoe and a bench.

The afternoon was warm, even hot, although his idea of hot had changed after years in Afghanistan.

Clint could tell from the shoreline and the other docks that the water was lower than normal, maybe by a foot or more. Still, it was a rich blue, which meant depth, and he wondered whether it was fed by springs as well as snow from the mountains.

He went inside and searched websites dedicated to building docks and lost himself in going from one to another, gathering ideas. It was not, he realized, as easy as he'd thought, which was a good thing. He needed a challenge.

It was well past eight when he closed the laptop. He'd made several designs along with a list of needed materials for each. He would take them over to the Mannings' the following evening.

He stood and the floor swayed beneath him. He grabbed the chair, knowing what was going to happen. He tried to concentrate, but the room was moving now. He needed to get to the bedroom, find his medicine. Lie down before he fell. The dizzy spells were almost always followed by a thunderous headache. He had hoped…

The hall swirled as he used the walls to steady himself. The foot, still sore as hell, didn't help. He reached the bed. Medicine and a glass of water were on a table next to it. He always left it there.

He lay down on the bed and some of the dizziness faded. Not all of it.

The ceiling still moved. Then the pain started…

CHAPTER SIX

CLINT WOKE FEELING as if he had been in a ten-hour battle. His head throbbed, his body too weak to reach the bathroom for a shower.

Light flooded into the cabin. Yesterday, before the dizziness came, he'd been feeling better about the cabin, about being here. He liked Josh. The man didn't say much, but he didn't have to.

He thought about Stephanie and wondered if she would be at dinner tonight. He didn't know why he was so attracted to her. She was far too serious for him, too cautious, too...unreceptive.

Maybe it *was* the challenge. Or maybe it was the brain trauma. Whatever it was, she was back in his head this morning, crowding everything out but the residue of pain.

He forced himself to get up and walk to the bathroom. There was some good news. Despite the doctor's warning that his foot would be worse today, it was better. Or maybe he was just putting it into context with the rest of his body.

He took a cold shower to wake up, then a hot one. He limped into the kitchen and poured a large glass of orange juice. He headed for the porch swing. The solitude was jarring. He recognized the irony of that, but since he was eight, he'd almost always been with others, first at boarding schools, followed by army training facilities and finally overseas. He was usually the center of things, something he'd learned in boarding school. To lead for fear of being left behind.

Now he was more alone than he had ever been and none of his mental tricks helped. Not the charm he'd developed, nor a nurtured optimism, nor an immediate goal. He had difficulty seeing anything but emptiness ahead.

He finished the orange juice, limped down the drive and crossed the road that ended in a little roundabout just beyond the cabin. He eyed the path up the steep slope of the mountain. Maybe tomorrow.

He went back inside, and for lack of anything else to do, he started checking out universities to finish his degree. His interest was in aeronautic electronics, but he didn't find a program that he liked. Maybe his heart wasn't in it. The thought of spending the rest of his working life in an office was deeply depressing. Although he had a natural curiosity about nearly everything and was a good student, the classroom had been the means of getting to where he wanted to be, and that was in the sky. He liked the outdoors, playing sports and testing himself physically. All that was at risk now.

He found one of Josh's books and took it to the porch. Maybe it would keep his mind from the future. And Stephanie Phillips.

STEPHANIE STARED AT the email from one of the few friends she had from the past. Her ex-husband was getting another divorce. That marriage had lasted two years longer than her own. The friend also said he'd made queries about her whereabouts.

A shiver of apprehension ran through her.

Mark Townsend didn't like rejection. He had practically destroyed her during their marriage and after the divorce. He had stolen her money, destroyed her reputation, made it impossible to practice in the Northeast. Wherever she went, he found a way of preventing her from being hired.

She'd found the position in Covenant Falls when a close friend from vet school told her of an older veterinarian in Colorado who was looking for someone to take over his practice. He'd inherited his family ranch and wanted to go back to full-time ranching, but didn't want to leave the community without a vet. He was willing to finance the sale for the right person.

She'd told Dr. Langford about Mark during their initial interview. One of the vet's daughters had experienced a similar problem, and he had recommended that Stephanie take her mother's maiden name legally. He'd cleared it through the state board and after working together for six months, he agreed to sell her the practice. He'd also suggested she retain the name of Langford Animal Practice. In today's electronic world, a dedicated searcher could find her, but she'd hoped Mark's new marriage would dim his vindictiveness toward her.

Now that his latest marriage was ending, she worried he might come after her again. Or would he concentrate his ire on his newest ex-wife?

How could she have been such a fool to marry him?

Maybe he couldn't find her. Or if he did, his power wouldn't be as great in Covenant Falls as it was in Boston. True, she wasn't a lifetime resident of Covenant Falls, but she was actively involved in search and rescue and was a member of the volunteer fire department. She also volunteered in causes that interested her, especially the community center.

Except for Eve, though, she'd avoided close relationships.

She closed the computer and glanced at her watch. She was running late for Eve's dinner, although she was glad she had conducted her weekly search. It was best to be prepared.

She regretted letting herself be talked into the dinner. She wasn't in the mood to be sociable. Especially not after reading the email about Mark.

But she *had* promised Eve.

She changed into a clean shirt but left on the blue jeans she'd worn all day. Darn if she was going to dress up for Clint Morgan. She did add a touch of lipstick. Just a bit. She brushed her hair and braided it back into a long plait. Ready to go.

Or not.

She almost wished for an emergency, and she felt guilty as hell about that. *No!* It was just that damned email about Mark. It reminded her of her own helplessness, her own sorry judgment. She hated the reminder.

Stephanie tried to look on the bright side. She would see her horse, Shadow, that she boarded at Eve's ranch, and Nick and the other two people she liked most in Covenant Falls.

"Stay," she told the two dogs as she grabbed her car keys.

Sherry whined, sensing she was ready to go. Styrker sat and held out his paw in entreaty. "Sorry, guys," she said. "You haven't been invited. There will be enough commotion without you."

At least she hadn't been asked to drive Clint to Eve's house.

Her cell rang. Her heart dropped. She *knew.* She just *knew.*

She looked at the name of the caller. *Eve.*

The phone continued to ring. She could ignore it, but Eve knew she always answered the phone in case it was an emergency. If she didn't answer, Eve would know why.

She answered. "I'm on the way."

"Can you run by the cabin and pick up Clint? Josh

is anointing steaks with his usual care, and my budget meeting ran late."

Stephanie sighed. There was no out. Not without making an idiot out of herself. "Okay. I'm leaving now."

She clicked off and went to the back of the clinic where she kept the van. She pulled up in front of Josh's cabin several minutes later.

Clint was on the swing on the front porch. He stood when he saw the van and ambled down the steps to the passenger side with only the slightest of limps, though she knew his foot must still hurt. She tried to deny the flutter in her stomach as he approached. He gave her a slow easy smile that would be devastating if she didn't know better. "Hi," he said. "I wouldn't be presumptuous in thinking you're my ride…?"

"Nope. Afraid not." Then she realized how that sounded. "Not presumptuous, I mean," she added halfheartedly.

His smile widened as he opened the door. "I'm happy to see you again, too."

She had no comeback for that.

"Josh said his house was chaos," he continued. It was more question than a statement.

"It is," she said more cheerfully. "It will probably drive you crazy." She hoped.

"After two wars, nothing drives me crazy."

"Watch out for the beagle. She's a kleptomaniac."

"I have nothing I wouldn't willingly surrender to a beagle."

"Don't sit on Fancy."

"I appreciate the lesson in etiquette, but who is Fancy and why would I sit on her?"

"Fancy is a small dog, and she sometimes sneaks up on the sofa just when someone is sitting down."

"I'll try to sit in a chair." He looked thoroughly amused. She wanted to slap him.

She decided to take another tack. "You're not limping." She realized the moment she said it that it was almost an accusation.

"Well, I still hurt if that's what you're wondering. Like the doc said…a couple of days." He shrugged. "I've had worse."

She was being petty. Ridiculous. He was just a man passing through town. A wounded man. A soldier like Josh. She owed him. The town owed him for his military service. It was the email; it had hit her like a sledgehammer.

She surrendered and described what would confront him at the Manning household. "Braveheart is a shy pit bull. He'll probably hide from you. Miss Marple is the larcenous beagle. Fancy is the homeliest dog you will ever see, but she thinks she's beautiful, and Captain Hook is a crotchety three-legged chihuahua who just might take a bite out of your leg."

"I think I was safer in Afghanistan," Clint said wryly.

"There's more," she said, unable to hide the slightest of smiles. "There's Josh's dog, Amos, who's a very disciplined ex-military dog unless he thinks someone is threatening Josh. There's also Dizzy, a cat with balance problems. And lord of the house is ten-year-old Nick."

"Tell me about Nick."

"He's a perfectly normal ten-year-old boy."

"You're not telling me something."

"Nothing more to tell." She would let him learn about Nick's endless curiosity himself.

He nodded, and she couldn't tell what he was really thinking. But a house full of animals probably didn't hold much fear for a guy who had been involved in wars for a number of years.

"How is the cabin?" she asked, struggling to be more sociable. *For Eve and Josh.*

"It's great. I had a visitor today."

"Who?"

"A Mrs. Byars, I think."

"Brownies?"

"How did you know?"

"She's famous for them. Her son died in Vietnam. She has a special place in her heart for veterans."

She turned into a driveway that led to a sprawling ranch house with a big porch. A barn stood next to it, and three horses grazed in a pasture. As they drove up to the door, a tow-headed boy ran out of the house followed by a troop of dogs. Only one remained at the door.

"I'm Nick," the boy said as he reached the van and Clint stepped out. "Josh told me to bring you inside. He's at the grill."

"I'm delighted to meet you, Nick," he said formally. "And your friends."

"I knew you would," Nick said. "Mom suggested I leave them inside, but they wanted to meet you, too."

"I'm very glad they did," he said solemnly.

Nick beamed.

Stephanie followed man and boy inside and watched Clint charm the shoes off Nick, which wasn't hard to do. Nick already worshiped his new stepfather and that was going to carry over to anyone who served in the military. To her chagrin, Clint sounded totally sincere as he talked to Nick and then bent down to let the dogs sniff his hand. Only Braveheart stood back.

It was hard to fool children and dogs. Mark had never even pretended to like dogs. That should have been a very loud warning bell, but when she'd asked him whether he had pets, he'd said he'd been too busy and it wouldn't be fair to an animal. That had sounded logical and even animal-friendly. *Get him out of your head.*

Eve met them at the door, a broad smile on her face. "Welcome," she said as the dogs sidled in alongside Clint. "I see you've met my motley crew."

"I have, and I've had a warning about the larcenous one."

"Just don't take off a shoe," Eve warned. "Would

you like something to drink? A beer? Or something else."

"A beer sounds great."

Eve's smile grew broader. "I've been anxious to meet you since Josh told me about your 'encounter of a bovine kind' with one of Steph's patients. I decided then and there that I was going to like you. What do you think about the cabin?"

"It's terrific. Far more than I expected. Your husband did a great job."

Eve beamed, and Stephanie sighed. No ally there.

"You sit here and get off that foot," Eve said. "Stephanie will bring you a beer. Nick, you go out and help Josh."

Clint did as instructed, and Stephanie gritted her teeth as she followed Eve to the kitchen. It was going to be a very long evening.

CHAPTER SEVEN

CLINT WAS BEMUSED. It *was* chaos here, but a comfortable kind of chaos. He enjoyed Stephanie's discomfort, as well. He was attracted to her. No question about that. His body alerted him to the fact every time he saw her.

Instinctively, he knew she felt the attraction, too, and was fighting it with everything in her. He didn't know why, but then, he had his own reasons to avoid any romantic entanglements. Last night's headache reminded him of his limitations. No blackout, but it had been a near thing. A month from now, he might still have them. Maybe a year, or forever, and what kind of job can you get when you can't drive or might pass out at any time?

For now, he would enjoy jousting with Stephanie and watching the fire in her pretty eyes.

She arrived with a bottle of ice-cold beer and handed it to him. "I'm helping Eve in the kitchen," she said. "Why don't you get acquainted with the dogs?"

He sat on the couch and three of the four dogs surrounded him. He suspected Stephanie thought it would unhinge him. He held out his hand to the dogs. The beagle came to him immediately, followed by the one called Fancy. In two more minutes, the Chihuahua hopped up into his lap. Only Braveheart sat at a distance, eyeing him as if he were an ax murderer. Maybe he channeled Stephanie.

The pit bull had scars, and one ear was half torn off. "Hey, Braveheart," he said softly. He held out his hand again. Miss Marple, the beagle, licked it. The Mexican Hairless nibbled at it. Braveheart looked unmoved.

"I know what you're thinking," he said. "I'm a stranger, and strangers are scary. I must be scary, but I like you. We both have some scars." Braveheart didn't move. Neither did he. "It's okay. Take your time."

Miss Marple rolled onto her back, and he rubbed her stomach. Then, to his surprise, Braveheart took a step toward him. Then another. Hesitantly. Very hesitantly. He was close enough to touch. Clint reached out to him. Braveheart shied away, came back still obviously poised to escape. Clint slowly leaned toward him and as gently as he could, rubbed the dog's ears. Braveheart inched closer. "Good boy," Clint said in a low, reassuring voice.

"I don't believe it," Eve's voice floated into the room.

He looked up and saw Eve and Stephanie, their mouths open, in the doorway to the kitchen.

Braveheart sat in front of him.

"Looks like you have the Braveheart seal of approval," Eve said. "That's a real distinction."

"Wow," said Nick, sliding in between them. "I just knew he would like you and you would like him."

"Josh thought you might like to join him outside," Eve said. "That's if you can stand on that foot."

"I can." He stood. "Nick, lead the way."

He took the beer and limped outside where Josh was putting steaks on the grill. Nick started to go with him, but Eve called him back.

Amos sat next to Josh, his eyes watching every movement he made.

"I like your wife," Clint said.

Josh smiled. "It's hard not to. Believe me, I know. I did my damnedest to chase her off, but nothing worked. She's the most determined woman I've ever met. And the kindest. Just try to say no to that combination."

"And Stephanie?"

"Like I said. She's Eve's best friend, which means she's good people, but she doesn't let many people get close to her. She's great with animals. I understand Braveheart here was a basket case when Eve found him beaten and nearly dead. For a long time, only she and Stephanie could approach him. Stephanie has magic with animals, not so much with people. She doesn't trust easily."

"So it's not just me?"

Josh chuckled. "It might be. Don't know anyone else who got kicked by a cow when they were with her."

"Stomped, not kicked."

"A valid distinction."

"I think so." Clint cleared his throat. "She said she's been here five years. Where was she before?"

"Back East. She doesn't talk about it much."

He was intruding. It was none of his business. He would be angry if Josh went around giving out information about him. "Sorry," he said. "I shouldn't have asked."

Josh raised an eyebrow. "Still interested in her?"

"I'm not in a position to be interested, and if I was, I don't think she is."

Josh didn't comment.

"Anyway, thanks for use of the cabin. I've been studying plans for a dock. You want a floating or fixed dock?"

"Going stir-crazy, already?"

"Just like paying my way."

"I got that." Josh flipped the steaks and seared the other side.

"As for the dock, whatever you think. Just let me know what you need and I'll have it delivered."

"That's a lot of trust."

Josh shrugged. "You were a chopper pilot, right?"

Clint nodded.

"That's a close bunch of guys. So were we Rangers. That was the worse part. Leaving my brothers behind." He paused, then added, "But they'll always be a part of me. I imagine it's the same for you."

He moved the steaks around, putting two farther from the hot coals. "Eve pulled me kicking and yelling back to life. There's a lot of strength in this town. It certainly has its own personality. No one minds their own business, and it drove me nuts. Still does. But it's because everyone—or most everyone—cares about everyone else. I'm proud to say that much of it is because of Eve. And Stephanie. Eve's in front because she's mayor, but Steph is right there with her. And that's probably the longest speech you'll ever hear from me."

Clint didn't reply. He didn't have to. They understood each other.

Josh removed the four huge steaks from the grill and piled them onto a plate. They were still sizzling.

"I'll take your beer inside," Clint said. He was salivating now. "The steaks smell great." He headed for the door and found that Nick had it wide open, waiting for them. "Good timing, Nick," he said.

The boy grinned.

Clint dodged around the beagle and Fancy and took the bottles into the kitchen.

Eve was finishing a salad while Stephanie placed baked potatoes on a platter. Clint put the two empty beer bottles on the counter.

"Can you open a bottle of wine?" Eve asked him.

"Sure."

"It's in the fridge. The wine opener is in the drawer."

Clint found both and deftly opened the wine and followed Eve's directions to a table, followed now by four dogs. This was mayhem, but a happy kind of mayhem with everyone contributing, including the guests. Belonging. Intended or not, he was no longer a guest or a visitor; he belonged. At least for tonight.

He'd once known how it felt to be part of a family. But that was a long time ago. Even then, it wasn't like this relaxed gathering where everyone pitched in, and kids and dogs were welcomed. The dinners at his house had been stilted formal affairs, even when his mother was alive. When his father remarried, he hadn't been welcome at all.

"Clint?"

He shook his head. "Sorry."

Nick pointed him to a seat on the far side of the table. "You can sit with me."

"Sounds good." He stood at the appointed chair, not wanting to sit until the others came in. Josh appeared carrying two plates, each containing a steak and baked potato. He put one on the table at Clint's chair and another across from him. "We have the rare ones," Josh said. "The ladies and Nick share the two medium ones."

He disappeared again and returned with a plate and bowl heaped with salad. Stephanie and Eve were right behind him with three more plates, each filled with a huge baked potato and steak.

Dinner was great. The steaks were perfect, as were the baked potatoes and salad. Eve kept the conversation going, telling the story of how Nick was bit by a rattlesnake bite and was saved by Amos who, in turn, was bitten. How Nick had been very still while Josh picked up the snake with a stick and threw it.

"And Mom shot it to pieces," Nick said.

"I'm impressed," Clint said. "Particularly that you stood so still. Maybe I should have been a Boy Scout."

"Why weren't you?" Nick said.

"My school didn't have a troop."

"But…"

"Not so unusual," Josh interrupted.

Eve changed the subject. She turned to Clint. "But do be careful," she said. "Josh thinks the snake had been wounded by a hawk or something and crawled under the porch for safety, but we do have snakes and other varmints around here."

She switched her attention to Stephanie who had been quiet. "How is Stryker doing with the rescue training?"

"He's finished the tracking program. We still have air-scent training to go. Then I have to find the right handler for him. Not easy to do."

"It won't be easy to let him go."

"No," she said. "But we need more search teams."

Eve turned to Clint. "I don't know if Stephanie told you, but she and Sherry are a search-and-rescue team. So far, they've found nine lost people, four of them kids."

"I'm impressed," he said. "I've seen handlers and dogs work. It's amazing."

Stephanie looked startled, then shrugged it off. "I'm just one of many."

"How long does it take to train a dog?" Clint pressed.

"Not as long as training the handler," Stephanie replied. "It took me more than two years."

Clint was truly interested. His unit had been borrowed at times to help in international disasters. He knew the training, and often heartbreak, that a team experienced.

"What made you get involved?" he asked.

"Sherry was already a rescue dog when I adopted her. Her owner was killed in an accident, and her mother wanted Sherry to go to someone who would continue to work her in rescue. It was a challenge. You said you joined the army because you wanted to fly. Why did you stay?"

Their gazes were locked, as if they were the only two people in the room. The intensity quieted the others. Her blue eyes were challenging. "I was good at it," he finally said.

"That's why I do search and rescue."

"I suspect you are *very* good at it."

"She is," Eve said. "She's also a volunteer firefighter with our fire department."

"A lady of many talents," Clint said.

"Not really," Stephanie said. "If you can do one, it's not that difficult to do the other. A lot of the skills are the same. Mapping, communications, first aid. Finding time for the training is the most difficult part."

"Do you have many fires?"

It was Eve who answered. "Maybe three or four a year in town, and our department also helps fight forest fires. Unfortunately, we've had a long drought, and the forest is like a tinder box. A careless camp fire or heat lightning, and we lose thousands of acres. Fortunately, we haven't had any near here, but our department has been called in on fires in other areas in the state."

"I'm impressed," he said.

Stephanie squirmed in her seat, and Clint was conscious of gazes on him. Speculative on the part of his host and hostess.

He took a sip of wine.

"Josh, did you know Braveheart let Clint pet him?" Nick broke the tension by asking the question.

"Nope. Now *I* am impressed," Josh said. "Sure took me longer."

"Can we have dessert now?" Nick said, skipping to yet another subject. "We're having Grandma's strawberry pie for dessert." He glanced shyly at Clint. "I hope you come over often, Mr. Morgan."

The comment made Clint grin. There's nothing like a ten-year-old boy to bring things into perspective.

Nick's face fell as he realized exactly how his words sounded, that he wanted Clint to return because he would get pie, not to see him.

"Yes, we can have dessert now," Eve said. "But I think we'll serve it outside so Clint can see our sunset." She turned to him. "Do you ride?"

"Horses?"

"Yes."

"Never had the opportunity, but it's on my bucket list."

"Good. We have two horses that are always in need of riding. We'll make a rider of you. Stephanie, why don't you take Clint out and introduce him to the horses? Nick can help me clean up the dishes and make coffee. When you get back, we'll have dessert."

"Nick can take him," Stephanie said. "I'll help with the dishes."

"Yeah, Mom," Nick said.

Eve shook her head. "It's one of Nick's chores."

Stephanie sighed. "Maybe Josh?"

"He has to make sure there's no embers left in the grill."

She stood. "Okay," she said with resignation. "I'll need a couple of apples."

Nick picked up several empty plates and disappeared into the kitchen. He returned with two apples and a knife that he handed to Clint. "We only have two apples. You'll have to split them. Beauty is my horse," he said.

"Should I give her extra, then?"

"Naw, it would hurt the others' feelings."

"I wouldn't want to do that." He followed Stephanie out the door. "Nice kid."

"He's a great kid."

"We agree on something."

"I don't know about that. You said 'nice.' I said 'great.'" But a shadow of a smile crossed her face.

She walked with him to the fence and whistled. Three horses ambled to them, the gray going straight for Stephanie, the other two eyeing the apples in Clint's hand.

"Mine is Shadow, the gray horse," Stephanie said, rubbing the animal's neck. "The pintos are Beauty and Beast. Beast is spirited. Beauty is the gentlest horse alive. Thus their names. Russ, Eve's late husband, bought them at a rodeo horse auction just before he died."

"When was that?

"Nearly five years now. Healthiest man in town, or so we thought. He was a football coach. Was in great physical shape, then he just dropped dead while running around the track with his team. A heart defect no one knew about."

"You knew him, then?"

She nodded. "I liked him. Everyone liked him."

She was talking more to him than she had. Maybe it was the excellent meal, or the wine, or the evening that was now cool. Maybe it was a sky that looked on fire.

He didn't ask any more questions. He wanted to, but he sensed her wariness.

He divided the apples. Her horse nuzzled her. He fed the other two horses more apple, keeping enough for her horse. "Should I feed Shadow, too, or do you want to?"

"You have the apple."

He cut several pieces from the second apple and fed them to Shadow, enjoying the feel of the soft muzzle and mouth. The horse nickered softly and nudged him for more.

When he glanced up, he was close to Stephanie. Too close. He could feel the heat from her body, or maybe it was from his own. Or maybe the combination of both. Mutual combustion.

Her eyes widened and her body stiffened. Her tongue ran over her lips, and it was such a sensual yet unconscious gesture that the heat inside him spread like wildfire through his body. He wanted to touch her. Hold her. Most of all, he wanted her wariness to fade away.

He shouldn't feel any of that. He was the temporary beneficiary of someone else's largesse. As long as he still had the symptoms from the brain trauma, he had little future. Besides, she didn't seem to like him much. And yet he was drawn to her in a deeper way than he'd ever been drawn to a woman before.

"Stephanie?" He didn't know what he was asking. He put a finger on her face and lightly traced a path from the thick eyelashes down the high cheekbones.

She stood absolutely still, her blue eyes fathomless as she looked at him.

Currents. They flowed between them. Strong and hot and compelling. He experienced a deep yearning he'd never known before, a connection that had always eluded him. He'd known attraction. Infatuation, certainly. But never anything this strong. It was almost as if they were linked by some invisible chain.

She shook her head. "No." It was a whisper, but enough to tell him she felt the link, too, and wasn't a bit happy about it. Well, he wasn't, either. He didn't need more complications in his life. But he still couldn't move away.

It didn't make sense. He didn't make sense. Confusion filled her eyes, too, and for a second she rested her head against his hand. He leaned down and his lips touched hers. Lightly. Then he stepped back. "I wanted to do that since I met you," he said.

"Why?" Her eyes were so blue, so direct.

"Damned if I know."

"We should ignore it."

"Yes." But neither of them moved.

"We have to get back," she said. "Eve will wonder…"

"And Nick wants his pie," he said.

"We can't keep Nick waiting."

"Or he'll be out here in a minute."

"This is ridiculous," she said.

He nodded. *Ridiculous that they were standing*

here and not making another move toward each other. But the signal had to come from her.

A door slammed and Nick ran toward them.

Clint lowered his hand and stepped away from Stephanie, who exhaled a soft breath.

"Mom's ready," Nick said. "She said go around to the back. I'll show you."

Nick went ahead and Clint obediently followed although every part of him wanted to do something else. He wanted to grab Stephanie and explore these feelings, but he knew that would not be welcome at the moment.

He also knew how unwise it would be.

Still, everything in him wanted to do it.

CHAPTER EIGHT

DESSERT WAS AGONIZING.

Stephanie tried to eat her slice of Mrs. Douglas's strawberry pie, but she was far too aware of the man next to her to appreciate it. She even dropped her fork when his leg accidently bumped hers beneath the table.

"Sorry," they both said at the same time.

She'd let him kiss her. And, God help her, she'd melted inside.

It had been the sunset, and the horses, and the wine. *It was the wine. Definitely the wine.* She chattered on about members of her search-and-rescue team. She never chattered. She saw Eve's gaze on her and took a bite of pie. It was her favorite dessert and it tasted like sawdust. She practically choked on it.

Clint, on the other hand, was eating like he'd been starving to death for years. If he felt any of the tension she did, he didn't show it.

That said a lot. *Drat.*

Fancy trotted over to her and sat, looking longingly at the plate in front of her. Then to her surprise she saw Braveheart sit next to Clint.

Clint touched the pit bull's ears, and Braveheart didn't flinch. He continued to rub the dog's ears, then moved his hand to the dog's back and rubbed it. Braveheart rumbled with contentment.

Eve's eyes widened. Josh raised an eyebrow. She, herself, had a hard time believing her own eyes. Braveheart had never, ever—as far as she knew— approached a stranger. And Clint Morgan *was* a stranger.

She dutifully finished the pie because she always did, and she didn't like the speculative look in Eve's eyes. Were her cheeks flushed from the kiss?

Lord, she hoped not. It hadn't meant anything. A sunset. That was all it was. That and the fact she had been startled.

"We should go," she said. "I have to be up early in the morning and I have to walk my boarders tonight."

"I'll help with the dishes," Clint said.

"You have a sore foot," Stephanie protested before Eve could reply. She suspected Clint wanted to prolong the evening. She didn't. Not when every time she looked at him, her senses went crazy.

"It's better."

"I don't think so. I've experienced it."

"Maybe I heal faster," Clint said as he gave Braveheart one last rub of his ears and looked up.

Stephanie suddenly realized Josh and Eve were staring from one of them to the other with bemused expressions.

"I'll drive him home if you have to leave," Josh offered after a silence.

"That's okay," Clint said. "I probably should leave now." He looked toward Eve. "That was the best meal I've had in a very long time. Thank you for having me."

"Thank Josh," Eve said. "He's the grand grill master."

"I have a great deal to thank him for." Clint stood. Braveheart sat right behind him. He scratched the dog's ears again.

"How did you do that?" Nick asked.

"Do what?"

"Make Braveheart like you."

"I don't know. Maybe he recognized a kindred soul."

"What do you mean?" Stephanie couldn't help but ask.

He shrugged. "It's nothing. I'm ready to go when you are."

She wanted to know more. He had said very little about himself since she'd picked him up. He talked. He was funny. Self-deprecating. But he didn't reveal much. He'd just said more in those few words than all those he'd uttered so far.

Her heart clenched, and she didn't welcome the feeling. She didn't want to know him better. He would soon be gone, and her life would return to normal.

Suddenly, normal didn't sound as good as it had pre-Clint.

Nonsense. She got to her feet. "Sure we can't help you with the dishes?"

"I have a system," Eve said. "You would just mess it up. And I expect Clint must be tired. He's only been out of the hospital a few days."

Her eyes twinkled, and Stephanie knew for certain she was trying to throw them together. They would have a discussion about that, but now she didn't have a choice without being churlish. She nodded.

Eve turned to Clint. "Would it be okay for me to stop over tomorrow? I have something I would like to discuss with you."

"Sure. Any time."

"About twelve thirty?"

He nodded.

"Good. And welcome to Covenant Falls. I'm delighted the cabin is being put to good use."

Stephanie found herself at the door with Clint close behind her. She'd seen a glint of matchmaking in her friend's eyes, and she was going to put an end to that. Fast.

But first she needed to drive Clint home.

They hadn't turned out of the driveway before she sensed Clint's gaze on her. She was, unfortunately, very aware of his presence. Too aware. The heat in the car was far greater than outside.

"I really like Eve," Clint said.

"Everyone likes Eve."

"And Josh," he said.

"Mmm," she murmured, not wanting to encourage him.

"And Braveheart."

She suspected now he was going to go through the entire Manning household.

She only nodded this time.

"And I like you," he added softly.

Her pulse quickened and heat flooded her—the same unwelcome warmth she'd felt earlier when his lips had touched hers. She felt it down to her toes. She sped up.

She didn't answer. She didn't know how. She had no quick quip this time. The words had been said softly and sounded as if he meant them. But words were easy.

He was silent the rest of the way. Did he feel rebuffed? Or had he said what he had to say or...?

She turned on the radio, to the country western station to fill the silence during the rest of the drive. But when she pulled up in front of the cabin, she relented. "I hope you like Covenant Falls."

He paused a few seconds before reaching for the door handle. "Thank you," he said, and the two words had none of the earlier teasing. It was said with feeling. She had been in the wrong again. Drat, but he was good at doing that.

He stepped out of the car. "Good night." He closed the door and limped toward the porch. She waited until he opened the door to the porch, then she stepped on the gas and drove away.

CLINT SPOTTED THE large box leaning against the front door of the cabin. He closed the screen door, unlocked the cabin door and carried the box inside.

He looked at the return address. One of his roommates from Ft. Hood. He opened the box. A guitar. He read the note. "Heard you lost your guitar in the crash. We took up a collection from all those you entertained and bought this at the pawn shop. It's not as good as the one you had, but, hey, every time you play it, think of us."

Clint removed it from the packaging and ran his fingers over the wood, then the strings. It was a damn good guitar, despite what the note said. It had scratches, but the sound was great, better than the one that disappeared after the crash. He wasn't a very good musician, but he could pick up tunes and melodies, and he was good enough for a room full of drunken soldiers back from deployment.

Most of all, he appreciated the gesture. The sender, Ted Endicott, was a chopper instructor and the only permanent resident of the house.

Clint played a few notes, a ballad, and then put it down. There was no one to play for.

He'd fought against the loneliness he'd felt since waking up in the hospital in Texas, far from his base in Kentucky. It had only deepened when he realized he was not going overseas with his unit, that he might never fly again. Everything important to him had died in that car.

He'd almost banished the loneliness for a few hours tonight. He had a lot in common with Josh, and he'd liked Eve tremendously. Stephanie made him feel alive again. And Braveheart... Braveheart had touched him. He sensed in the dog the fear and loneliness Clint tried to hide from everyone.

He put the guitar back in its case and checked his watch. It was ten, and he hadn't gotten much sleep the previous night. The pain had been too severe. He took off his sandals. His foot wasn't quite as swollen, or as discolored, but it still hurt when he put weight on it.

He would take a bath, soak the foot, then go to bed. He thought about tomorrow and made a mental list of things to do. It gave him more of a sense of purpose. He would finish his plan for the dock in the morning. Maybe he would try to walk into town and see what the hardware store had in stock. Something to do. He was not good at idleness. He'd always been active: training, always training, and sports. As great as the cabin was, he knew he had to make an effort to keep moving.

STEPHANIE WALKED HER two canine boarders longer than usual. She took them down Pine Street and found herself nearing the park bordering the lake on the east. She'd left Stryker and Sherry at home;

these two needed attention, and she'd taken her own dogs for walks before she had picked up Clint.

From the park, she saw the lights from the various homes along the lakefront. There was the barest of light filtering through the pines from the last cabin, the one where Clint lived.

She sat on one of the benches and considered the evening, and why Clint Morgan flustered her so. Her experience with men, thus far, had been disastrous. She had wed at seventeen to escape an abusive father, but was a widow within six months. During that time, she had taken a job as a vet tech. It was a move that probably saved her life.

She loved her job. Animals were simple. Treat them well, and they treated you well. She trusted them as she trusted few humans. Exceptions were Eve and Josh and a few other town residents whom she'd known for years.

She admitted it. She was a terrible judge of men. Her first husband was killed in a drug deal gone bad and the second had been an abuser whose charm died soon after the wedding vows.

And then Clint Morgan had come to town and kissed her, and she had melted. She wanted something she couldn't have.

The strength of that want was intense.

Lord knew he was attractive. That alone wouldn't have affected her like this. She knew how much ugliness good looks could hide. She had been blinded by it once. But there was something open about Clint.

She had watched him carefully when he spoke to Nick and touched the dogs. She'd searched for a sign of deviousness, of pretense. Instead, there had been a gentleness about him that completely undid her.

It didn't make any difference. She was never going to risk herself, or her practice, again. She had worked way too hard for her independence and self-respect. She wasn't about to throw it away for a stranger passing through.

"Come on, guys, let's go home. You can play with Stryker and Sherry for a while."

She let them play with her two dogs for thirty minutes, then put the two boarders in their run, made sure they had plenty of water and added a treat provided by their owner. They would be picked up tomorrow by their family.

She climbed the stairs to her apartment, Stryker and Sherry on her heels. She checked the phone for messages and stopped breathing for several seconds. A call from Boston. The name was "Unavailable." No message.

She was not going to call the number back. But she would ask a vet friend in Ohio to check out the number. She didn't want anything coming from her office or even from the state. At least her personal cell phone had not been called. Her clients had the number for emergencies, and she was never without it. It, too, was listed under the name of Langford Animal Practice. If anyone had thought that strange, they hadn't mentioned it.

Maybe the call was just a salesman, she told herself. Or a political survey. They often didn't leave names, just hung up when no one answered.

She took a hot bath, but rather than relaxing her, it brought back the heat that ran through her body when Clint had kissed her, her befuddlement at how much she enjoyed it. But then the kiss had been over. She'd expected some mention of it when she had driven him home, but there had been none.

Maybe he wanted to forget it as much as she did.

JOSH TURNED OFF the light and got into bed. He kissed Eve on her nose, then took more time with her mouth. "Love you," he said.

"Ditto," she replied. "I think tonight went well."

"Except Steph was as prickly as a cactus."

"That's because she likes him."

"You think?"

"She sure is trying to fight it, but she would have been a lot nicer if she didn't like him."

"That doesn't make sense."

"That's because you're a man."

He thought about that for a minute. "True. But if she's prickly because she likes him, why were you nice to me when we met? I was rude and…"

She put a finger to his lips. "Because I knew I liked you, and she doesn't know she likes him yet."

"Damn, woman, that really doesn't make sense."

Eve laughed. "I'm glad he wants to build a dock."

"I have a hunch it will be a good one."

"Why?"

"He showed me a couple of designs. He's been doing his homework."

She took his hand and held it tightly. "Did you see how Braveheart stayed with him?"

"Couldn't miss it. Nick was pointing it out every minute."

"Why do you think Braveheart responded the way he did?"

"I think Clint might be more wounded than he appears," he said. "Braveheart sensed that. Remember how he reacted to Amos?"

"And Amos to Braveheart. They both recognized the pain the other had."

Amos, lying in a dog bed next to them, stirred and wagged his tail at the sound of his name, then barked. "Go back to sleep," Josh ordered. "This is between my wife and me."

"You think he knew what we're saying."

"I wouldn't be surprised."

"I think I might do a little meddling," Eve said.

"I don't doubt it. Not for one nanosecond," he said, then kissed her. And more.

Minutes later, she asked, "What do you think about loaning Braveheart to him for a few days? He's probably lonely in the cabin."

Josh sighed. "He won't be alone for long, not if I know this town."

She gave him a disgusted look. "You know what I mean."

"Well, ask him."

"No, we have to give him a reason to take Braveheart. I think he's a lot like you. Doesn't like to think anyone thinks he needs something."

"That's convoluted."

"No, it isn't. He needs to feel needed. Just like you, although you wouldn't admit it." She stopped, then grinned. "Tell me, are all men so dense?"

"Are all women so meddlesome?"

"I hope so."

He sighed. "I'm sure you will come up with something. Poor Clint. And what about Nick? He won't want to give up Braveheart."

Eve waved a hand. "Temporarily only, and for a good cause. I think he'll approve. He really liked Clint."

"He likes everybody."

"True, but he particularly likes helicopter pilots."

"What about poor old grunts like me?"

"You're fishing for compliments," she said. "You know he adores you."

"What about you?"

She showed him exactly how much.

CHAPTER NINE

CLINT WAS READING when he heard the sound of tires on the gravel outside. Twelve thirty.

Eve Manning was right on time and he welcomed the break. He was getting damned tired of his own company.

He walked onto the porch and held the door open for her.

"Hi," she said. "We really enjoyed having you with us last night."

He didn't quite know what to say. He'd enjoyed it, as well, not only because he liked the Mannings, but because Stephanie had been there. "It was a great dinner," he finally said. "Thank you."

She wouldn't meet his eyes. Her fingers twitched. This did not fit her at all. "What can I do for you?" he finally said.

"I wonder if you could do us a favor," she said. "The plans for the dock are..."

"Not the dock. Josh is taking Nick on a camping trip tomorrow. They haven't been alone together much, and Nick used to go with his father..."

Clint didn't think he was going to like what was coming. She was too hesitant. It couldn't be good.

"Stephanie's leaving early tomorrow morning to conduct a search-and-rescue evaluation near Denver. She's taking Sherry, but is leaving the other dog, Stryker, with me." She hesitated, obviously reluctant to go on. "Well, Braveheart is afraid of him. I thought…hoped you could keep Braveheart this weekend. He really seemed to like you."

Clint's mouth fell open. *Him. A dog.* Hell, he didn't know anything about dogs.

"I know it's an imposition, but I'll bring food with him and all you need to do is keep his water fresh. He's housebroken and easy to look after. It's just I have so many animals already and can't give him the attention he needs."

That was certainly true, the part about so many already.

He couldn't say no. He owed the Mannings for use of the cabin, for their hospitality and open acceptance without asking questions. He thought about the sad-looking pit bull with the scars.

"Sure," he said.

"I just happened to bring him with me," she said.

Clint began to get suspicious. He certainly wasn't in a position to keep a dog. Not for more than a few days. He could do that, but if Eve Manning was expecting him to be a permanent owner, she could forget it. He couldn't take care of himself these days, much less a dog.

She was already at her pickup. She opened the door and pulled a reluctant Braveheart down with a leash. When the dog saw him, what was left of his tail did a timid wave.

"He'll probably just hide behind a sofa, but he's not afraid of you. You can't possibly know how rare that is," she said. "He needs to go out in the morning, afternoon and just before you go to bed. Cars scare him to death. In truth, nearly everything does, but he does seem to trust you…"

Her voice trailed off as he knelt and Braveheart came to him. Licked his hand. Clint felt oddly pleased that this timid dog trusted him. He rubbed the dog's ear because it seemed the right thing to do. The dog grinned at him, actually grinned.

"I'd better go," Eve said. "I have a meeting at city hall, then a lot of errands. Thanks a lot for taking him. He really is intimidated by Stryker's energy."

Clint just nodded as the mayor went back to the pickup and returned with a rather large bag of dog food, a water bowl and a leash. She also pulled out a big dog bed from the bed of the truck.

Clint's antenna went up a few more inches. Or was it feet?

Eve put everything on the porch. Clint suddenly remembered what Josh had said last night. *I did my damnedest to chase her off, but nothing worked. She's the most determined woman I ever met. And the kindest. Just try to say no to that combination.*

He was beginning to see what Josh meant.

CLINT WORKED ON the dock design until midafternoon then, stiff from sitting, he decided to walk Braveheart.

Knowing that Braveheart was fearful of most everything, he decided not to take him into town, which had been his intention before becoming a dog sitter. Instead, since his foot was much improved, he would walk down to the park, take a look around. He could use the fresh air and exercise.

There was no one on the road, nor in the park, but then it was midday on a school day. He found a seat at a picnic table, sat down and looked around. The park was filled with trees, their leaves changing from green to varying shades of scarlet and gold. A rich smoky aroma perfumed the air. Crystal-clear blue water lapped at a sandy beach. Playground swings swayed with the slight breeze. There were three structures in the park: a sprawling building with a sign declaring it the Covenant Falls Community Center, a pavilion with more picnic tables and a covered bandstand.

A monument was located at the entrance to the park. He rose to inspect it. A bronze soldier holding a World War II–era rifle stood above a metal scroll listing the town's fallen soldiers from the Civil War through the country's current engagement in Afghanistan. The total was a sizable number for a small town.

"You must be the veteran who just moved into Josh's cabin."

Clint spun around. He'd been so wrapped up in his own memories he hadn't noticed someone approaching him.

An older man in jeans and a blue shirt thrust out his hand. "I'm Bill Evans. I'm one of the councilmen, and I used to run the general store. I'm retired now, but I volunteer at the community center." He smiled. "Welcome to Covenant Falls."

"Thanks." Behind him, Braveheart whined softly.

"Sorry you had an unfortunate start here."

"You heard about the cow?" Of course he had. Everyone had. At least he didn't ask about the dog with him. Yet.

"Are you going to stay with us a while?"

"I'm not sure how long."

"I see you have Eve's pit bull."

"Just for a couple of days."

"Well, come over to the center Monday night. There's a room there reserved for our vets. I'm one. Vietnam. We play a little poker, drink a little beer. Some of the wives send snacks. There's a pool table that was donated and a television for when there's a game on."

"Is all that legal?"

"Hell, the ex-police chief, the current police chief, and the mayor's husband attend. Just penny-ante poker. No wives or husbands. Just vets. Chance to talk if you want to. Or not. If you just want to play poker, bring some change."

"Sounds good."

"You need anything, just let me know."

Clint watched him leave. How many times had that been said in this town?

"Come on, Braveheart," he said. "Let's go back and get something to eat. I have more work to do."

STEPHANIE WATCHED AS five dogs and their handlers/ trainees stood together Saturday morning, each handler with a different piece of clothing belonging to a volunteer "lost person."

At Stephanie's signal, they would give their dog the clothing to sniff, then send them in search of the owner of said clothes. Thank God for the volunteers who were "lost." They often spent hours waiting to be located. She always suggested they take a good book with them and, in cool weather, wear layers of clothing. They had left an hour earlier after being told to make it difficult. Go through a stream and don't leave anything on the trail.

Each "victim" was accompanied or followed part way by another volunteer who would then split off. The dog had to decide which person to follow.

At her signal, the five trainees allowed their dogs several minutes to sniff the clothing, then said, "Find." The dogs headed out, each owner trailing at the end of their lead. Like the "lost" volunteers, they had GPS units with them; Stephanie didn't want to lose either group.

This was Phase Five in certifying handler-and-dog teams. They had previously passed shorter tests.

First a short distance, then progressively longer ones. Now they had a two-mile search over rough terrain.

There were several breeds this time: two golden retrievers, a German shepherd, a giant schnauzer and a Labrador. When the last team was out of sight, Stephanie returned to where the other evaluators gathered. The day was an unusually fine one with clear skies and moderate temperatures. She would have preferred a rainy one for the test. It would have been more difficult. But it wasn't the end of training for these candidates. There was never an end to training. There were other evaluations in bad weather, courses in first aid, in canine first aid, area search, trailing, First Response Disaster, avalanche rescue, map reading, compass use, radio communication and more. Much more.

The problem now was the wait. Too much time to think. She had brought Sherry, who was sitting nicely with other evaluators, but she'd left Stryker, who wasn't sufficiently trained yet, with Eve.

Stephanie wasn't good at small talk, even if the conversation was about dogs. She was often too blunt. She didn't mean to be, but she always said what she thought, which was not always diplomatic. Case in point: Clint Morgan. She'd bristled with him from the first moment they met. She'd been rude, sarcastic and unsympathetic. But then he was a grown man. He didn't need sympathy.

Josh certainly hadn't. And neither, it seemed, did the newest resident in town.

She banished thoughts of Clint. She was tired. The clinic had been crammed with patients yesterday until 7:00 p.m., then she'd collapsed in bed. She hadn't been able to sleep and, even though she had known it wouldn't help her relax, she had watched several inane television shows before finally nodding off. She had awakened at 5:00 a.m. and driven three hours to the testing site. Dr. Langford would cover for her if there were any emergencies.

After this search was finished, there would be others for less-experienced handlers. Tonight she was holding a session on canine first aid. On Sunday, a physician was holding an all-day session on CPR and human first aid. She planned to stay for that, then drive home around dinnertime Sunday. It was a busy weekend, but she was doing something she loved.

But now Clint Morgan intruded on her thoughts. Especially that kiss at the corral. It had burned her to the core. Even now, frissons of heat ran down her spine as she replayed it. A sweet gentleness spiked with a sensuality that still made her ache. She'd never tasted them together. Did it have the same impact on him? Probably not.

What was he doing today? And dammit, why did she care? She didn't. He was just the newest puzzle in Covenant Falls. Why try to solve it when he didn't plan to stay? An hour passed. Then thirty more minutes. The first call came in.

Dave Elliott and his German shepherd had found

their victim. Three others then came in. The fifth handler and her dog, the giant schnauzer, had not reported in yet.

It was still too early to worry, and the handler, a young graduate student, was one of the best trainees. She had a phone and GPS and her victim might have been more creative than the others.

Then the call came. Handler and victim were coming in.

Every team had passed.

It was a good beginning of the day.

CHAPTER TEN

CLINT WOKE UP early Saturday to a loud snoring. For a moment, he almost believed he was back in Afghanistan sharing quarters with other chopper pilots.

Within seconds, he readjusted his thinking. The room was neatly painted with new blinds and tan curtains. This was not a crowded tent on a base in the middle of Afghanistan.

The snoring continued. Braveheart was sprawled out next to him. All four legs stretched out in different directions.

He couldn't help but smile. The dog had not left his side since Eve had brought him the previous day. Clint put his feet on the floor. Braveheart woke, startled, then gave him an intent stare as if trying to determine his intentions. Catching sight of the scars on the dog's body, Clint realized Braveheart had plenty of reasons to be fearful. An unfamiliar misting clouded his eyes.

Guys in his unit often fed stray dogs in Afghanistan, but he had stayed away from them. He feared getting attached, then having to leave it behind. He knew how that felt. He urged the other guys on, though, and often gave them his rations or money to buy food for them.

He wouldn't be keeping Braveheart, either. He was Nick's, and it would be incredibly stupid and destructive to get attached. He had sworn off stupid and destructive.

Still, he reached out and scratched the dog's stomach. Braveheart groaned with pleasure and licked his hand. Clint's heart melted.

He headed for the bathroom, Braveheart following him. "A little privacy, please," he told the dog and stepped into the shower. The plea had no effect, and the pit bull was still waiting when Clint stepped out of the shower.

"Okay, breakfast." He must be crazy talking to the dog as if he were a person. Crazy, or lonely as hell without his fellow soldiers. The previous day, he had fed and given the dog water. He had tried playing with him, but Braveheart would have nothing to do with chasing branches or the several dog toys Clint had found neatly placed in a cardboard box in the closet. The dog had just kept staring at him with big, brown eyes. It was unnerving. He had absolutely no idea why the dog seemed attached to him.

He also had absolutely no idea how he felt about it.

Clint made coffee and whipped up an omelet. It was one of the very few dishes he did well. He threw in ham, cheese and onions, and gave Braveheart a piece of cheese.

Or tried to.

Braveheart just looked at him.

"Okay," he said. "Dog food, then." He poured two cups of the dry food Eve had brought into a big bowl, then mixed the pieces of cheese into it, and set it down.

Braveheart sat, then sprawled in front of it, eyeing but not eating. It seemed like he was guarding it.

"You want one of my famous omelets, instead?" Clint asked, flipping it over. He added more cheese, then expertly scooped a quarter of it up and added it to Braveheart's dog food. "Since you're only going to be here a few days, I suppose it's okay. Kinda like me going to a good restaurant once in a while.

Braveheart sniffed it, then started eating.

"A dog with a good palate," Clint observed. "You were holding out for something better, huh."

Braveheart waved his stubby tail as he finished the omelet and started on the rest of the food.

"Or maybe not?" Clint said as the dog food disappeared as rapidly as the omelet had. Apparently, the dog wanted dessert first.

He must be nuts talking to a dog.

Clint transferred the rest of the omelet onto his plate and sat at the table. Braveheart stopped eating and looked plaintively up at him.

"Sorry, this is for me."

He poured himself a cup of coffee, ate the omelet, then made a list of things to do. He would phone in the list of dock materials to the hardware store to find out what they had and didn't have. But first he needed to know more about the lake's bottom.

He quickly washed the dishes, dressed in jeans and a pullover shirt. He rolled up the jeans above his knees, then hunted through the house for a long, straight stick. No luck. He went outside, Braveheart trailing behind, and finally found a reasonably straight branch that had broken off a large tree.

Then he went down to the lake and stepped into the water. Freezing, but he waded up to his knees, pushing the stick down as far as it would go. The lake bottom was sandy and seemed free of rock. The stick went fairly deep so he knew he would need footings. He returned to dry land, where Braveheart waited. "Coward," he said. The dog wagged his stub of a tail.

Clint made a mental note to ask the owner of the hardware store what he would recommend for the footings. This afternoon he would go and get prices for everything. He probably needed to cut the grass, too.

He and Braveheart walked back to the cabin where he washed and dried his mud-clad, chilled legs. However, it was the kind of beautiful morning that made birds sing with more sweetness. A fresh cool breeze swept in from the lake, and the sky was as pure a blue as he'd ever seen. Not a cloud in sight.

He poured another cup of coffee, grabbed the guitar and ambled onto the porch. He strummed several notes, then played one of his favorite melodies. Braveheart proved to be a noncritical audience.

There was a sense of peace here that encouraged sloth-like behavior. He had always been in a hurry, first to make the grades to get into the army, then to get into the helicopter training program, then to be the best he could be.

Time to smell the roses.

Or the scent of pines. He'd never had that time, never wanted to have it. And yet, it was pleasant. For a while.

A short while.

He glanced at his watch. Only 1:00 p.m. Might as well trek into town now and talk to the hardware store owner, discuss the list of materials with him.

"What about you, Braveheart? Do you want to go into town?" Clint was still bewildered at Braveheart's attachment to him, especially since everyone said the dog rarely responded to anyone other than Nick. But he was appreciative for the company. He was aware of the various programs to match shelter dogs with vets, and now he was beginning to understand why.

When a person has little or no family, the army *becomes* family. It had for Clint. Now there was a huge void in his life. It felt like he'd lost his identity. And after nearly two decades of owning that identity, it was difficult to build a new one.

"Is that your problem, Braveheart? You don't know where you belong? Damn but that name is too long. I'm going to shorten it to Bart. Just between you and me. Okay?"

The dog licked Clint's hand.

"Tell you what, Bart, I'm going to walk to town, reconnoiter it. Maybe try that diner Josh told me about. Talk to the hardware guy. Look around a bit. Do you want to go?"

Braveheart, alias Bart, tipped his head as if trying to figure out what Clint said and if he should answer.

"Okay, we'll try it. If you get worried, we'll come back. Is that good for you?"

Clint slipped into a dry pair of jeans, figuring he would be less conspicuous in jeans rather than slacks. He ran a comb through his hair. He needed a haircut. Maybe next week. No rush. No rush for anything.

That was damned depressing. He pocketed the small bottle of pills, then picked up the dog leash.

"Come on, Bart." The name was close enough to Braveheart that the dog should understand.

Bart stood and waited patiently while he attached the leash.

"Off on a mission," he said.

Bart seemed amenable.

Clint took that as approval.

IT WAS AN easy walk for someone army-trained even with his injured foot. Although a chopper pilot, there was always the prospect of being shot down and having to make his way to safety. He'd stayed in shape and could easily walk twenty miles or more, even after five months off duty.

He was not made for inactivity. The months of his recuperation and stay in the hospital had worn on him and the past few days of staying off his foot had increased his need for exercise.

His first stop was the hardware store.

The owner welcomed him with a broad smile. "I'm Calvin Wilson. Great to have you here in Covenant Falls. Josh said you would be coming in about the dock. He's kept me in business for the last few months." He grinned.

Clint nodded. "Clint Morgan. I made a list of what I think is needed for a four-foot wide, twelve-foot-long dock." He handed the list to Wilson who scanned it.

"Good stuff," Calvin said. "I know Josh had been planning to add a dock, but with the wedding and a new family and all, it got relegated to last place. The bottom of the lake is mainly sandy, which is good for a fixed dock. The pilings will need to be about six feet into the sand. I have a water pump and hoses you can borrow to jet water from the holes. But you'll need help. Can't do it alone."

"When can you have the materials?"

"You need chemically treated pilings. I don't have any. It will take several days for delivery. They can be here next Friday if you give me the go-ahead Monday. I can get some guys to help you." He handed Clint a cost estimate. The prices were more than fair. "Thanks," he said. "I'll clear it with Josh on Monday."

He wandered down the street. Bart stayed next to him, but hid behind him when anyone stopped to say hello, which almost the entire town did. He was beginning to understand what Stephanie had meant about the town.

When he reached Maude's, a tall, well-fleshed older woman, stepped out. "You must be the fellow staying in Josh's place. I'm Maude. Come on in and have a piece of cake. We're famous for our lemon cake."

"I have Eve's dog with me."

"One of them, anyway," she said. "I'm surprised you have Braveheart. He's usually…timid."

"Mrs. Manning asked me to look after him this weekend. Josh and Nick were going camping."

"Would say come on in anyway, but I'm nearly full. Stay here, and I'll bring you several slices of cake to take home."

Two minutes later, he was walking back to the cabin with a box clutched in his hands. He would gain twenty pounds if he stayed in this town long. He passed Stephanie's office. A sign on the door stated "Closed through Sunday. Call Dr. Tom Langford in case of an emergency." There was a number attached.

He continued on past a real estate and insurance company, then a grocery store. If Bart wasn't with him, he would have gone inside, though he still had more food than he needed at the cabin. Eve had done a great job in stocking it.

Several more people stopped to welcome him. The nurse from the doctor's office crossed the street. "Looks like you've recuperated."

"Good as ever," he replied. "However, I'm staying away from cows."

She grinned. "The doctor will be glad to hear it. How do you like Covenant Falls so far?"

"Haven't had time to see much."

"Seen our falls yet?"

"No."

"Someone should take you there. You should ask Stephanie."

"I'll do that," he said. He was beginning to think there was a conspiracy to throw Stephanie at him or him at Stephanie. It seemed to include everyone but Stephanie.

"That's Braveheart," she added in an almost accusing voice. It seemed everyone knew Braveheart, as well as the fact he was staying in Josh's cabin.

"So it is," he said without elaborating again. And then he relented. "I have temporary custody."

She tipped her head in question.

Clint remembered what Josh had told him about the town. Incredibly nosy. He had received confirmation today.

"I'll tell you, just you," he said in a low conspiratorial voice. "Josh and his boy went camping. Stephanie left her dog with Eve while she's somewhere doing search-and-rescue exercises, and Eve said she needed help. Now," he said, "I think something else might be afoot, but I haven't a clue what it might be."

The nurse chuckled. "I wouldn't be surprised," she said. "Well, I have to get back to the office, but I'm glad to see you up and walking."

How long would it take for his conspiracy theory to circle around town? He smiled and continued on. He passed the drug store and looked across at the city hall. Two police cars were parked in front. Why did a town this size have its own police department? Crime couldn't be rampant in a town called Covenant Falls.

A few minutes later, he met two men who welcomed him and a young lady who tried to flirt with him. "I'm Beth," she said. "Beth Malloy. I work for Stephanie as her vet tech." She glanced at the dog. "That's Braveheart," she said.

For all the attention Clint was getting, he might as well be leading an elephant down the road rather than a shy dog. "It is," he admitted.

"But he won't go with anyone but Eve and Nick. I can't..." She stopped suddenly, apparently afraid of admitting a failure in the canine area.

"I seem to be the exception."

"Wow."

Wow, indeed, he thought. He still didn't know how or why he had gotten roped into this, and why it seemed to be the most interesting news in Covenant Falls. Except, maybe, that he had been kicked by a cow.

"Anyway, welcome to town," she said. "It's nice to have someone new here. I've been meaning to bring over some cookies."

He didn't know what to say except maybe she should ask her folks first, but that might be hurtful. She was way too young for him. Pretty but young. Not-past-twenty young.

He held out the box. "I already have more than I can possibly eat," he said. "Maude just gave me this cake. Mrs. Byars brought over some brownies. Some cookies landed on my doorstep. Your mayor filled my fridge with all kinds of food. But thank you for the thought," he added gently. "And thank you for the welcome."

"Is Braveheart going to stay with you?"

"No. No. Just today and tomorrow." He suspected now that Eve feared he might be lonely. She was right. But it was something he would have to get used to. And it was no one's fault except his own.

Braveheart—no, Bart—nudged him. "It's time to go, but it was nice meeting you, Beth. Give my best to Stephanie when you see her. You might tell her my foot has healed."

"I heard. Not from Stephanie. She doesn't say anything about anyone, but…"

"It's all over town," he finished for her. He didn't add he already knew that.

"I can drive you to the cabin," she offered.

"Thanks, but I really need to walk and so does Braveheart."

She nodded, and he turned and headed in the direction of the cabin again.

His pace quickened. He'd tired of being the center of interest. And community interest was not just centered on him, but also on poor Bart. Did everyone know that much about every one of Eve's dogs? Josh had warned him, and Stephanie had certainly hinted at it, but no way had he figured interest would be this intense. Of course, part of it was the dog. He couldn't believe the dog preferred the name Braveheart, as well-intentioned as the naming might have been, to Bart. He chuckled. Apparently, Braveheart was as notorious as he was. Why? Who knew? He didn't know much about small towns. He'd been born in Chicago, and spent his first eight years there before being shipped off to boarding schools.

Now he had a lot of questions about Covenant Falls. Why hadn't it grown when it had so much natural beauty? Why did Stephanie move to the middle of nowhere and keep the former vet's name for her practice? And, most of all, why did he want to know, when he was staying only a short time? A few weeks at most. He couldn't live off someone else indefinitely.

It was that pesky curiosity of his. It always got him in trouble.

He was hailed by several residents of Lake Road as he neared the cabin. He returned the waves. Mrs. Byars was sitting on her porch. An older man sat next to her, a cane at his side. A romance there, maybe.

There were several fishing boats on the lake. He thought about calling out, asking about the fishing. But he didn't want to have the same conversation he'd had several times in town. Bart needed his refuge, and he wanted to taste the cake, to determine for himself how good Maude's Diner really was.

He opened the screen door to the porch and unlocked the cabin door. Bart dashed directly to his water dish, then went to the window where Clint had placed the dog bed. He sprawled in it and stared outside.

"Looking for Nick?" Clint asked. The dog stared back at him.

Sighing, he peeked into the box Maude had given him. There was at least a third of an entire cake in it. He cut a large slice for himself and a tiny one for Bart. He wasn't sure it was good for the dog, but just a bite shouldn't hurt him. Bart licked Clint's hand in appreciation and quickly disposed of the treat. Clint took his slice and went outside to the swing. And, yes, the cake was as good as advertised. He went back inside and got a second piece. Bart followed him back to the porch.

It was good having the dog with him. Company with few complications and fewer demands. He scratched Bart's ears and was rewarded with a moist kiss on his hand. It was going to be hard to see him go. He was startled at how hard.

CHAPTER ELEVEN

STEPHANIE TOOK A hot shower in her hotel room and fell into bed late Saturday night. She was beyond tired. Not getting any sleep last night hadn't helped, and the session tonight on canine first aid lasted far longer than she'd intended. The handlers were attentive and eager for as much information as she could give them.

That was good. The bond between handler and dog was close. Absolute trust was essential. The handlers here, she thought, had what it took to be in search and rescue.

She scratched Sherry who promptly turned over on her back and waited for a tummy rub. Stephanie hoped Stryker was behaving himself at Eve's house. There was no one she trusted more to take care of the dog.

She read for a few moments. It usually helped when she was too tired to sleep. The words blurred together. The earlier, anonymous phone call haunted her. She'd called her friend George and asked him to check it out. He said he would and told her then that Mark's current wife was divorcing him. Was that why someone from Boston had called?

And then there was Clint Morgan. His face wouldn't disappear in the night. He made her laugh. His quirky humor had affected Eve and Josh, too. She knew they liked him, and he had so easily made himself at home.

Nick had been won over also, but that was to be expected. He was only ten and liked nearly everyone. He practically worshipped his new dad, and Clint was a veteran like him. Not only a veteran but a helicopter pilot. Braveheart's show of support had probably only added to his hero worship.

But she was not ten years old and should know better. She thought of Rick, her first boyfriend and husband. He'd been the bad boy every girl thought she could tame. All he needed was a good woman. *Wrong.* Then there was the disastrous second marriage.

At least she'd had some sweet memories of the first.

And now her nice, uncomplicated, organized world had been turned upside down in the past few days, first by her reactions to Clint Morgan, then the phone call that brought back all those feelings of helplessness and fear.

Everyone couldn't be wrong about Clint, especially Josh who was skeptical of people in general. But then, half of Boston thought Mark a saint. He gave to good causes, was a patron of the symphony, a big donor to political figures. However, no one knew what occurred inside his expensive, impeccably neat house. She didn't know anything about the wife who was now divorcing him, but she had to think he was trying to destroy her, as he had tried to do with Stephanie.

She tried willing herself to sleep. She had a full morning of additional evaluations, these ones shorter in length for less-experienced handlers and dogs, then she wanted to attend the first-aid session.

The task, though, would be almost as difficult: victims were hidden in caves, barrels and holes to make it difficult for the dogs.

Then she would head back home with an equal amount of dread and anticipation that she couldn't quite tamp down.

Drat it. Sleep continued to elude her. Images of two men dominated her mind. She gave up, picked up the book again. A romantic suspense. The heroine needed to find money stolen by her dead husband or her kidnapped son would die. She had thought her husband died in an accident, only to find her foundation crumbling beneath her when, instead, she discovered he'd been a thief and had been murdered.

The story hit close to home, but at least this fictional heroine would win in the end.

Sunday morning

CLINT ROSE WITH the sun. Sometime during the night, Bart had sidled his way up onto the bed again and was snoring.

"Okay, feel at home," Clint said to the sleeping dog.

He didn't know whether it was allowed at the Manning house or not. He'd never shared a bed with a dog before and found it strangely comforting. He was no longer alone. For a brief time, anyway. It was pretty pitiful that the void was filled by a dog.

He got out of bed. He'd slept unusually well. Maybe it was the fresh air, or maybe the long walk, or maybe Bart. The more he looked at the dog, the more he felt Bart was just the right name for him. He wasn't the courageous Scottish hero, and a name wouldn't change that, although Clint understood the sentiment behind it.

Bart was just a dog trying to adjust to a life without violence, pain and fear. Much like some people. And it wasn't easy for a human who at least knew some of the whys. A well of empathy filled him. He gently rubbed the dog's ears, waking him. Bart groaned with pleasure. Then he licked Clint's hands, and Clint felt he'd just been given a trophy.

"Come on, Lazybones," he said. "We're going for another walk this morning. We are going to attack that mountain behind us. Your Josh said it's safe enough if I'm careful, and I have you for assistance."

He fixed breakfast for both of them. An omelet for him. Dog food topped with an egg for Bart. He was halfway finished when Eve called with an invitation to dinner with her in-laws. "You'll like them. He's the town pharmacist and owns the drug store.

Mom's the one who made the strawberry pie. I expect she'll bring something. She always does. It will just be the four of us. Pot roast."

Home-cooked food. Sounded great, and he was tiring of his own company. But he didn't want to give up Bart. Not yet.

"What about Ba...Braveheart?"

"Why don't you bring him with you? How is he doing?"

"Making himself at home. He's eating good." Damn, he was going to miss the dog.

"Good. I'll see you in a few hours. We'll send someone to pick you up. Oh, and it's definitely casual dress."

"Looks like we have an invitation," he told Bart who tipped his head in question. "Of course, it's your home so you won't be a guest."

He took another swig of coffee. "Let's go exploring," he said.

He got the leash, and Bart stood still while he attached it. Then he filled a large travel cup with the rest of the coffee and headed toward the mountain. It was early Sunday, but a couple of men were already fishing from a row boat. He returned their wave and started up the path that wound its way up the small mountain that led to larger ones.

Aspen leaves were turning to gold, and although the morning was warm, a breeze made the walk more than tolerable. With Bart at his side, he followed the path until he reached the lookout Josh had mentioned and he gazed down over the valley below. The houses were miniature from this view. He saw several church spires. The streets were nearly empty. A pretty, peaceful town, the kind that were in old movies.

Before coming to Covenant Falls, he hadn't known they still existed.

He sat on a rock and finished his coffee. What in the hell was he doing here? He didn't fit in. He'd never fit into anything but the army. Band of brothers. They had that right. God, how he missed them.

He waited until he heard church bells, then started down. He would read for a while, then change clothes and wait for his ride.

It was about thirty minutes after four when a silver car turned into the driveway. Clint was waiting on the porch, strumming the guitar. Bart was still his shadow, reluctant to leave him for a moment.

"Come with me," he said to Bart as he stood, tucked the guitar inside the cabin, locked the front door and opened the screen door. Maybe it was a good thing Bart was going home. He was getting altogether too attached to the dog.

The man got out of the driver's seat, approached and grasped his hand. "I'm Jim Douglas, the pharmacist in town. Eve was married to my son, and my wife and I consider her our daughter. Glad to meet you, son. Welcome to Covenant Falls."

"Thank you, sir. I'm Clint Morgan."

"I hear Josh has already put you to work, and I

see Eve foisted Braveheart on you. Beware of my daughter-in-law," he said with a huge, affectionate grin. "She's very good at snaring helpless victims in her causes."

Clint nodded. "I'm discovering that, but maybe you're wrong about Braveheart. Eve said it's time for him to go home."

"I'm rather shocked she let you have him even for a couple of days. She's very protective of Braveheart. She's the one who found him nearly dead." He held the car's back door open for Braveheart so he could jump inside. "He sure seems to have taken to you."

"We kinda took to each other."

"You a dog person, then?" Jim Douglas asked as started the car.

"I guess I'm a Bart person."

"Bart?"

Clint thought fast. "Nickname. Just dropped the middle between 'B' and 'art.'"

"Bart, huh? I like it. Don't know if Nick will, though. He thought up the name."

"I hear he went camping."

"He's been wanting to go since Josh first arrived here. He's a Boy Scout and really missed doing things with dads like the other kids. Now he can brag about going camping with an Army Ranger."

"He's a lucky kid." Clint meant it. When he was eight, he had wanted nothing more than to be a Scout and go camping with his father. Never happened.

In minutes, they were at the Manning home. Eve

came out to meet them. "I'm so glad you could come," she said. "Come meet my mother-in-law. She took over the kitchen."

Clint opened the backseat for Bart who stepped down hesitantly. He walked over to Eve and sniffed her outstretched hand, then returned to Clint's side.

Her eyes widened, then she gave him a smile that belied her next words. "I might sue you for alienation of affections. What did you do to Braveheart?"

"Bart," corrected her father-in-law and the dog looked up at the sound of his name. "Mr. Morgan here shortened the name. It fits him."

Clint shrugged. "It just kinda slipped out."

"Whatever you did or said, it did wonders. I haven't seen him this…content. He's even smiling."

"He's a good dog," Clint said.

"Well, come on in. Dinner's nearly ready."

When he entered, the other dogs, including Stephanie's other dog, Stryker, greeted him as a long-lost friend. Oddly, Braveheart seemed to have no problem with Stryker. Clint thought Eve had left Bart with him because he was afraid of the other dog. He decided not to say anything.

The pot roast practically fell apart, and Clint could have eaten the entire bowl of gravy on his own. Instead, he limited himself to a huge portion over mashed potatoes.

Conversation was good, too. He liked Abby, Eve's former mother-in-law, or were in-laws still in-laws after the death of a spouse? It really didn't matter because the affection between the three of them was very real. Jim Douglas regaled him with stories about Covenant Falls and how it was founded in the mid-1850s by a Scottish trader. Then he turned to local politics. Eve had just been re-elected mayor, Jim said with as much pride as if Eve were his own birth daughter. Clint envied their closeness.

"And your family?" Jim asked.

"Scattered," he said to avoid any other questions.

There was another pie, this time filled with chocolate that melted in his mouth. But it was the warmth around the table that touched Clint, that made him ache for what he'd missed.

"We have to go," Jim said regretfully. "I have to go to the store and do some paperwork. Clint, I'll take you home."

"You two go on," Eve said. "I'll drive him home."

"The dishes," Abby protested.

"Clint can help me with them."

The older couple left, and Clint and Eve worked together as if he'd known her for a long time. "I noticed," she said, "that Brave—*Bart* hasn't left your side."

"We kinda understand each other," he said as he dried the last dish.

"I noticed. I don't think his gaze has left you since you two came inside. I think he's afraid you're going to leave him."

"This is his home."

"Oh, he likes us. But dogs pick their own person

and sometimes there's nothing you can do to change that. It's obvious he's picked you."

"He's Nick's dog."

"He's *one* of Nick's dogs. The thing about Nick is he has the biggest heart I know. He wants everyone to be happy."

"I'm in no position to adopt a dog," he protested. But that wasn't the real reason. The real reason *was* Nick. What kind of man takes a boy's dog?

"Well, keep him overnight," she said. "He's not going to let you go, not if he has any say in it. Maybe he'll come home tomorrow with Nick here."

He knew he should say no. He also knew he couldn't.

A CALL CAME Sunday afternoon as Stephanie was loading her car for the drive back to Covenant Falls. It was on her cell phone, and when she saw the number, she answered immediately.

"I asked a detective friend to check on the number," George said. "It came from an attorney's office in Boston. Name of Matthews and Garland. It's a small firm, not one I would expect your ex-husband to use. My source checked further and found out that they're the attorneys for Townsend's wife."

"Thanks," she said. "I owe ya."

"You pulled me through veterinarian school. You don't owe me a thing. Let me know if you need any additional help."

"Say hi to Sandy for me. And Teddy."

"Theodore. He insists on Theodore now. Says Teddy sounds too much like a bear. He's seven going on eighteen."

She laughed. "Just think, you're almost escaping the terrible teen years."

"You have a point. Keep me posted."

She hung up. She suspected now the new wife's attorney might be having problems with Mark and hoped they could get some ammunition from her.

No one had listened to her before. There was no reason to think they would now. Except now there were two of them, not just one. But she had fought hard to get loose from Mark's tentacles and she wasn't going to offer herself up to his machinations again.

She would continue to ignore calls from that number and, for that matter, from any area code in Massachusetts unless she knew it had something to do with her practice. It might be burying her head in the sand, but so be it. She had buried those five miserable years—three as Mark's wife and two recuperating—deep inside.

Instead she concentrated on the weekend. It had been a good one, spent with people who loved dogs and wanted to make a difference. The evaluations had certified four of the five in the final phase of training. The fifth handler had been very close. The dog just needed a bit more work.

She had a real sense of accomplishment, something no one could take away. Her practice gave her a livelihood, and she loved the animals under her care, but search and rescue filled a deep emotional need. Nothing was as satisfying, or empowering, as finding a lost and endangered child or adult. Sherry felt it, as well. She always had a huge grin on her face as she accepted thanks from a grateful parent, relative or friend.

Stephanie was halfway home when she saw a puppy huddling on the side of the road. The traffic wasn't that heavy on a late Sunday afternoon and she pulled to a stop on the side of the road. It was always risky trying to rescue a dog this way. Too many times, a scared animal ran into traffic to escape a new threat.

She reached in a package of dog treats she always carried with her for her own dogs and for rescues like this. She took out a handful and very slowly approached the dog. She threw a tidbit on the ground. It was not so far as to hit the dog, but close enough the dog could smell it and hopefully recognize it as food.

After a moment of indecision, the puppy approached the treat and gobbled it down. She threw another a bit closer, tempting the puppy to come nearer. Then she sat on the ground and held out a treat in her hand.

The puppy paused, then came closer, sniffed her hand and gingerly took the treat.

After it finished, it gazed at her with big puppy eyes. It was a small, still-growing, nondescript, Heinz 57 dog. Maybe four months old. It was very thin, and there was no collar. Dumped, no doubt, by someone who had found a dog was more trouble than they had expected. She talked to it in a soothing voice and waited until it took another step toward her and let her touch her.

She gathered the pup in her arms and carried it to the van. She let Sherry sniff her, then settled her down on a blanket in back of the seat. The dog shivered with fear. She released the canine seat belt, and Sherry rose from the front right seat and lay next to the puppy, licking its face.

Stephanie started the van. The last thing she needed now was another dog, but no way could she leave it on the road to starve or get hit by a car. She doubted whether she could foist her on Eve, who had already adopted two of her finds. She should be able to find someone.

She was a pretty dog, kind of like a female Benji with thick, bristly hair. A bath would determine her color, although it looked a mixture of tan and black. She would give the pup a bath and shots and shop around for a family. Something to keep her mind off her other problems.

Stephanie arrived home an hour and a half later. The little dog was still shivering as she carried her into the clinic and conducted tests for heartworm and other diseases. Luckily, none were positive. Next came a flea bath. She would save the shots for tomorrow. Let her get settled. Stephanie found a collar that would fit, and took her outside, encouraging her when she went about her business.

The puppy followed her as she found a wire kennel and carried it upstairs to her apartment. She reached the top and looked back. The pup stood at the foot of the stairs bewildered. So it hadn't lived in a home with stairs, or perhaps it had been a yard dog.

Sherry, forever the caretaker, looked on with concern, then bounced up the stairs and stared back at the puppy, obviously expecting the dog to follow her example.

The dog stayed stubbornly at the bottom.

She could carry her up, but Stephanie didn't want to do that. She wanted to know how quickly the dog learned.

She went back down the stairs and sat on the lower step, urging the dog to jump to the second step, then the third. She moved up with the dog. The last two steps were taken with more confidence. She was a smart little dog.

She temporarily called her Lulu. The name would do until she found her a family. Lulu followed her into the bedroom as Stephanie placed papers on the bottom of a kennel, then added a soft blanket. She then went into the kitchen to get the three of them supper.

The dog gulped down a small bowl of dog food. So did Sherry who also kept an eye on what she obviously considered her new charge. Stephanie wondered how Stryker would react to having a new dog in the apartment. Usually, he was good with other animals. She would know tomorrow when she picked him up from Eve's.

She fixed herself a fat sandwich and allowed herself a glass of red wine.

Then she checked the practice's phone. Another call from Boston. This time, there was a message. She hesitated before clicking the play button, then decided reality was better than her imagination. She pressed the button.

"Dr. Phillips. I'm David Matthews, an attorney in Boston. I represent Susan Townsend, the wife of Mark Townsend. If you are the former Stephanie Roberts Townsend, we would very much like to talk to you." He concluded with a phone number.

She erased the message. She had no intention of returning the call or ever getting involved with Mark Townsend again. Not in any way.

She had a second glass of wine. She seldom did that, particularly at night. Sherry, detecting that something was amiss, hovered near her while she undressed and put on an old oversize T-shirt.

"Okay, Lulu, bedtime," she said as she picked up the newcomer. She cuddled her for a moment. "You're okay now," she said softly, then put her in the kennel beside her bed.

The newcomer whimpered for a few minutes, then settled down and went to sleep.

Lucky dog. She knew *she* wouldn't get any sleep. Not tonight. If she didn't reply to the phone call, what would David Matthews do? Would he try to track her down here? If so, it would be for nothing. Still, she wondered about Susan Townsend. What had Mark done to her? What had he done to other women?

She turned out the light. It was past midnight, and she had appointments beginning at 8:00 a.m.

Tomorrow will be a regular day. A normal day.

CLINT TOOK BART up the mountain again to watch the sun go down. It was spectacular as scarlet, crimson and gold stretched across the sky before fading into a rich dark blue. To the west, the sun sank below a snowcapped peak.

Serene was the word. Peaceful. He knew, though, he couldn't linger on the mountain. He needed to get down while there was still some light.

As he and Bart descended, they bumped into a young couple, maybe seventeen, on the way up. They looked startled to find him, then the boy said, "You must be that new vet in Josh's cabin."

Clint was mentally counting the times he'd heard that. "Guilty," he said. He thought this was the tenth time, or maybe the eleventh. Had Josh Manning ever become used to the curiosity syndrome of Covenant Falls? They did look curiously at Bart, but evidently didn't know as much about the dog's background as other residents did.

When Clint reached the cabin, he removed his shoes, grabbed a soda and his guitar and went out to the porch. He was hooked on the smell of pine and the million stars lighting the evening sky. He started playing a melody that was haunting him. Maybe because it made him think of Stephanie and the mystery around her. She was so many different people: tender with animals, a good friend to Josh and Eve, committed to helping people yet so self-contained. She had a great grin when she allowed herself to show it. But it wasn't often with him. And he didn't know why.

Bart nudged him, and Clint put the guitar down and rubbed the dog's ears. He knew he shouldn't, but he couldn't stop himself. He liked hearing the deep rumbling in Bart's throat. And he probably shouldn't be calling the dog Bart. He didn't want to confuse him. But, damn it, he thought of him as Bart. He looked like a Bart.

He was going to miss him. It was amazing how attached he'd become to the dog in just three days. But there it was. Maybe it was his need for company. Any company.

Rationalization did not help. Maybe he would get a dog of his own, although part of his attachment to Bart was the fact that Bart was attached to him. The pit bull had accepted him unconditionally. He hadn't cared that Clint had made the world's dumbest mistake, that he didn't feel whole, that the future he'd planned was gone. He was just happy to lie next to him.

Clint knew, though, that it shouldn't be enough for him. He needed to get his act together.

He took the guitar inside and grabbed a mystery book off the shelf. He had nearly a week before the dock materials would arrive. He started to read, but his thoughts kept going back to Stephanie and how the sparks flew in those pretty eyes when he baited her.

He read for an hour with Bart keeping watch next to him. He was in the third chapter when his cell rang. He looked at the name listed. *Eve Manning.*

He answered.

"Hi," Eve said in her cheerful voice.

"Hey, what's up?"

"I just got a call from Josh. He and Nick are on their way back from camping. Josh wants to get together with you about the dock. Is there a good time tomorrow?"

"Whatever is good for Josh."

"Let's say around ten. If it changes, he'll call you in the morning."

"Sounds good," he said and hung up. Then he looked at the dog. With Nick coming home, Bart would be leaving. "I'll miss you."

Bart gave him that steady, earnest look, his eyes intent on communicating. Clint went inside and turned on the lights. There was a small television in the corner, and a satellite dish in back, but he'd never been much of a watcher except for sports, and even then he would rather participate than watch.

He'd always preferred a softball game with his buddies, or a game of poker or darts. He opened his laptop and checked email.

There were five messages from his buddies in Afghanistan. No casualties, but a close call. There were rumors they would be pulled out soon. The deployment was coming to an end, and the army would be downsized. Several members of his unit feared they would lose their planned career in the army. Some were already contacting possible employers.

He emailed them back, thanking them for the guitar. Had a new bed companion last night, he wrote. No, it's not what you think. I didn't get lucky. It's a seventy-pound pit bull I'm keeping for the guy whose cabin I'm using. It's a great cabin with mountains on the doorstep. I don't know how long I'll be here. Building a dock for the owner, then who knows. Kick their ass out there!

He sent it, read some of the online news sites, but became depressed.

Bart whined.

"Okay, out you go, then bed and a book."

Bart whined again, and Clint felt the first sudden, sharp pain of a headache.

Bart lifted a paw and touched his knee in some kind of entreaty. Clint wished he spoke pit bull, but he didn't. He didn't know canine-speak at all. "Sorry, guy," he said. "I don't have a clue what you want."

Obviously frustrated, Bart pawed at him again.

He leaned down to rub Bart's ears, but it didn't stop the dog's nervous, heavy breathing, nor the insistent pawing on his lap.

Clint was hit by a headache then, the sudden sharp pain spreading throughout his head. The pills were in his pocket. He took one and swallowed the rest of the soda. The earlier he took the pill, the better the result.

He tried to breathe slowly as the pain deepened. Bart whined again beside him. Clint understood. Bart had sensed the attack. Somehow he had known before it hit.

"Off to bed," he said. He stood, swayed. Damn. Two attacks close together. Wasn't good.

He made his way into the bedroom, stripped to his Skivvies and lay down, letting the pill work.

Bart came to the edge of the bed and stared at him with worry in his eyes.

"Come on up," he invited, and Bart awkwardly jumped onto the bed and snuggled next to him as if his proximity would help. He swiped a wet tongue along his arm.

Clint rubbed Bart's stomach in return. The dog was a pitiful specimen with all his scars and insecurities. But, damn, Clint's heart melted when he looked at him.

And tonight, at least, he wouldn't be alone.

CHAPTER TWELVE

STEPHANIE WOKE WITH a start and glanced at the clock. Later than she intended. She had a very crowded schedule since she hadn't had her usual Saturday hours.

She'd finally gone to sleep last night, but not easily. And the only reason she had any at all was the fact she'd had damned little the last two nights. She felt hungover, but not from drink. The sense of dread hadn't gone away since that last phone call.

Sherry jumped off the bed, and Lulu made plaintive little cries.

"It's okay," she told the pup. "I'll take you outside in just a few minutes."

She slipped on a pair of jeans, a bra, a T-shirt and a white professional coat. Then she attacked the curly mess she called hair. She ran a brush through it, pulled it back and secured it with a rubber band. No one was coming today to see how she looked.

She looked at the clock again. Beth should already be downstairs and making coffee. Her first appointment was in twenty minutes. Mostly shots this morning. Annual exams. Follow-up appointments. She had several scheduled spays this afternoon.

She was lucky to have Dr. Langford as a backup when she was called for a rescue or was otherwise unavailable. But he'd earned his retirement, and she hesitated to call on him unless absolutely necessary or she needed his advice on a medical problem. Still she couldn't do her rescue work without him.

She picked up Lulu. She had just a few minutes to get the two dogs outside in the backyard. She would keep Sherry with her and Lulu would have to go in the kennel upstairs.

She carried Lulu downstairs with Sherry following behind.

Beth's eyes lit as she saw the pup.

"Who's this?"

"I really don't know. She was hitching a ride on the highway."

"She's thin."

"I think we'll fix that." Stephanie glanced at her watch. "We have a few minutes. Why don't you run over to Maude's and get a couple of doughnuts for us while I take the dogs outside? Thanks for making the coffee." The aroma told her it was ready.

Beth headed for the door.

"And Beth," she added, "if there's a call from a Mr. Matthews or any call from someone outside Colorado, tell them I'm not in, and you don't know when I will be."

"Right," Beth said, but she looked puzzled. And troubled. "Is there anything wrong?"

"Just someone I used to know and really don't want to see again."

"Okay," Beth said in an uncertain voice.

"And please don't say anything to anyone. Hopefully, the caller will give up and not try to contact me again."

"I promise," Beth said. "Cross my heart. I won't mention it to anyone. Not even Mom."

That would be difficult for Beth, but Stephanie knew the girl would try.

She hated to put her in that position. It was cowardly of her. Especially cowardly to ask her not to say anything.

Drat it. She couldn't do it. Surely, she had grown a backbone in the years since she had left Mark.

"Forget what I just said," she told Beth. "If someone wants to talk to me, I'll get the phone unless I'm with a patient. If I am, then take a message."

Beth looked vastly relieved. "I won't say anything unless you tell me I can," she said.

"I don't want you to lie to your family," Stephanie said.

"I won't, but neither is there a reason to say anything I don't know."

Stephanie nodded. She had hired Beth out of high school after the girl had volunteered to help with the animal rescue group Stephanie and Eve had started. Beth had convinced her family to let her foster dogs and cats and had enlisted other kids to talk their families into doing the same. She loved animals, and for Stephanie, that was the most essential qualification. In the following two years, Beth had become a fine vet tech. Stephanie urged her to go to college and vet school, but her assistant didn't have the drive to do it. She wanted marriage and a family more.

Stephanie wasn't sure how Beth was going to find one in Covenant Falls. Most of the young men left town as soon as they graduated. Selfishly, Stephanie wanted to keep her at the practice forever.

"Who's first this morning?" she asked.

"Mrs. O'Connor and Honeybun. Honeybun has been limping more than usual."

Honeybun was a very elderly cat who was already defying the feline life expectancy. Mrs. O'Connor was in with her every other week, partially, Stephanie thought, because Honeybun was her only family.

"Okay. I'll take these two out. Sherry's already adopted Lulu."

"Lulu?"

"Or whatever the new owner decides to call her."

"You are an optimist, Doctor." With that, Beth ducked out of the office with a big grin on her face.

The day was too busy to worry. Stephanie slightly upped the arthritis medicine for Honeybun who, otherwise, was doing admirably for seventeen. Then there were exams and shots, a follow-up exam for a dog that had been hit by a car. Doing well. Mrs. Cassidy brought in her son's rabbit who was acting strangely. Turned out the rabbit was about to be a mother. Mrs. Cassidy thought she had two lady rabbits. *No.*

The afternoon was filled with the scheduled spaying of four dogs. She did those for a token cost because too many people in town were just barely getting by. She considered it a community service.

She would be lucky to be through by 7:00 p.m. Then she would stay downstairs with the animals that had been sedated. She would sleep on the cot there. *Good. No time to think.*

The day went fast. There were always at least two clients waiting, and then there was an emergency: a cat fell from a second-floor window that had been left open. By some miracle, it had survived, but one of its legs was broken and had to be set.

At 2:00 p.m., Eve called her. Stephanie grabbed the phone while standing at the counter giving a patient a prescription.

"Hi, how was the evaluation?"

"Good. All but one were certified, and he should be soon."

"That's great. Ready for Stryker?"

"Has he been a problem?"

"Nope. I parceled out Braveheart."

"To whom?"

"Clint."

Stephanie was appalled. "Why did you do that?"

"I thought he needed company. Of course, I didn't

tell him that. I just said I needed help since I was keeping Stryker for you."

"How did Braveheart feel about it?"

"He seemed quite pleased. He went willingly into the house and even accompanied Clint on a trip to town. And Clint brought him to our house for dinner, and Braveheart obviously wanted to leave with him."

"Are we talking about the same dog?"

"Yes."

"How does *Nick* feel about it?"

"He's willing to share Braveheart for a few days. He really likes Clint."

"Good for him," Stephanie said with a decided lack of enthusiasm. The last person she wanted to hear about now was Clint who seemed to dazzle everyone.

"We can keep Stryker another night," Eve said. "I imagine you're busy."

"That would be great." She paused, then added, "I found a puppy on the road."

"Should I alert a foster family?"

"She's really cute," Stephanie tempted. "And scared."

"No, no and no," Eve said. "But…"

"What?"

"Maybe Clint…"

"No!"

The silence was deafening.

She needed to explain. "We don't know how long

he will be here, and he has no permanent home. It would break all our rules."

"It would be temporary only," Eve said.

"Lulu needs something permanent."

Her friend sighed. "I'll ask around, then. And I'll bring Stryker over on my way to the office tomorrow."

"Thanks. I have appointments until after six so I couldn't pick him up until then."

She hung up before Eve offered anything else about Clint Morgan.

But then she glanced out the window and stiffened. Clint was standing with Josh outside the office. He wore a light blue long-sleeved shirt with the sleeves rolled up. Lord, but he was fine-looking. Electricity flickered and danced down her spine. Its heat pooled in her stomach.

Nonsense! She turned away. There was another patient in the waiting room, and she was standing here like a smitten schoolgirl. Missy, a black cocker spaniel, was waiting for her annual exam.

Beth was in the treatment room doing the preliminaries. Temperature. Weight. Checking the eyes. Missy was still for the examination although her eyes never left her owner.

Twenty minutes later, Stephanie had finished. The tests were all negative, and with Beth's help, she'd administered all the shots. Beth filled out the county form for the rabies shot while Stephanie talked to the owner. "She's in great shape for her age, but she does have some arthritis. There's a prescription that would help. She'll feel better."

The appointments continued until 6:00 p.m., then she gave Lulu her shots. She made Beth leave at six thirty and finished her paperwork at seven. She wearily went upstairs, made a sandwich and drank a glass of milk.

The phone rang. She looked at the ID. It was the Boston attorney. He wasn't going to quit. Resigned, she picked it up.

"Dr. Phillips?"

"This is Dr. Phillips."

"You're a hard lady to track down."

She didn't answer. It wasn't a question. Or maybe it was.

There was an uncomfortable silence, then, "I'm David Matthews. I'm an attorney representing Mrs. Townsend. I understand you were also married to Mark Townsend."

Again no question. No need to reply.

"*Are* you the former wife of Mark Townsend?"

She'd decided during her exchange with Beth that she wasn't going to lie. Neither did she intend on getting involved.

"Yes."

"Can I ask you why you divorced him?"

"I didn't divorce him. He divorced me, at least according to the state."

"I would very much like to come to Colorado and talk to you."

"Why?"

"He beat the hell out of his wife, but he contends her lover did it. Problem is she didn't have one. She just wanted a divorce. From the records of your divorce, I take it you went through something like that."

She cut to the chase. "What do you want from me, Mr. Matthews?"

"We would like you to testify for her."

Stephanie swallowed hard. "I've spent years trying to forget every moment I spent with him and the following years when he tried to destroy me. Why should I give him a chance to do it again?"

"Because he'll keep destroying good people."

"How do you know I'm 'good' people? I could be exactly what he said I was."

"Because I do know Susan Townsend. She's a close friend of my sister, at least she was before she married Mark. Then Townsend thought my sister wasn't good enough for them to know. I checked around trying to find you. It wasn't easy. I had to go through layers and layers."

"Didn't that tell you I didn't want to be found?"

"It did. But we need help. I don't know what he did to you, but I do know what he did to Susan. Isolated her. Chose her friends, her clothes. Insults. Then small slaps that grew into larger ones."

Stephanie was silent. She had gone through the first steps. The isolation. The belittlement. The theft of her business. He had hit her, too, and that was when she had left. Her father had hit her mother, and Stephanie had always sworn it would never happen to her.

But it had, and she *did* leave, hell with the consequences. She'd known fighting would be an uphill battle after Mark had found men who swore to having sex with her. He was the betrayed spouse in Boston's eyes, not the man who'd stolen the proceeds from the sale of a veterinarian practice she'd inherited. And she hadn't had the resources for a long legal battle…

"Dr. Phillips?"

"I can't help you," she said. "I have a practice that requires all my time. I'm not getting into that quagmire again."

"He nearly beat her to death."

"Call the police."

"He's convinced them she had a lover and he's the one who did it, that she's lying to protect him. Sound familiar?"

"And just as ridiculous. The police actually believe he has two cheating wives? Doesn't say much for him, does it?"

"I don't know about the police, but certain high officials in the department back him."

She believed every word the attorney said. It was the way Mark worked.

"I'm not sure what you want me to do," she said. "My reputation is certainly ruined in Boston, apparently enough for your client to have dismissed it and marry him. I can't say I have a lot of sympathy."

There was a silence. "I understand how you feel, but…"

"I don't think you do. Look. I fought that battle and lost. By the time I quit, I was the whore of Babylon. He contacted every place I applied for a job and did his best to make sure I wouldn't work as a veterinarian. He even tried to have my license revoked."

"Will you just talk to Susan?"

She hesitated. She would be opening a door she didn't want opened. Mark would find out where she was and make her life miserable once again. If he thought for one second she might be helping his wife, there would be hell to pay.

Coward! She flinched at the word. But she had paid and paid and paid for her stupidity. *He can't hurt you now.* People in Covenant Falls knew her and they didn't know him. She owned the practice. No one could fire her but herself.

Practically own it. Dr. Langford still held the note. It was almost paid off, but not completely.

She wasn't physically afraid. She'd learned to take care of herself. She'd learned independence, and she was quite sure that gentle Sherry wouldn't let anyone touch her. But she wasn't sure what Mark would do. From what the attorney had said, his violence had escalated.

"I can't make the trip up there. I have too many obligations here."

"We'll come down and talk to you."

"What is she like?" she asked.

"Pretty. And quiet. A little shy. She has a very popular, outgoing sister and I think she always felt in her shadow. She was literally swept off her feet when Townsend showed interest. He showered her with attention." He paused, then added, "There's the child. A daughter. He's trying to take her away from Susan by calling her an unfit mother."

Stephanie closed her eyes at the thought of Mark having custody of a girl. He really did not like women. She'd come to understand that. It hadn't been her who had infuriated him as much as her sex.

You will not get involved.

Stephanie capitulated. "I'll talk to you, but that's all I'm promising. I really don't know what I can do. He pretty much sullied my reputation. And Covenant Falls isn't very convenient. We're out of the way. You'll probably have to fly into Denver and rent a car. I can tell you now, I won't go back. I can't afford the time, and I never want to see him again."

"Anything we can learn could be helpful. She's pretty much alone. Her family blames her for the breakup. She's not getting any help there."

Stephanie sighed. "Let me know when you'll arrive."

"Is there a hotel there?"

"There's a bed-and-breakfast. Not very fancy but clean. You wouldn't want to stay in our only motel."

He asked for the name of the bed-and-breakfast and the phone number. Then, "Would the day after tomorrow be okay?"

She hesitated. No day was good. But she remembered how she felt when she had tried to leave Mark. No one had been there for her. No one had believed her.

"Okay, but on one condition. Mark won't know about it unless I agree. I want your promise."

"You have it, and thank you. It will probably be later afternoon, but I'll call you when everything is arranged."

She hung up, not bothering to say goodbye.

Sherry and the new pup seemed to sense her disquiet. They nuzzled her. Sherry licked her hand. "I like you, too," Stephanie whispered to them.

They were all she needed. Damn if she would ever give another man power over her. Ever.

CHAPTER THIRTEEN

CLINT TOOK BART for a walk. It was a grand fall morning. There was that slightly smoky smell, and a sky so blue it hurt.

When he returned to the cabin, he made breakfast for Bart and himself and enjoyed a second cup of coffee. Then Josh called.

"I have a meeting this morning at the bank," he said. "Might take a while. Can I change the meeting time from 10:00 a.m. to noon and pick you up for lunch at Maude's? We can talk about the dock and then walk over to the hardware store and order the materials."

"Sounds good," he said. Really it didn't. It meant Bart would probably leave after lunch. The thought was painful. It was staggering to think how much he would miss the animal after just a few days. Maybe it was the solemn way with which the dog regarded him, or the joy in Bart's eyes when his stomach was rubbed. Or maybe just the comfortable companionship, something Clint hadn't known he needed, but now knew he did.

"I talked to Mr. Wilson at the hardware store

Saturday," Clint continued, "and he gave me some advice on the materials needed. All we have to do now is order them. He said he would loan us the equipment I need."

"Good. How is Braveheart doing?"

"We just took a walk. He seems happy."

There was a silence, then, "That's great. I'll see you later."

Clint walked out to the edge of the lake. He'd picked up a measuring tape at the hardware store and now he measured where the first land posts should go. He marked the spots. It was the footings in the water that would require more than one person. He could handle the ones on land.

Bart watched as he dug the dry holes. Clint relished the labor, and the cool fresh air, so different from the fiercely hot Afghanistan desert. The lake sparkled, cool and clean and inviting.

Satisfied that he had finally done something constructive by taking the first few steps toward building the dock, he returned to the cabin.

He drank a glass of water. He'd been in Covenant Falls a week. Building the dock would probably take six or seven days, depending on who helped him. Then he would need to make some serious decisions about his future. These last few days had given him a soft landing from the despair he'd felt in the hospital.

But aimlessness taunted him. Dr. Payne had told him to expect it. Clint had spent half his life as a soldier, a pilot. When he wasn't in the field, he was training for it. His friends had been training with him. Some had come and gone, some had been killed. Some had been with him a long time. But he'd always been surrounded by people with a like mind. They wanted to be the best at what they did. They played hard, loved hard, fought hard. They shared the same shattering memories. Losses. Fear. And adrenaline. It was who they were. Who he was.

Who he had been.

The loss of that identity was a huge hole. Bart filled a tiny little corner, but there was a still gaping hole. Josh and his wife had been a godsend. Josh didn't say much, but there was that silent recognition. Josh had defeated the alienation Clint was experiencing, the feeling that no one understood, or could understand, how difficult it was to walk back into a civilian world.

And then there was Stephanie. She hadn't left his thoughts over the weekend. Search and rescue. The acerbic vet had a heart. Unfortunately, it seemed to be for those in need of rescue, and he hadn't qualified.

He was puzzled by his own interest. He'd never been more intrigued by a woman. His marriage had happened in a burst of exuberance just prior to a deployment, a need to come home to something. There had never been magic. He knew that now. He'd known it on his wedding night. He especially knew it when he didn't receive much mail from his bride, but a great deal from friends about her activities with other pilots. He knew it when his heart wasn't broken at the news. He took pride in one thing, though: he was a realist. Ever since he was a young boy, he'd never really believed in anyone. The exceptions were the men and women that flew with him.

Clint checked his watch. Twenty minutes before Josh would arrive. He showered and changed into clean clothes. Maybe he would see Stephanie in town.

He fetched the materials list and design and went outside on the porch, Bart on his heels. He sat on the swing and scratched the dog's ears. "I'll miss you." Bart licked his hand and looked at him soulfully, as if he understood.

He thought about calling Stephanie, ask her for lunch or dinner, or breakfast or a coffee break or whatever. All she could do was say no, and he wasn't a schoolboy anymore. He just wanted to explore those odd feelings, to know whether she felt any of them. *Probably not.*

Simple fact was he couldn't get her out of his mind. Smart. Independent. A tender heart under that acerbic cloak. And pretty. Make that attractive. Very, very attractive.

He wished he knew more about her. No wedding ring. Had she been married before? Something had made her wary of men. Or maybe it was just him. He intended to find out.

Maybe he could pry some information from Josh.

As if summoned by the thought, the crunch of tires sounded on the gravel outside. Josh's Jeep approached with Amos sitting in the front seat. "You have to stay here this time," he told Bart. "I don't think he meant to take you to lunch, although you're a very good dining partner."

He herded a reluctant Bart inside and walked out to meet Josh. Amos jumped into the backseat and Clint took the front seat. "I see you started on the holes," Josh observed as he drove out onto Lake Road. "By the way, I have a canoe I bought when I first came here. It's yours to use anytime. And fishing equipment. There's a lot of fish in that water."

"I've seen fishermen out there and envied them."

"Done much fishing?"

"Not much opportunity, but a little."

"Me, neither," Josh confided. "Always seemed too sedentary to me, but I'm beginning to appreciate the art involved. And now a little quiet time is good." He glanced at Clint. "How's Bart doing? Eve told me you shortened his name. She likes it. So does Nick. So it's kind of official."

Clint didn't reply. It wasn't his decision. Nothing about Bart was his decision. And yet keeping the name made him feel more connected to the dog. *Not good.*

He envied Josh for his ability to drive. When would he be able to drive again without endangering other drivers? If he were the only one at risk, he would say what the hell, but he wasn't going to risk others. He'd almost killed the truck driver on that Texas road.

"Going stir-crazy?" Josh asked.

"Maybe a little. I had enough rest in the hospital."

"How long were you there?"

"Three months, two weeks of them in an induced coma," Clint said. "Then rehab while they tried to figure out why I continued to have headaches and blackouts. They're not quite as frequent now, but still bad enough to keep me from driving and maybe killing someone."

"No family? And you don't have to answer if you don't want to. I sure as hell didn't when I first arrived."

"No problem. There's not one I want to claim."

Josh nodded. "Got it. I had one of those, too. You're invited to our twice-a-month get-together for vets. It's not a meeting, just an informal gathering. Some from Vietnam. One from the Korean War. Most are from the Iraq and Afghanistan."

"I met Bill Evans in the park," Clint said. "He told me about them. Sounds good."

"They're good for all of us, no matter when we served. Time to vent, or relax, or both."

"I'll be there," Clint said.

"Bill is one of the regulars. As you probably know, a lot of vets live in this town. There's not many job opportunities, and the wide world sounds pretty good to young guys without a future here, so they join the military. Then they get back and they can't talk about it to friends and relatives." Josh's jaw tightened. "It's worse for lifers like us. After years of training and war, you don't think you're fit for anything else. It's not easy to become a civilian after all those years."

"You did it."

"It never really leaves me. It's always somewhere inside my head. I never feel I deserve this. Not when others are dead. And I still have night sweats."

"You were wounded over there. I wasn't. I don't..."

"Hell, I know what chopper pilots did, the chances you took to save our asses. I don't give a damn how you were injured. You guys are heroes to the grunts. I wouldn't be here today if it weren't for a chopper pilot."

Josh's words hit home and, for the first time since the car accident, some of Clint's guilt slipped away. "I figured I would put in my twenty years, then try to find a job as a chopper pilot here in the United States. That's out of the question now. At least until these damn blackouts end." He changed the subject. "You mentioned you were starting a construction business."

"Contracting, but to make it work we have to bring people into the town. Right now, we're set to remodel the one remaining motel in town. It's in rough shape. Then we're going to try to bring in tourists, some new businesses. We really need a clothing store. The last one left eight years ago.

Maybe with new businesses we can keep some of the younger residents here."

They arrived in the business area and Josh parked the Jeep in front of Maude's. They headed inside, Amos at Josh's heels. Maude's, Clint noted, was like those cafés in other small towns across America. Mismatched tables and chairs. Worn wood floors. A counter with seats. Cheerful yellow curtains. Flowers in a jar on every table. Worn paper menus. It was about half-full.

Maude hurried over to them.

"That cake was quite the best I've ever had," Clint said.

She beamed. "First meal is on the house," she said.

"I don't think you did that for me," Josh grumbled.

"Actually, I think I threw in a steak for Amos at one time or another," she countered.

"That was for Amos, not me."

"I appreciate it," Clint broke in with a wide smile.

"Two steaks?" Maude asked. "Medium rare, right? And a hamburger for Amos?"

"Right," they both said at the same time and grinned at each other.

"Flatterer," Josh whispered after she disappeared into the kitchen.

"Well, it *was* a great cake." Clint pointed at Amos. "And how do you get him in here?"

"Maude considers him a service dog." Josh didn't have time to say anything else. One by one, or two by two, diners strolled over to say hello and introduce themselves. Clint tried to remember as many names as possible. He'd perfected that skill long ago. It was a skill that put him in good stead with most people.

The steaks were as promised. As soon as they finished, Josh paid the bill for his steak and they started for the hardware store. In another fifteen minutes, they had ordered all the materials for the dock.

"The treated lumber should be here Friday afternoon," Calvin Wilson said. "I'll come help Saturday and bring a couple of men. My son can manage the store."

"I'll take care of the bill," Clint said. "What's the total?"

Calvin looked at Josh, who nodded.

Clint was grateful. Josh knew where he was coming from. What he needed to do. He didn't want a free ride. Never had. The cabin was a godsend, a sanctuary where he could come to terms with what happened and what should happen now.

They walked back to Josh's Jeep, passing Stephanie's office. Clint glanced in and saw her talking to what must be a client. She wore a white coat, and her curly red hair was tied back. Then she turned, and he saw the recognition in her face and maybe, just maybe, her glance remained on him a second longer than necessary. She took a step forward, then turned away from the window.

"Any other stops?" Josh asked.

Clint shook his head. "I imagine you have other things to do."

"Everything's taken care of for the day. The morning's meeting was to finalize financing for the motel. My partner, Nate, is finishing specifications. Like I said earlier, the building is in rough shape. It's deteriorating and is mostly a by-the-hour business now. It's just outside the city limits and an eyesore and trouble spot."

"Why did you get into contracting?"

"Well, I inherited the cabin. It needed rehabbing badly. I discovered I liked building and fixing things more than blowing them up. Another vet here helped me replace the flooring. He'd been a building foreman before his company went bust. With a new city council ready to promote growth, it all seemed to fit. Speaking of the town, do you want to see our claim to fame?"

"Sounds good. I must admit to a certain curiosity when Covenant Falls didn't seem to have a falls," Clint said. He sure as hell didn't have anything better to do.

"It's about twenty minutes away."

Clint waited until they were driving out of town. "Tell me more about Stephanie."

Josh chuckled. "Stephanie is hard to explain. She's a damn good vet. As you know, she's very involved in search-and-rescue activities and she's on the volunteer firefighters team. The guys in it give her high marks. She can do anything they can, and she never complains. She has friends, more than she knows, but I think Eve is the only person with whom she's really close. I do know I like her tremendously. She was the only person in town who tolerated me when I first came here."

Clint laughed. "When she picked me up in Pueblo, she told me you were going to meet me at the cabin to give me the keys and probably tell me the best way to piss off the town. She said you did a great job of doing that when you first arrived."

Josh grinned. "I did. I was really messed up when I first came here." He glanced at Clint. "But since you asked, I've never seen her so…flustered as when you're around. You certainly have some kind of effect on her."

"I don't know what that means exactly. In a good way, or bad?"

Josh shrugged. "Don't ask me to explain women."

They didn't talk again until he turned off on a dirt road and drove up its winding path. They reached a parking area. "There's a path to the waterfall."

"The 'falls' in Covenant Falls?"

Josh nodded. "The falls is a hidden jewel. Not many tourists know about it. The so-called first family, descendants of the man who founded Covenant Falls, wanted the town to stay small. The problem is when there's no growth, there's no jobs, and when there's no jobs the young people leave and the old ones die. Most of the people here are descendants of the original settlers.

"Eve wants to change that," Josh added. "Much to my surprise, I discovered I do, too. So does the majority of town, which is why they reelected Eve mayor. They're tired of watching their kids move half away across the country or go into the service."

Clint heard the rushing of water and he looked down into a canyon and at the river roaring through it.

"This way," Josh said and guided him along a path that wound around a stand of trees. It ended in a parklike setting with picnic tables. Beyond that was the waterfall. The falls were spectacular, tumbling and rushing into the river below.

"I see what you mean," Clint said. "It would make one hell of a tourist attraction. I can't believe no one comes here."

"It's off the beaten track, but it's perfect to anchor a wilderness expedition business. Camping, climbing, fishing, hunting. We even have abandoned gold mines. But we need accommodations first. The town has a great story to tell and we can take tourists on some of the early trading trails up to an abandoned mining camp. There's great fishing in the streams running off the river.

"Problem is Covenant Falls is well off the main highways and after one brief effort to bring summer tourists here, the town gave up."

"What happened?"

"Some summer cabins were built here and bought by a group of people in Denver. My cabin was one of them. But then the recession came, and home prices plummeted. There was some vandalism and a drowning. The cabins and cottages around the lake were sold at bargain prices and mostly bought by people who already lived here. The town just got smaller until Eve was elected mayor on a pro-growth platform. She was stymied by a non-growth council that blocked nearly everything she wanted to do. The chairman of the council has since resigned, Eve was reelected and now she has a council that also wants growth."

It made sense to Clint. "The view's great. And I like the idea of an adventure company."

Josh sighed. "I don't know if it will work, but it was a dream my buddy and I had. He owned the cabin."

Clint remembered that Stephanie had said Josh had inherited the cabin.

It brought his mind back to the woman who occupied his mind all weekend. "The scarch-and-rescue work. It's all volunteer, isn't it?"

"Yeah, and it costs the members a lot of money for equipment and the necessary training. It really is a labor of love." Clint stared out over the canyon. "Stephanie is trying to convince Amos and me to join, but right now is not a good time. She's also looking for a handler to train Stryker."

Working with Stephanie certainly had an appeal, but he knew she would never go for it. No reason she should. He had no experience with dogs. It was just that he and Bart happened to hit it off. No reason to think that extended to other dogs.

"I don't think Bart is necessarily a good indication," Clint said. "I've never had much to do with dogs, and I don't plan to stay here long. As you said, jobs are rare, and if I can't fly choppers, I have to find something else. I keep thinking about finishing that degree in computer engineering, but to tell you the truth, I don't like the idea of being inside every day."

"I understand. I feel the same way. Let me know if I can do anything to help."

"You already have. God knows I felt alone the day I was released from the hospital. I hate to admit it, but I needed someone to kick my ass."

Josh smiled. "Eve kicked mine." He glanced at his watch. "I need to get back."

Clint nodded. "Thanks for bringing me. I've been wondering about the falls part of Covenant Falls."

"You should get Stephanie to tell you something about the history."

"I'm not sure she would want to do that."

Josh shrugged. "Worth a try."

Clint looked at Josh suspiciously.

Josh blinked, obviously trying to appear innocent.

They reached the Jeep. "I think Stryker is staying with us another night so if you could keep Brave— Bart tonight..."

"I can do that."

"Good. Oh, and you can bring Bart to the veterans' get-together, if you can coax him out. I think he'll be okay if you're with him. I always bring Amos. He belongs there, being a retired military guy."

"Would the other guys mind?"

"Hell no. You should see the way they fawn over Amos."

"Maybe I'll do that."

Thirty minutes later, they arrived at the cabin. After Josh drove away, Clint opened the front door. Bart stood, wagging his tail tentatively as if not quite sure he should.

Clint dropped to his knees. "Hey, guy," he said. "Let's go inside and get you dinner. We have an engagement tonight."

Bart wagged his stubby tail and looked up hopefully at him.

Clint rubbed his ears. He knew he shouldn't. It wasn't good for either of them to get so attached. But one look at those anxious, worried eyes caused him to increase his efforts until Bart moaned with dog ecstasy.

Damn!

CHAPTER FOURTEEN

STRYKER DASHED INTO Stephanie's office and covered her with kisses, then inspected Lulu who stood bravely and tentatively wagging her tail. Stryker inspected her, then licked her. Acceptance.

Eve smiled guiltily. "Beth said I could come on in."

"Welcome to my chaos," she said.

Eve knelt next to Lulu. "So this is the new orphan."

"Cute little thing, isn't she?" And Lulu *was* cute, after her bath. She was a mixture of white and tan and several different shades of brown. Her hair was short and bristly. She was the ultimate mixture of many breeds, and her eyes were bright and curious.

"How old is she?"

"I would say about four months. And I know four things about her. She's a survivor. She's never climbed stairs. She gets along with other dogs. She knows the difference between inside and outside. In other words, she's either extremely smart or has already been housebroken. But there's no chip, no collar. I'm sending out emails to vets in the area in case someone's looking for her, but I'm not hopeful. If I don't hear anything back in ten days, I'll put her up for adoption."

"Hold off on that," Eve said.

"Why?"

"We might have a problem with Bart."

"Who's Bart?"

"Braveheart," Eve said.

"Sorry, but I'm a bit confused."

"Well, he seems to have attached himself to Clint Morgan."

"He loves Nick."

"Yes, he does, but he's never given his heart to Nick."

"Don't tell me he's given it to…Mr. Morgan. And what about 'Bart'?"

"It seems Clint shortened the name. We all approved, Nick included."

"I've been away for two days and the world has gone mad."

"No, just realistic. You saw it that night at our house when Bart hovered around Clint. I'm taking Nick to the cabin this afternoon and it will be up to Bart as to whether he wants to come back with us."

"And if he doesn't?"

"Nick and I agree Bart gets to choose. But Josh, who has had a crash course in dog, said Clint took Bart to the vets' meeting last night, and he wouldn't stir from his side. Not even for Josh."

"Isn't it going to be very hard on Nick if he decides on Clint?"

Eve frowned. "He loves Bart, but he wants him to be happy, and he realizes Bart is one of five at our house. He knows all our dogs are fosters and we keep them until we can find a good home. We just never have, and they all became ours. But it may turn out that Bart is one of those one-man dogs, and he has found *his* one."

"That's crazy. We don't really know anything about him. He won't be staying and…" She stopped suddenly.

"We may be worrying about nothing," Eve said. "Bart might want to come home with Nick, but if he doesn't, maybe we could add another dog." She ran her hand over Lulu's head. "She's a sweet one."

"Have you talked to Josh about this? About maybe adding a new dog?"

"We talked about Bart's attachment to Clint."

"It's only been a few days," Stephanie protested. "And we…you…really don't know much about Clint Morgan. You know our rules about adoption. We inspect a house, make sure whoever is adopting has provided for a previous animal with proper vet care."

Eve's gaze settled on her, and Stephanie squirmed. "What is it about Clint that unsettles you? I thought you would be happy we might have a home for Lulu."

"Nothing unsettles me," Stephanie lied. "I just don't know him well. None of us do."

"Josh wouldn't have offered the use of the cabin if he hadn't checked on the man pretty thoroughly."

"Don't you think he might be a little...too affable?"

Eve's eyebrows raised. "Too affable? He's pleasant, good with kids and dogs. Funny. Josh said he paid for the materials for the dock. He's apparently responsible and..."

"He's *too* perfect," Stephanie blurted out. "I know about too perfect. I married a 'perfect' man, and he..." Her voice trailed off. Although she and Eve were friends, she hadn't said much about her marriages. She felt too much the fool in both cases. Too vulnerable. She had worked hard never to be vulnerable again. And now the recent calls had disrupted her confidence. The fact wasn't that she didn't trust easily. She didn't trust at all.

Except maybe Josh because he hadn't been perfect at all when they had first met.

He'd been as damaged as she had been years earlier. They had been kindred souls, although there had been nothing romantic between them. More a recognition.

And now she had to tell Eve some of her story because tomorrow she would be involved again in Mark's world, and she had no idea what he would do.

"You know that I was married to a man named Mark. He was charming, too, just like your Mr. Morgan. Respected. I had a small vet practice in Pennsylvania. I worked all the time to keep it above water.

"Then I met Mark who was attending a seminar in a hotel not far from my practice. We had lunch, and he was the most charming man I'd ever met. To make a long story short, he wined and dined and courted me. He asked me to marry him and promised me the moon. I knew he was a prominent banker in Boston, and I worried I wouldn't fit into his world. But I was in love with what I thought he was."

Eve nodded, encouraging her to continue.

"He convinced me to sell my practice and invest the proceeds. Wasn't much, but it was mine. And then he set about changing me. I was not good enough for him as I was. First my hair, then my clothes. Only his friends could be mine. Verbal abuse came next. Then physical. When he hit me, I left him. He promised that if I tried to divorce him, or said anything, he would make sure I never worked as a vet again. He almost succeeded. Might have if not for Dr. Langford. Mark smeared my reputation as much as it could be. Vindictive doesn't even cover what he did."

Eve's face paled. "And the proceeds from your practice?"

"Disappeared in a 'bad investment.' You wonder why I'm not as eager to embrace Clint Morgan as you are. I don't know him. I'm suspicious of most men, and particularly charming ones. Second, I've been receiving phone calls from an attorney in Boston. He's representing Mark's current wife.

He's doing to her what was done to me. They want my help."

"Oh Lord, Steph, I'm sorry. What can I do?"

"There's nothing. But if I agree to help them, I can expect retribution. I wanted you to know in advance."

"Are you going to help?"

"My first reaction was no," Stephanie said. "But then that may let Mark win again. I don't know if I can do that. I'm going to listen to them. The lawyer and Mark's wife will be here tomorrow."

Eve touched her arm. "You have friends here, Stephanie. Josh, me, Tony Keller. He's still police chief and a really good one. Then there's Nate and all the people you've helped. You have a fortress here, my friend."

"He's my problem, not yours."

"He *will* be, if he tries to cause trouble here."

"But now you know why I don't jump on the Clint Morgan bandwagon. I don't trust charm. Even if I did, he'll not be here long. It would be more than stupid to get involved."

"That's what I thought about Josh."

"Don't try being a matchmaker with me, Eve. I've had two strikes. I don't intend on going for an out."

"Clint's a soldier, Steph. He's not a banker. And Josh is a good judge of character. Clint's exactly what he seems to be."

"You think?" Steph shook her head. "Doesn't matter. I like my independence. I won't risk it. I'm really happy about you and Josh. I think you two are great together. It's just not for me."

"Okay," Eve said. "But that doesn't affect my problem with Braveheart. So keep Lulu available, okay? She really seems to be a sweet dog. We need one ordinary mutt around."

"Will do."

"Remember, Josh and I—and Tony—are only a call away."

Stephanie nodded. "I've learned to take care of myself."

"No such thing with a sociopath. This man sounds like one. Promise you'll keep me posted."

"I will. What about lunch? My next appointment is at 2:00 p.m. I was going to do some paperwork, but a patty melt sounds better."

"I was hoping you would suggest that."

WHY IN THE HELL did he agree to teach seniors to how to use a computer?

Sure, he'd taught younger chopper pilots, but then he knew choppers inside and out. Knew every screw that went into them, and he was teaching younger guys every bit as eager to be good pilots as he had been.

Civilians? Now that was a different story. Bill Evans had lulled him into agreement after several beers and a game of poker. And Clint was feeling pretty good. No headaches in a couple of days. No weakness. He liked the guys at the center, especially Nate and Josh. So he had agreed.

His first class was at 2:00 p.m. He decided to walk to Maude's for lunch first.

The café was crowded. Every stool at the counter was taken, along with every table.

Maude approached him. "We're full, thank the good Lord," she said, "but Eve and Stephanie have the back booth. Is that okay?"

"If it's okay with them," he replied. Life had suddenly improved.

Maude hurried to the back, then returned. "It's okay," she said. "Do you know what you want?"

"A burger, fries and iced tea," he said.

"Gotcha. Medium rare?"

He nodded and headed for the back booth. Eve was moving to the end of the seat in the booth. Stephanie sat in the middle of the opposite bench. They were halfway through their meal. He quickly sensed where he was supposed to sit, and it was not beside Stephanie. It suited him. He could look at her, although she didn't seem overjoyed to see him. She was obviously still wary of him.

"I hope I'm not interrupting anything," he said.

"Absolutely not," Eve said. The words were not echoed by Stephanie.

"I heard you'll be teaching Harold Stiles and Mrs. Aubry today," Eve said.

"I don't quite know how that happened," he said with a grin. "I was happily drinking beer one minute and the next someone volunteered me. Don't you have some real teachers who can teach?"

"Mrs. Aubry wouldn't go unless a stranger teaches it. She's terrified she will look foolish or dumb to her neighbors. She's been a widow fifteen years and she won't leave Covenant Falls, but she wants to contact her children and talk to them online. Harold is a farmer who heard he could get better prices online. He's a bachelor who is shy around women. Neither could be talked into taking a class. I think they both feel more comfortable around a stranger than to show weakness among their friends."

"Well, I have Mrs. Aubry at two this afternoon, and Mr. Stiles later in the evening. I explained to Bill Evans that I don't know how long I'll be here, and that I've never taught anyone other than a fellow soldier, but I would give it a try." He turned his attention to Stephanie. Her striking blue eyes challenged him, and he felt the now familiar jolt of attraction. "Hi." *Lame. Very lame.*

"I hear you're taking care of Braveheart," Stephanie replied, the usual tart note in her voice.

"Just until this afternoon. Eve and Nick will be picking him up then."

"Probably around six," Eve said. "Nick has a Scout meeting after school."

He nodded. *He's not yours.*

"How long do you plan to stay in town?" Stephanie asked.

"Not sure. At least until I get Josh's dock built,"

he said. "Eve said you taught a search-and-rescue session this past weekend. How did it go?"

"Good." The answer was short, not inviting other questions, but her eyes were a vivid blue and very alive.

"How did you get involved in rescue work?"

For a moment, he didn't know if she was going to answer, then she shrugged. "A woman who lives on a ranch about thirty miles north of here raises retrievers and has trained several for search and rescue. Her daughter was a certified handler, but died in a car crash. I was the vet for their dogs and the woman wanted Sherry, her daughter's dog, to continue in rescue work. I'd always been interested in it. So I said yes. Sherry was already trained, and I already had a lot of the required skills, so it was a good match."

She flushed when she stopped speaking. It was obvious she didn't like talking about herself, and after hearing her explanation, he felt an enormous guilt that he'd been reluctant to spend a couple of hours teaching several elder citizens how to use the computer.

"I would like to go with you some time," he said. She blinked. "Why?"

"I was in that business myself for a number of years. Search and rescue."

"And kill," she said.

"That, too," he said mildly. "But it was the other part I liked about my job."

Regret immediately crossed her face. "I was rude," she said. "And wrong. I'm sorry. God knows I respect what you all do out there."

"An apology isn't necessary."

"Yes, it is. I just had some bad news and I'm taking it out on you."

"Good."

"Why is it good?"

"Being irritated at me will take some edge out of the news." He wanted to ask what it was, but he was pretty sure he wouldn't get an answer.

"No, it won't. I'll just feel more guilt." This time there was a hint of a smile.

He was aware then that not only Eve was watching with avid interest, but so were those diners within hearing distance.

His food arrived.

"I have to go," Stephanie said. "Patients." She put money on the table and stood. She nodded to both of them, then took off at a fast walk.

"Something I said?" he asked Eve.

"No. She's just backlogged from this weekend." Eve ate a French fry. "Thanks for agreeing to teach today."

"I don't know how good I'll be at it."

"You'll be good. You have an easy manner about you."

"Stephanie doesn't think so."

Eve frowned. "She does, and that's the problem."

"I don't understand," he said, truly confused.

There was a mutual attraction between them. They had kissed at the corral! Why was she fighting it so hard?

Eve shrugged. "She'll work it out. Now eat that burger before it gets cold."

Clearly, she wasn't going to say more. He took a bite and it was as good as the steak had been yesterday.

MRS. AUBRY APPEARED in the computer room on the dot of 2:00 p.m.

Clint had had time to walk to the cabin and bring Bart back with him. He didn't want to leave him alone all afternoon, not when he had to give him up later in the day. And no one he'd met thus far had objected to his presence.

The community center had twenty computers, ranging in age from ancient to ten new desktops with printers.

Before the arrival of his first student, Clint had taken several minutes to look at the computers. Basic. He played with one for a few minutes before Mrs. Aubry appeared in the door with a hesitant look on her face.

She had dressed for the occasion. She had to be in her late seventies, and didn't make any attempt to hide it. Her hair was gray and pulled back into a knot at the back of her head. She wore what might be her Sunday best: a pink cotton dress with sleeves.

"Mrs. Aubry," he said as he stood and went over

to where she waited at the door. "I'm Clint Morgan. This is Bart beside me. I hope you don't mind I invited him along, too. He gets lonely by himself."

Some of the hesitation in her face eased. "That's just fine, young man. I like animals." She didn't move. "I'm not very good at fancy electronic things," she said with a tremor in her voice.

Clint knew what he shouldn't say. He shouldn't say it was easy, because that would make her even more afraid that she couldn't master something "easy." Instead, he pulled out a chair in front of one of the new computers. "Why don't you take this seat, ma'am, and we'll just play on the computer for a while?"

She sat, and he took the seat next to her. "How much do you know about computers?" he asked.

"Nothing. My daughter ordered one for me so I could email her and my grandchildren. They're in Florida. But there were no directions so it's been sitting in my dining room."

"If you like, I'll come over to your house tomorrow and set it up for you," Clint said.

She looked hopeful, but then the worry lines on her face returned. "It's too much trouble."

"No, it isn't," he said. "And to tell the truth, you would be doing me a favor. I'm getting mighty tired of my own company in that cabin. And if you like, I'll bring someone with me."

"No need, young man. Eve vouches for you. That's good enough for me."

He spent the next hour showing her how to set up an email account and trade photos. Then he showed her all the possibilities of the internet and discovering information. "What do you like to do?" he asked.

"Gardening?"

"What about cooking?"

"I don't cook much for myself any more. It's just one person."

"Okay, let's look at meals for one person. See that line? Type in 'meals for one person,' or 'quick meals for one.'" He watched as she hunted for the correct keys to type in the words, then beamed when a number of selections came up.

"You can use any combination of words to search for information," he explained. "For gardening," he said, "just type 'plants, Colorado, shade.' Or 'sun.' You can find anything in the world on this machine. You can play bridge or poker, though I wouldn't recommend the latter," he added with a grin. "You can go to a faraway place, or you can read many different newspapers for free."

The hour was up far quicker than he had imagined. "Where do you live, ma'am?"

"On Oak Street. Two twenty-five."

"How does 10:00 a.m. tomorrow sound? I'll hook everything up and set up your email. You can email your daughter immediately."

She hesitated. "I don't want to impose."

"Mrs. Aubry, it isn't an imposition." And it wasn't. He liked her, and her pleasure was contagious.

"Eve was right. She said you were a very nice young man."

He knew his face was coloring. "And you are a very nice lady," he said. "The computer will take you to a lot of places."

"Well, then if you're…sure?"

"I'm sure."

"Thank you," she said a little shyly. "I was really afraid I couldn't figure this out, and everyone would see that. I'm not good at technical things. It seemed easier not to try. I wasn't sure about coming today. I almost didn't." She looked like she was ready to cry. "Thank you," she said again.

"Thank *you*," he said and meant it. He felt useful. It was a gift.

CHAPTER FIFTEEN

STEPHANIE FINISHED WITH her appointments early. Her 5:00 p.m. appointment was cancelled. She decided to go over to Eve's ranch and ride Shadow. Riding always helped her to think. Always gave her a sense of peace, and she desperately needed that now.

She had been unforgivably churlish at lunch today. She'd always supported the troops. She respected the hard job they did, and she was aware of the consequences of doing that job. How could she have said what she did?

It was something that could have come from Mark. But she'd resented Clint breaking in on her conversation with Eve, even if it had been Maude's doing. She resented him looking so damned irresistible. She resented the frisson of heat that ran down her spine when he had looked across the table at her. She resented how her heart beat just a little faster when his lips turned into his wry smile.

She didn't call Eve before arriving. The barn was always open, the horses free to roam the pasture whenever they wished. She had a bargain with Eve and Josh. They boarded her horse, and she provided vet services to their animals. The arrangement worked out splendidly for both.

When she parked the van, Shadow galloped over to the fence. She let Stryker and Sherry out, then headed to the corral to feed Shadow and the two other horses carrots. Stephanie climbed over the fence and led Shadow into the barn, saddled him and rode him back into the pasture. She leaned down and opened the gate, then closed it after they passed through.

Shadow happily stretched into a trot, and Stryker and Sherry ran beside them. Stephanie headed toward a riding trail that bordered several other ranches on the north side of Covenant Falls and led up into the national forest. This was the freedom she loved. Her horse. Her town. Her mountains. Mark couldn't touch her here.

As for Clint, he was an acquaintance, and he would be gone soon, and that pesky attraction gone with him. Her life would be back to its contented normal. *Safe.*

Still, she wondered how he had fared with Mrs. Aubry. The widow owned a cat and lived alone. She was timid, hesitant and reluctant to join any group. Apparently, her husband had been controlling and convinced her she couldn't do anything well. At least that was what the daughter had told her on one of her few visits to town. The daughter had tried to get her mother to move to Florida, but Mrs. Aubry refused. She'd been born in Covenant Falls and she would die in Covenant Falls.

Damn it, Clint Morgan would probably win her over, too.

Stephanie lightly touched her heels to Shadow's sides and he joyfully started to canter. This was her world, and she wasn't going to let Mark destroy it. Or, for that matter, Clint Morgan.

CLINT KEPT BART with him as the time for his next appointment approached. The dog seemed content at his feet although he always kept Clint between him and any newcomer.

Like Mrs. Aubry, Harold Stiles arrived right on the dot at the appointed time. Covenant Falls citizens obviously believed in being prompt. As he had with Mrs. Aubry, Clint asked whether Bart was a problem.

"No, sir," the man said. "Got a bunch of dogs myself." Even if he hadn't known from Bill Evans, Clint would have immediately recognized the man as a farmer. He was thin and wiry, his face dark from the sun, and Clint had felt the calluses on the man's hand when shaking it.

Like Mrs. Aubry, Harold approached cautiously, uncertain about seeking help from an outsider. Clint had a long history of soothing or pacifying superior officers after he, or other members of his unit, got in trouble. Hell, a farmer didn't stand a chance.

His newest client asked to be called Harold rather

than Mr. Stiles, and Clint obliged. The farmer had been keeping all his records, sales and purchases on paper because that's the way his father had done it. But his usual suppliers were going out of business, and he realized that he needed help to survive in the current economy.

The man was smart and caught on quickly as Clint showed him how to find suppliers, check prices and establish accounts. Then he discussed various financial software programs that would help with bills, accounts receivable and taxes. Harold didn't have a computer, so Clint checked out several on-line marketplaces for computers and found a few he thought would fit Harold's needs.

They visited several websites in search of the best price. Harold, Clint discovered, was no one's fool. He knew how to pinch a penny. After Harold finally selected one, Clint offered, as he had Mrs. Aubry, to help set it up in his farmhouse. Harold, now convinced he was going to save a lot of time and money, eagerly accepted the offer.

Clint and Bart left the community center a little after five. A number of children played in the park while two men roasted hot dogs in permanent grills. Balloons proclaimed the event a birthday. Several balloons boasted a big number six.

Adults sat at the picnic tables talking. One of tables was heaped with gaily wrapped packages, another with buns, bowls of food and a large cake. The sound of laughter was like music.

Bart pulled him away from the celebration, and he realized he had come to a complete stop, staring. Several of the adults waved at him, and he waved back. One of the men at the grill signaled for him to join them, and maybe he would have if Bart, shivering, had not pulled him in the opposite direction.

Plus, Eve had told him she would be at the cabin at six. It was a fairly short walk from the community center. Too short because he would have to relinquish Bart at the end of it.

They had just arrived at the cabin, and Bart had just gobbled down a piece of cheese when Clint heard the sound of tires on gravel. He peeked out the door and watched as Eve stepped out of the pickup. Nick, dressed in a Boy Scout uniform, hopped down from the other side of the pickup.

With a sense of dread, Clint opened the screen door and invited the two inside. Bart wagged his tail but didn't go over to Nick.

"Hi, Bravchcart," the boy said. The dog stood and walked over to him, licked his fingers, then returned to Clint's side. Nick's face fell. He looked at his mother.

"I'll get his leash and things," Clint said. "Unless you would like a soda first?"

"That would be nice," Eve said.

"I only have one kind of soda," Clint said, as Eve and Nick entered the living room. Nick sat on the edge of a chair.

"Anything would be fine."

They were all stiff. All uncertain. He headed to the kitchen, Bart following. He opened three cans of soda and returned to the living room, handing one to each of his visitors and taking one for himself.

"Mrs. Aubry called me," Eve said. "She said you were the nicest young man and very helpful." She tipped her head slightly in question. "She said you offered to come over to her house and set up her computer."

"The setup can be confusing," he said. "It often takes an engineer to figure out the instructions. If, that is, they come with any."

"That was nice of you," she said with a satisfied smile on her face.

He wasn't sure how to feel. Teaching—if he could call it that—certainly wasn't flying choppers. But the time had gone by fast, and Mrs. Aubry's shy smile and Harold's appreciation warmed him inside. He'd felt useful for the first time in months. "I liked her."

Nick put his drink down and approached Bart. The boy gave the dog a huge hug. "He's always been so afraid," he said. "He doesn't seem afraid with you."

"We get along," Clint said simply.

"How did you do that?" Nick asked. "He usually doesn't warm up to anyone. It took us months before he stopped hiding under the bed."

"I don't know," Clint replied.

Nick regarded Braveheart sadly. "Mom thinks he wants to stay with you."

Clint started. "I'm not sure he knows what he wants to do. He obviously loves you."

"I love him, too."

"I know," Clint said. That was obvious. He wasn't sure where this conversation was leading, but he sensed Nick's distress. "I'm not going to take your dog."

"Stephanie has a puppy she found on a road," Nick said. "She thought we might want it. Mom says five dogs are enough."

"More than enough," Eve said. "Let's say limit."

"What do *you* think?" Clint asked Nick, now understanding what was going on.

"I want what's best for Braveheart," he said in a tearful voice.

"I don't think I'm best for Braveheart," Clint said. "I have no real home. No steady job. I can't take care of him like you can." But it would hurt like hell losing his companion. Bart didn't care what had brought Clint to Covenant Falls or the uncertainty of his future.

"Why don't we leave it up to Braveheart?" Eve said. She put the soda can down and stood. So did Nick.

"Come on, Braveheart," the boy said. "Let's go." He walked to the door.

Bart didn't follow. He moved closer to Clint.

Nick opened the door. Bart made a soft crying noise but didn't move.

Eve put her hands on Nick's shoulders. "Tell you what. Why don't we leave him here a few more days, then maybe he'll be ready to go home."

"No," Clint said. "I'll go out with you. I'm sure when he's been home a few days, he'll be just fine." He'd be damned if he was going to take a dog from a boy.

Nick's face brightened. "Mom said you started calling him 'Bart.'"

"I did," he admitted. "I just kinda shortened it."

"I like it," Nick said. "I'll call him Bart, too. He's not so timid now. Bart is a nice, strong name."

Clint put the leash on Bart and walked him to the door, Eve and her son following behind. He walked him to Eve's pickup and boosted the dog inside, then helped Nick up. As he closed the door, he saw Bart's face, and he winced. He didn't know dogs could have expressions, and maybe it was his imagination, but he thought he saw betrayal.

He stepped back as Eve paused at the door on the other side and mouthed, 'Thank you." Then the pickup was gone, and Clint was alone.

He went back inside. He needed a drink. A beer. Unfortunately, there was none. He compromised with another soda, grabbed his guitar, went out to the porch and strummed. He needed sound to fill the silence, the emptiness in the cabin. The emptiness in him.

IT WAS DUSK by the time Stephanie finished her ride. She led Shadow into the barn, unsaddled him and rubbed him down. Then she checked to make sure he had fresh water and food.

The moment she fastened the gate to the pasture, her mind turned to tomorrow, and her stomach churned. She looked toward the house, but neither Eve's pickup nor Josh's Jeep were there.

She opened the van's door for the dogs, and they jumped inside, vying for the front seat. Stryker won this time and stuck his head out the window as she started out of the driveway. Sherry settled on the thick rug on the floor.

She needed to get back. Lulu was in her crate, although she had food and water. And yet she didn't want to go back to her apartment. She was still too restless, too uncertain about tomorrow's meeting with the attorney and Mark's wife. Just the call had revived the bad memories she'd tried to suppress.

She drove to Maude's, rolled the windows down and left the dogs in the van as she went into the café. It was nearly empty with only one young couple lingering over coffee. She ordered two hamburgers and iced tea to go. "Am I closing you up tonight?"

"Heavens, no. I'll be here at least another hour."

"You work too hard."

"I could say the same about you. You need a young man."

Stephanie choked out a laugh. "Like I need a third leg."

Maude grinned and disappeared into the kitchen. Stephanie took a seat and stared out the window. The street was empty. The lights were on in the police area of city hall, but the rest of the street was dark. It was nearly eight, and she was antsy. She decided to drive down to the lake and eat there rather than her apartment above the office.

Maude returned with a bulging paper bag. "Here you go. I added a slice of pie I had left over. You look too thin."

"I love you, Maude." She took the bill, noticed the pie wasn't included, and added a very substantial tip. She left before Maude could protest.

The trash cans at the park were full, the obvious remnants of a child's birthday party. Two young couples sat on the swings, talking and holding hands. She turned her eyes away and headed for a table close to the beach. Both dogs trotted at her side.

The night was perfect, even if she was alone. Unlike big cities, the stars didn't have to compete with hundreds of streetlights and neon signs, and they sparkled like jewels sprinkled across a dark blue velvet cloth.

She loved Colorado nights. She had grown up in Pittsburgh. In a walk-up apartment in a mixed-nationality part of town where gangs dominated. There was always noise. Always danger. Always temptations for a kid desperate for love and safety.

She sat down at a table and unwrapped the food. She divided the meat from one hamburger between the dogs and relished her own burger. She was finishing the slice of pie when she saw a figure walk down Lake Road and turn into the park. He looked very much alone, and she knew from the lanky stride that he was the man she'd been trying to avoid.

She also knew the instant he saw her and turned in her direction. She still had most of her iced tea left. She thought about tossing all the wrappings into the bag and escaping, but that would be too obvious. She'd already decided she was never going to run again. Not to or from anyone. Tomorrow would be a test.

Apparently, tonight would be one, too.

Clint looked impossibly appealing. Out of place in his khakis and blue shirt with the sleeves rolled up. "Hi," he said.

"Hi," she replied softly.

"I was out for a walk. I didn't expect to see anyone here."

"I don't usually come here at night." She must look terrible. She was in her riding clothes: worn boots, tight breeches and short-sleeved shirt. Wisps of hair had come loose from the clasp in back. No lipstick. And she smelled like horse this time.

He didn't seem to notice. He looked down at the two dogs, contentedly sitting next to her.

"Say hello," she said to the dogs. And both held out their paws to be shaken. Clint knelt and shook them. "They're really very striking together."

She nodded, not sure whether she wanted to cut

him off or continue the conversation. There was something about him tonight. Not cocky or clever or quirky. Instead, she saw lines in his face, loss in those dark brown eyes. Vulnerability. Uncertainty.

"Do you mind if I join you for a few minutes?" he asked.

She did. *She didn't.* "It's a public bench," she replied. It was ungracious and she was immediately remorseful. "Where's Braveheart?" she asked.

"He went home with Nick." The tone of his voice told her a great deal more. His sadness struck her to the core.

"Do sit down," she said. *Bad idea.*

He visibly relaxed and sat a few inches away. Then he gave her that wry smile that was so attractive.

"I hear you play the guitar pretty good," she said.

"Who told you? My neighbors? Does it bother them?"

"They like it."

He shook his head. "This town has the most amazing…communication system."

"You mean they are remarkably nosy. No need to be diplomatic. They take great pride in the fact. For instance, I also know that Ruth Aubry thinks you walk on water. Haven't heard from Harold Stiles, but I rather imagine I will. I heard you had a session with him. It's very nice of you. Mrs. Aubry is a very lonely woman, and Eve said she had never heard her sound so happy."

He shrugged. "I liked her."

"Are you going to continue mentoring?"

"I think I'll be pretty busy with Josh's dock starting Friday. And then, I have to start thinking about what I want to do with the rest of my life."

"Any ideas?" She was truly curious.

"I was considering computer engineering." He wasn't amusing now, and he wasn't facile, and she found she liked him even more. "I have a lot of university credits already. It would take maybe another year."

"Is that what you want?"

"Honestly?"

"Yes."

"I can't really see myself in an office, but the only other thing I know is flying, and I may never be able to do that again."

"Where would you go?"

"That's another good question. My credits are at the University of Maryland. A lot of guys take on-line courses there. I can probably get some or most transferred to another university, but I have to wait for a new semester. I also have to apply for my military education benefits. Right now I'm seized by indecision and I don't much like that in myself."

That she understood. She remembered only too well how she'd felt when she couldn't find a job as a vet. How would she feel if she was told she could never again work with animals? She knew. Empty. Useless.

She had her practice, and her friendship with

Eve and Josh and a few other people, but she'd consciously kept people at an emotional distance since Mark. She sensed Clint Morgan did the same except he covered it better. She also understood something else. "Eve and Nick took Bra…Bart home?"

"They did."

"You really liked him, didn't you?"

"Yeah, he kinda got to me." He gave her that lopsided smile that had so intrigued her on their first meeting. "I never had a dog before. Well, I don't have one now, but I enjoyed his company."

"Dogs do that to you," she said. "Why haven't you had one before? You seem to be so natural with them. It's not something you can fake. They would detect it in a minute."

"I went to private schools until I graduated from high school, then I went directly into a special army program for helicopter pilots. I was in the service seventeen years. An army base and frequent deployments are not good for animals."

He was close to her. Too close. His dark eyes were expressive and the hollow sound in his voice too piercing. Contradictory images, she knew. Hollow and piercing. And yet they seemed to fit.

She tried to look away from those eyes. Upward. The moon was big. Not quite full, but getting there. And bright, as bright as newly minted gold. The color reflected on the water and a few wandering wispy clouds gave it movement. Soft music came from a portable radio being played by one of the couples on the swing. She tried to concentrate on that, not the tall, lean and ever so attractive man sitting next to her, the man she was beginning to understand.

That smile and ready wit hid something both painful and raw. There was a lot he wasn't saying. Nothing about family. Nothing about his childhood except private schools. A loneliness ran strong and deep inside him. She had tamed hers. She had buried it in her practice and volunteer work. He had nothing now, and she knew exactly how that felt because after her divorce, she'd lived in that never-never land.

She didn't want to recognize it, but it was there between them, same as the strong attraction. No matter how hard she fought the pull linking them, it grew fiercer every time she saw him, and now it threatened to overwhelm her. *Go now.* She needed to get some sleep and be alert tomorrow to meet with the attorney. Yet, she couldn't seem to move.

The need was too strong. Too elemental. Too vital. She felt the heat of his body, and every nerve in her body was sensitized. The air sizzled. His lightest touch sent currents of heat racing through her.

His fingers stroked her cheek. Gently as if she were a fragile piece of glass. Her gaze met his, and she wondered at the vulnerability she saw there. She thought about the way he'd said Braveheart had gone home. She knew that Eve had played with the idea that the dog really belonged with Clint, that for whatever reason, the two had bonded in a way that Braveheart hadn't with anyone else. The somber note in Clint's voice told her he had refused to keep the dog, and not because he didn't want him. It was because of Nick.

All her defenses shattered. There was a decency in him that she hadn't trusted in the beginning. And when she'd started to believe, she'd fought accepting it. It didn't go along with her past experiences.

He was nothing like Mark. Nor was he like Rick who'd transferred all his rage into deadly activities. She had loved him like only a lost sixteen-year-old girl could when an obscenely handsome boy saved her. Temporarily.

"You have the most remarkable blue eyes," he said.

She relaxed against him. His fingers followed the lines of her cheek, then touched her lips. She nibbled the tips of his fingers.

She knew this was not the time or place. The fact they were…romancing in the middle of the city park would be all over town tomorrow.

But she was loath to lose the warmth that surrounded her like a cocoon.

"I have to go," she said. She didn't want to. She was befuddled by longing. She wanted more of his touch. More of his gentleness. She'd never known that before. But this was a public place. Rumors would be running through town like a virus.

And there was the fact, of course, that he was a temporary resident.

He looked at her with questions in his eyes, questions she couldn't answer. She didn't know what would happen in the next few days with Mark. She steeled herself. Now was not the time to get involved with anyone, particularly someone who evoked the kind of emotions Clint did from her. She needed to think clearly.

"I have a dog you may like," she said, switching to the impersonal, practical Stephanie that she'd worked so hard to maintain. "Lulu. I found her on the highway Sunday."

"Ah, you trust me with a dog. Progress."

"I'm getting there," she said, surprised when she found her hand in his.

"As for Lulu, I thank you for trusting me with her, but I'm not really in a position to take one. I was just keeping Bart…Braveheart…for Eve and Josh. It was little enough to do after living in their cabin. We got along fine, but I knew it was temporary."

We got along fine.

Casual words, but he was hurting because of Braveheart. He was an expert at hiding any sign of emotional pain. She certainly had noted how adverse he was to recognize physical pain. She should have figured it extended to the other kind, as well, but she had been blinded by her fear.

He hesitated, then said, "Come to the cabin with me," he said. "Just for a drink? A soda? A glass of water?"

She wanted to. The air had thickened with desire.

Shafts of electricity spiraled through her. She wanted more of his touch. More of that tenderness. Every fiber in her wanted to go with him. But then she remembered her appointment tomorrow. Her own terrible judgment in the past.

"I can't," she said. "I really do need to go home," she said. "I have paperwork and the dogs to feed, and Lulu needs attention."

"Then have lunch with me tomorrow," he said.

"And have the entire town talking?" she said, desperately trying to inject a note of levity to dispel the overwhelming sexual tension hovering between them. "Maybe it's tempting for that reason, but I have visitors coming in from out of town, and I'm not sure when they'll arrive."

"Tempting is good for whatever reason," he said with a half smile that sent her heart reeling. "And I hate to tell you, but from what little I know of this town, I suspect everyone is already talking." He kissed her nose. "I've wanted to do that for a long time. It's a very delectable nose."

"It's a very plain nose," she said.

"Nothing about you is plain." He stroked her hand. "Maybe some other time?"

She should say no. She should shut this down now. She had no room in her life for someone else. And she had no idea what would come of tomorrow's meeting and what damage Mark might wreak if she agreed to help Mark's wife. "I don't think that's a good idea."

"Why?"

"You don't plan to stay here, and I'm not very good at relationships," she said frankly. And, unfortunately, truthfully.

The young couples at the swing departed, the music trailing behind them. Clint touched her hair and played with a curl, then rubbed the back of her neck. His tenderness nearly undid her. He had awakened her body from a long slumber and it craved the feelings long denied it.

He lightly touched her lips with his.

Her arms went around his neck, and his kiss deepened. The raw passion between them was so potent she could barely think. Damn, she wasn't thinking at all. Just…feeling. *Sensations. And aching. Aching like she'd never known.*

And it scared the hell out of her.

She jerked away. "We can't. Everyone will know."

"And that's so important?"

"Yes. No." The latter was the truth. She didn't care about what the town thought about a simple kiss. Or even a not-so-simple one. She cared about the life she'd carved out her for herself here. She cared about her independence. She cared about losing her heart.

She couldn't afford another disaster.

She moved away from him. "I *do* have to go."

"What are you afraid of?" he asked in a low, gentle voice.

She couldn't answer. She couldn't say "you" because that would admit there was something there between them, something so strong that she still hadn't moved when she should be running like hell.

"I don't want to get involved with anyone," she finally said.

"Why?"

"You're here just for a short time," she said, seeking a more logical reason than fear. "It makes no sense to start something. It's not...practical."

His fingers moved to the back of her neck again. "And you're big on practicality?"

Go. Go. Go...

She swallowed hard, then summoning all the self-control she had left, she moved away from him and stood on trembling legs. "I try to be," she said in what she feared was not a very convincing tone.

"I don't give up easily," he said.

"Neither do I," she replied and walked away, forcing herself not to look back.

CHAPTER SIXTEEN

STEPHANIE COULDN'T SLEEP that night. She couldn't stop thinking about the kiss. Her body wouldn't let her. She'd wanted him, and she had come so close to accepting his invitation.

She still wanted. She knew she would want him tomorrow and next week. And, she feared, many weeks after that.

Her lips still felt the warmth of his. His second kiss. The first at Eve's corral had been gentle like a spring rain; this one had been a tornado, tearing apart all reservations. Tenderness had turned into raw, naked need. On both their parts.

She winced as she thought about how she'd basically run away. But the fear was too ingrained in her. Fear of being wrong. Fear of loving and losing not only her heart, but the self-respect that had taken her so long to rebuild.

After she'd left him last night, she had retreated to her backyard. She sat for a while in a lawn chair, staring up at the stars. So bright. So eternal. So immune to feelings that afflicted mere human beings.

Lulu had jumped up on her lap and cuddled as the

night grew deeper. Sherry and Stryker took a piece of grass on each side of her. Her protectors. At midnight, she'd gone inside.

But this was a new day and she had a busy morning. She went through the appointments, all, thank God, benign ones. Checkups and vaccinations. She had no appointments during the afternoon. Nothing unusual about that. She usually tried to keep Wednesday afternoons free. That was the time she caught up on paperwork, ordered medications and sent bills.

Beth usually helped her, but at noon Stephanie sent her home early and she put the closed sign on the door. Susan Townsend's attorney called and said they expected to arrive at the bed-and-breakfast at 1:00 p.m. They wanted to meet her at 2:00 p.m.

Stephanie suggested they come over to her office. It would be the most private place in Covenant Falls.

Just before two, she took Lulu for a short walk, then put her in her kennel. She was in the office when she heard the front-door bell ring. She opened it and greeted the man and woman standing at her doorstep.

She brought them inside the waiting room. Sherry and Stryker had come to the front door with her and, as instructed, they were on their best manners. Both sat and wagged their tails in welcome.

"Thanks for seeing us," David Matthews said while shaking her hand. He was a tall man in his midforties with a nice face and a friendly smile. She imagined he would be good with a jury; he'd certainly been convincing on the phone. Prior to their phone conversation, she'd been determined never to be involved in anything to do with Mark again.

Susan Townsend reminded her a little of herself ten years ago. She was a redhead, too, with blue eyes. Her hair was cut stylishly short and she wore expensive slacks and a silk blouse, but her manner was diffident as if convinced she had little of value to offer. She appeared shy, but whether that was due to Mark's remarkable ability to beat people down, or her natural demeanor, Stephanie did not know.

"I am so sorry I believed what he said about you," Susan said in a voice laced with nervousness.

"I believed everything he said, too," Stephanie replied. "He can be very convincing." She gestured to her dogs. "Meet Sherry and Stryker. They both love visitors. Sherry, say hello."

Sherry held out her right paw. Both newcomers solemnly shook it.

"Stryker?"

Stryker did not always respond as trained, but today he did, and he raised his paw. He barked happily after both visitors took it. Stephanie relaxed. They had passed the Sherry and Stryker test.

She led them upstairs into her apartment. "Can I get you coffee, tea or a soda?" The attorney asked for coffee, Susan a glass of water.

After fetching the drinks, including coffee for herself, she brought the plate of pastries she had bought at Maude's. "I didn't know whether you had time for lunch. These were baked this morning by the best cook in this part of Colorado." She paused, then added, "I know you didn't come here for food. I'm just not sure how I can help you."

The attorney spoke first. "I know from Susan's experience that what you experienced must be painful, but anything you can tell us about your marriage would help. There were rumors…"

"I bet there were. But before I go into that, I want to know why you came to me, why you need information from me and how you propose to use it if I give you any."

"It depends on what you have to say. But I promise I won't repeat or use anything unless you give me permission."

She studied him for a long time. "Let me hear your story first."

Susan looked at the attorney, and he nodded.

She started to speak in a low voice. "Mark and I have a daughter," she said. "Melissa. She's three. He has temporary custody. Not because he really wants her. He never had much to do with her unless there was company around. It's a weapon to make me stay. There's a custody hearing in two weeks. Right now, I'll lose. He says he can prove I'm an unfit mother, that I've had affairs and that I'm mentally unstable, none of which are true."

"He told me he didn't want children," Stephanie said. "That was after the marriage."

"He didn't. He wanted me to take birth control pills. I did because I wanted to please him, but I'm one of the three percent for which they didn't work. My pregnancy came as a surprise to both of us. I was happy. He wasn't. His verbal abuse became worse, then he started hitting me after the baby was born. The last time, I thought he was going to kill me. He always called his personal physician who came to the house. No medical records, and I was too frightened to go anywhere else. He said he could prove I'd been unfaithful and take Melissa and I would never see her again. I remembered all the gossip about you, and I started wondering."

"Whether it was true?" Stephanie asked. "It wasn't."

"I know. I came to understand how controlling he was, how abusive. That he could do what he did to you is only proof that he could ruin my life, as well, and worse, take Missy. But I knew I couldn't stay. His rages were getting worse. If he killed me, what would happen to Missy? His mother…"

"Oh, I know about Mother Dearest," Stephanie said. "Mark could do no wrong."

Tears streamed down Susan's face. "He won't let me see Missy. I don't even know where she is. I don't have a chance against him. I thought, maybe, you could help."

Stephanie believed her. It followed the trajectory of her time with Mark. She didn't want to talk about it because she hated remembering how weak she'd been, how powerless. Wouldn't she be exactly that if she didn't help another of Mark's victims?

"I can tell you what happened to me, but I don't know how it will help."

"Anything that tells us more about Mark Townsend would help," the attorney said.

She told them the whole unvarnished story, not sparing any detail.

She'd kept it bottled up for years, but after the phone calls, she had realized she couldn't keep it private any longer. He'd been the bogeyman in her closet too long. He had kept her from trusting. From loving. From living. She'd become a prisoner as much as if he had locked her in a room. She'd not known how he'd dulled her life until last night when Clint had kissed her.

When she came to the end of her story, she shook her head. "I was offered this opportunity in Colorado. I didn't tell anyone in Boston, just moved here and legally changed my last name to my mother's maiden name. I knew he would come back into my life at some time. He's not someone who lets anyone go. Not without hurting them very, very badly. With me, it was taking away my career. With Susan, Melissa.

"Someone needs to stop him," she continued. "I'll do what I can. I want to warn you, though. I've received several phone calls from an unlisted number in Boston. I didn't answer precisely because I think it may be him, and I didn't want him to find me."

"Do you think we led him to you?" Susan asked.

"Maybe, maybe not. I always knew he could find me if he really tried. However, I would check all your phones. I know he tapped mine when I was in Boston. He was able to block every attempt I made to find a job."

The attorney's face darkened. "Would you testify? In court?"

"If I think it will do any good. But he smeared me so badly in Boston, I don't think anyone will believe me."

Matthews shook his head. "I don't know. Let me think about it. Thank you. You certainly confirmed all my thoughts about him. If he was violent with you and Susan, he must have been violent with others. Now we know there's a pattern. There must be others. Maybe not wives, but girlfriends."

"Good luck," Stephanie said. "He's ruthless, a liar, and won't stop at doing anything to protect his image."

David stood. "We appreciate you seeing us. If we can find one more woman, maybe we can expose him." He cocked his head to the side. "You really think it's Townsend who is calling you?"

She nodded. "Anyone else would leave a message. Well, anyone I would want to answer."

He swore. "I'll have my investigator check our phones as soon as we get back." He glanced at Susan. "Can we take you to dinner someplace? I promise not to discuss this anymore. Maybe that restaurant you mentioned earlier. We're staying here tonight since our plane isn't scheduled to return to Boston until tomorrow afternoon."

Stephanie saw Susan shiver as David said the words. She didn't want to go back. Stephanie glanced at her watch. Four o'clock. She owed them at least that much since it had been a long trip, maybe for nothing. And their enemy was her enemy.

"Did you rent a car?"

He nodded.

"What about a picnic? We would have to take your car since I only have a van with two seats. I think we all need fresh air."

The attorney and Susan looked at each other and nodded.

"I'll call Maude's and ask her to fix a basket. I would suggest fried chicken, although she also has great steaks and hamburgers."

"Chicken sounds good," the attorney said.

"Vegetables?" Susan asked.

"Maude has a very good veggie plate." She called Maude. "I have a couple of Easterners here. I'm going to take them up to the falls and thought we would have dinner there. Fried chicken for three and a veggie plate. Iced tea and three slices of your best pie."

"Friends of yours?"

"Yep."

"Be ready in twenty minutes."

Stephanie was already feeling better. The falls

would clear her head, flush the bad memories away. Hopefully, they would give Susan a few moments of pleasure, as well. No matter how bad some days were, particularly when she had to put animals down, she would head for the falls and breathe in the mist.

CLINT SPENT WEDNESDAY morning setting up Mrs. Aubry's computer. He made sure she knew how to use it and helped her send her first email to her daughter. He also left a set of easy-to-follow instructions and a list of websites he thought she might enjoy.

He arrived back at the community center just in time for an appointment with Ethel Jones who had heard from her friend, Mrs. Aubry, that he was, quote, "a lovely man." There had been nonstop phone calls after that. He apparently had become the most popular man in Covenant Falls.

Mrs. Jones wanted free recipes. She didn't have a computer because it was a "newfangled fad" that would eventually disappear. But she would love to have free recipes and, if he taught her, she could come to the community center once a week until she found the perfect cherry-pie recipe. She intended to win the city competition this year.

Just after her was Herman Mann, an elderly, bearded man who lived in a cabin somewhere up in the mountains. He had bicycled in to pick up a few supplies and heard about "the teacher" at the community center. He didn't have an appointment, but Clint had the time. The old gent wanted to know more about the history of the boarded-up gold mine not far from his cabin. Clint sat him down at the computer, showed him how to look up gold mines in Colorado and watched him wander through the choices.

An hour later, he was still sitting there, lost with Mr. Mann in the stories of those mines. He thought it might be interesting to hike up there. Maybe after the dock was finished. He recalled that Josh had mentioned a travel adventure business. Abandoned gold towns would definitely be a draw.

He didn't mind these hours of instructing, or mentoring or whatever it was. He was picking up bits and pieces of knowledge ranging from recipes to gold mines, and he'd always had a curiosity about almost everything. He had time on his hands until the materials for the dock arrived, and he missed Bart even more than he thought he would. He didn't much like being alone in the cabin, however comfortable it was. And he was rather enjoying meeting the townspeople, all of whom apparently had just become enchanted with computers.

It was four thirty. He decided to go to Maude's for dinner. He walked the three-quarter mile over there. It was already filling up. Maybe some of the guys he'd met Monday night would be there. He'd especially liked Nate and Tony Keller. Both, he knew, were bachelors.

He was just opening the door to Maude's when a strange car drove up, and Stephanie stepped out and headed for the door, a tall man following her. Clint held the door open for both of them. "Having dinner?" he asked as he eyed her companion. Tall. Good-looking. Midforties or so. Jealousy gripped him.

"Taking out," she said. She walked to the counter where Maude was just packing food in a box. The man paid for it, and the two left together. His gaze followed them. There was another person in the backseat. He didn't see Sherry or Stryker as the man drove off.

"Damn," he uttered under his breath. Suddenly, dinner did not seem like such a good idea. He didn't see Nate or Tony. He went to the counter. "I'll have a hamburger and iced tea to go," he told Maude.

The woman looked at him sympathetically. "Stephanie has visitors from out east. Man and woman. They're staying at the local bed-and-breakfast. I expect Stephanie wanted to show them the falls."

Ah, how he enjoyed the Covenant Falls buzz line. Not Stephanie and another man. Maude's explanation was obviously meant to be comforting. Which probably meant someone had seen him and Stephanie together last night.

Maude gave him his sack of food and he started home. Alone.

He walked past the park, past the bench where

he had kissed Stephanie, and she had kissed him back. He ached to hold her. Would she let her defenses down again?

And he missed the quiet presence of Bart, and hoped with all his heart that he was happy to be back with Nick.

"Ah, Bart," he whispered. Damn. Now he missed both Bart and Stephanie.

CHAPTER SEVENTEEN

THE FALLS WERE exactly what Stephanie needed. Susan, as well, if the smile on her face was any indication. The sheer breathtaking beauty of the falls blocked, at least temporarily, the ugliness of their conversation. The mist freshened the air.

Maude had made a special effort with their dinner. The box was piled high with chicken, veggies, salad with fresh strawberries, potato salad and pie. More food than Stephanie had ordered. The wine she had brought was crisp. They feasted with the sound of the falls as musical accompaniment. It was as if they silently agreed to speak no more of Boston. Instead, Stephanie regaled them with the history of Covenant Falls and its denizens, all in an affectionate way. Sometime during the conversation, they moved to a first-name basis.

"You make me want to move to Covenant Falls," David said. "No suits, no ties. No traffic jams. No crime."

"Well, we do have our occasional crime. Our police chief was killed about five years ago by bikers passing through. And then recently we had a rogue police officer, but for the most part, we're a very peaceful town." She ran her fingers along the soft grass. "Probably the biggest problem—for me—is the town's insatiable appetite for gossip or, as the mayor more politely puts it, an endless curiosity. No secret is safe. For long."

"And the nightlife seems quiet," Susan said.

"It is that, although we have several bars that the owners prefer to call saloons. One, which is located outside the city limits, is rough, but it caters mostly to cowhands from nearby ranches. They like to raise hell on payday."

David laughed. "I'm glad to know it isn't perfect."

"It's far from perfect, but it suits me. Mark wouldn't last long in Covenant Falls. People here are pretty good on ferreting out the frauds." *They like Clint. Eve likes Clint. Josh likes Clint. Everyone who has met Clint likes him. But then most of Boston considers Mark a model citizen.*

"I'm sorry we've involved you," David said.

"I involved myself. And I rather imagine that Mark already knows about your visit."

"Are you worried about your safety?" Susan asked.

"Not physically. Not anymore. I'm in search and rescue. I'm also a volunteer firefighter. There's a lot of fitness necessary. I've taken self-defense classes, too. I'm pretty good at karate. And I'm a good shot. Mark doesn't do direct confrontation unless he's sure he can intimidate. He knows, or should know, or will find out, he can't hurt me, not anymore. He might try something more subtle, try to destroy my practice, but people know me here. Not him. Come to think of it, I wouldn't mind if he did try something. I've let him be a bogeyman in my life long enough."

Susan hugged herself. "Do people here know about Mark?"

"They know I've been married. None of the details. That might change now."

"Not from us," David said. "But I can't say what Mark will do if he learns you're talking to us." He frowned. "The fact that you and Susan have similar coloring and frames worries me. It could mean he has a fixation that goes beyond normal. I'm going to ask my investigator to check on other women in his life. In the meantime, be careful."

Stephanie nodded. "It's hard, if not impossible, for anyone new to go unnoticed in Covenant Falls, and the mayor is a friend. So is the acting police chief who, incidentally, also lives at your B and B. You might run into him."

"I don't know how to thank you," Susan said. "Just talking to you helped. I'm just sorry that I didn't talk to you before I married him."

"He's charming. Wealthy. Respected. I can't believe you and I are the only ones he's victimized. If there's enough publicity, maybe others will come forward."

It was getting dark when they left. "Mark will not let you go easily," she warned Susan. "Good luck."

"We'll keep in touch when we get back to Boston tomorrow," David said as he dropped Stephanie off at her office. "Thanks for talking to us. It helps. I'll let you know if anything else develops."

Stephanie waved goodbye and went inside. She checked the office phone. One missed call. No message. She didn't recognize the area code.

She took the dogs outside, all three of them. Lulu was becoming attached to Sherry, and that reminded Stephanie she needed to continue to look for a home for her. Eve was out now that Bart was back with Nick. There was Clint, of course, but she didn't think that was the right fit.

She got some treats and taught Lulu how to shake hands. The more tricks, the easier it would be to place her. By the end of thirty minutes, the puppy had caught on. She was a fast learner.

She fed all three dogs. It was only nine o'clock and she was restless. She poured herself a glass of wine. *Forget Mark.*

Think Clint. And the kiss that was like no other.

Where was he now? Alone? She'd heard from one of her clients this morning that every widow in Covenant Falls had shown a sudden interest in computers. She smiled. He apparently had infinite patience. More proof that he was not like Mark. She couldn't imagine Mark teaching anyone anything. Even his subordinates at the office. He'd expected perfection and if he found it lacking, the employee was fired.

Her cell phone rang. She answered it. A pause. Then a hang up.

The ID simply said, "Private Caller." Calls on both her business and private phones. She didn't like that.

Maybe it was time to call Tony Keller and alert him there was a remote possibility of trouble. She would do it first thing tomorrow. No sense bothering him at night.

CLINT PACED THE CABIN. He'd read for a while. Tried to watch the television. There was a satellite dish in back and a varied number of stations, but after surfing through them, he gave up in disgust.

Some of the overseas posts had satellite television, and he and his buddies usually confined their interest to sports. Tonight, he couldn't find any that interested him. Hell, the Super Bowl probably wouldn't interest him now. He was too preoccupied by a missing dog and an elusive woman.

Damn it, he was jealous. That was an uncommon sin for him, mostly because he never cared enough about any woman. It was love them and leave them, and he usually liked women who felt the same.

What did Stephanie want? He didn't know, though he knew the attraction sizzling between them had grown stronger. So why had she run?

He wished he knew more about her. For all that this town liked gossip, he'd heard precious little about their vet. Apparently, because she gave so little away.

He had more computer appointments in the morning. Bill Evans said the phone had not stopped ringing and the man was thrilled. Clint wasn't so sure he was, although he'd enjoyed his "students." He had never lived in a small town, particularly an insular small town, and he was fascinated with the people he'd met. Most of them, or at least the ones he'd met, would do nearly anything for their neighbors and their town. It was so different from large cities where even next-door neighbors often didn't know each other.

He was too restless to stay still. He needed to walk. He only wished he had Bart with him. He hadn't realized how much he'd bonded with the dog. He missed waking to Bart's snoring, and the way the dog would lie on his back asking for his stomach to be rubbed. He missed the way Bart stayed at his side.

He walked to the park and, still restless, he walked into town. It was after eleven, and everything was closed. A police car drove by, stopped, then the deputy said, "Oh, it's you, sir. I've seen you around. I'm Cody Terrell."

"Just taking a walk."

"No problem. By the way, my granny's coming to see you tomorrow. I offered to show her how to use a computer, but I think she was afraid I would think less of her if she didn't catch on. I wouldn't, of course. She can do a lot of things I could never do. You'll probably see what I mean tomorrow." He tipped his hat. "Good night, sir."

Clint grinned. He would look forward to seeing the cop's "granny." He continued on, walking on the sidewalk, until he was in front of city hall directly across from Maude's. It was closed, of course. Stephanie's office was several doors down from Maude's, and the lights were on upstairs. She was home. Were her visitors staying with her? He was tempted to throw a stone just below the window like some fool in a movie. A crazy idea, and he quickly dismissed it. With his luck, he would miss and hit the glass and be arrested by Officer Cody Terrell.

Then he noticed someone else looking at Stephanie's building. The man was on the other side of the police station, back in the shadows. A big man, holding a camera with long lens. He snapped photos of shops along the street, but lingered on Stephanie's office. Clint watched for several minutes, then decided to act.

He strode over to the man. He was sure he hadn't seen him in town before. "What's so interesting?" he asked.

"None of your business."

"I think it is. I live here. Do you?"

"That's none of your business, either."

"I think I'll go over to that building you're photographing and let the occupant know someone's taking photos of her house. A big guy with a Boston accent. Maybe she knows you. Or," he added, "maybe I'll go to the police station. It's not far behind you."

The other man cursed, then tried to walk away.

"No, you don't," Clint said as he grabbed him. "Not until you answer me."

The camera fell from the man's hands. He cursed and swung at Clint.

A mistake. Clint had received military training from the best. He ducked and hit the guy in his mid-section. It hardly made a dent. His assailant, moving faster than Clint thought possible for a big man, brushed it off and threw a punch that hit Clint's chin. Pain shot through his head. The punch also moved them out of the shadow and onto the visible lawn of the courthouse.

The man leaned down to pick up the camera, and Clint knew he intended to run. He tackled him, bringing him down despite the man's twisting and turning. Clint's hand brushed a holster on the man's belt and realized he had a weapon on him just as his opponent directed a blow to Clint's shoulder. Clint grabbed the man's wrist, standing as the stranger stood. Then he threw the man off balance, and swung a lucky punch on his nose. Blood spurted.

His opponent didn't stop to inspect it. Furious, he struck out again, hitting Clint just below the eye, then aimed for his midsection. It was a glancing blow and Clint remained on his feet. So was the other guy who threw another punch, this time going for Clint's chest. Clint dodged and the man's fist barely struck his side. He kicked out, his leg contacting with the guy's right leg, sending him to the ground. As the man fell, his leg twisted awkwardly, and Clint knew instantly it had broken. Swearing, the stranger writhed on the ground. Clint heard a siren and then a shout. "Police. Stay where you are!"

Clint's body stilled. Flashlight beams nearly blinded him.

Patrolman Cody Terrell approached cautiously, gun drawn.

"He has a gun," Clint told Cody. "And, I think, a broken leg. And maybe a broken nose." Cody searched the man, finding the gun. He took it while the stranger swore.

Cody was joined by Tony Keller. "I was in the office when I heard the siren. What happened here?" Tony asked Clint.

"I was walking past city hall when I saw him skulking around and taking photos of Stephanie's office. I asked what he was doing, and he took a swing at me. I defended myself."

The man on the ground groaned, then said, "Not true. He swung first."

Keller looked at Clint. "You don't know why he's here?"

"Not a clue. Is he one of your residents?"

"Not that I recognize."

Keller kneeled next to the injured man. "Care to enlighten us as to who you are and why you're here?"

"I want a doctor," the man said.

Keller examined the injured leg. The skin wasn't broken, but the man was clearly in pain. "Could be broken," Keller said in a conversational tone. "Who are you?"

"Bolling. Karl Bolling."

"Identification?"

"In my pocket."

Keller removed a wallet from the man's back pocket. Cody held the flashlight so his boss could read it. "PI, huh. Boston. What are you doing in our town?"

"I wasn't breaking a law." Bolling tried to move and groaned. "I want a doctor," he insisted again.

"Maybe not for taking photos, but let's see, we have a clear assault case." He glanced at Clint. "You do want to press charges, don't you?"

"Yes, I think I do."

"Why are you here, Mr. Bolling?" Tony asked courteously, but Clint heard a definite edge to it.

"That's privileged," Bolling said. "And I wasn't breaking the law by taking photos. He just saw me and swung."

Clint raised an eyebrow. "Not true."

"His word against yours," Keller told the detective, "and I know whose word will be believed here in Covenant Falls. And as far as I know, PIs don't have confidentiality anywhere in the country. Speaking of the law, do you have a Colorado carry permit for that gun?"

Bolling didn't answer.

"Didn't think so. I'll add illegal possession of a gun to the assault charges."

"I want my camera back."

"I'm confiscating it for now," Tony said, then used his cell phone. "Doc, I have two casualties here at the courthouse. Nothing major. Looks like a broken leg and maybe a broken nose in one, and one hell of a black eye in the other. Okay if I bring them over? The broken leg is in custody. The black eye is Clint. Yeah, he's in trouble again. Okay. Five minutes."

He hung up, then made another call. "Mayor," he said after a few seconds. "This is Tony. Thought you would like to know there's been an altercation on the courthouse grounds. Haven't sorted it all out yet, but your new tenant is involved." A pause. "No, it's not serious, but he has a shiner. Because of his concussion, I want Doc Bradley to see him."

He listened for a moment, then added, "The other fellow apparently was taking photos of some of the stores with, according to Clint, special attention to Stephanie's building. He was doing it surreptitiously, also according to Clint, and when he confronted the guy, Clint was assaulted. Turns out the assailant is a private investigator from Boston. He also had a .45 with him. Looks like he has a broken leg and broken nose." A pause, then, "Okay. I'm going to have the PI patched up and take him to jail unless Doc thinks he needs a hospital."

Clint saw Bolling glare at Tony. Clint, however, was liking the police chief more each second.

Stephanie emerged from her building. She glanced around, saw Clint and rushed directly to him. "The dogs were going crazy. What—" Then she saw Clint's face. "What in God's heaven happened to you?"

Tony broke in. "He saw someone taking an interest in your building and asked a few unappreciated questions. Turns out the man is a private investigator from Boston who doesn't want to share why he's sneaking around at night taking photos of your building. He hit Clint who responded in like manner."

Stephanie looked at Clint, then Tony. "A private investigator?" she echoed.

"That's what his identification says. He thinks that entitles him to withhold information as to why he's here. It doesn't."

She went over to the wounded figure on the grass. "Mark Townsend sent you." It was a statement, not a question. "What did he want?"

The man glared at her. "If I don't get a doctor, I'll sue the town for every cent it has."

"And what jury is going to award that to you?" Tony said. He gestured to the other two officers. "Doc should be ready for us now. You two had better get a wheelchair from his office for Mr. Bolling here. Call me on my cell when Doc gets through with him and I'll take Clint over."

"I want an attorney," Bolling said, wincing as he moved.

"I'll give you a list of local ones. You have one call, so choose carefully."

He turned to Stephanie and Clint. "I think we need to talk."

"We can go to my apartment," Stephanie said.

"You okay, Clint?" Tony asked.

Clint nodded.

They walked across the street to Stephanie's office. She led the way to a hall, then up stairs to a door. When she opened it, three dogs clamored for attention. Clint leaned down and scratched ears. The smallest one tried to climb his leg.

"No, Lulu," Stephanie said, and the pup sat. She turned to Clint. "I'll get some ice for that eye. And you have a cut on your cheek. It's bleeding. I'll get a bandage until Doc can take a look at you."

Clint touched his cheek where the second blow had landed. He imagined he was going to have one hell of a black eye. There was blood on his hand, but not much. Probably not more than a scratch. Still, he liked Stephanie's concern. He looked around the living area. A comfortable sofa and two large chairs dominated the room. The building was old, but the interior of the living quarters looked well kept and comfortable. Lots of bookcases. Several magazines were tossed carelessly on a coffee table.

She returned with an ice bag full of ice, a wet cloth and a bandage. She wiped the blood from his cheek and applied the bandage. "Coffee or something stronger?" she asked the two men.

"I'm on duty," Tony said. "Coffee. Black."

She turned to Clint. "And you?"

He needed to stay clearheaded, although he dearly wanted something stronger. "Coffee. Black for me, too."

She brought two cups of coffee, handed them to the men, then sat down.

"Cody said you pack one hell of a punch," Tony said, looking at his eye.

Clint shrugged. "Army training."

Tony turned to Stephanie. "The guy was trying to get away. Clint wasn't having it."

"Thank you," she said to Clint, her slight smile warming him, then she looked at Tony. "I was going to call you in the morning."

"Something to do with this?"

"Most likely."

He looked at Clint. "Do you mind if he stays?"

She shook her head. "I wouldn't have known about the investigator if he hadn't noticed him." She looked at his wounded eye. "He earned it."

Clint felt as if he'd just been awarded a medal.

Tony waited for an explanation.

She sighed. "It's a long story."

CHAPTER EIGHTEEN

STEPHANIE WASN'T SURE this was the best thing to do, especially bringing Clint into her problems. And her life.

But he might well be in some kind of trouble, or danger, because of her.

She had no doubt now that Mark must be involved. The anonymous phone calls, Susan's visit and now a Boston investigator were just too much to be coincidental.

Clint had thwarted a plan of Mark's.

"I think the PI was sent by my ex-husband, Mark Townsend," she said. "He's an investment banker in Boston." She took a deep breath. She didn't like to admit what an idiot she'd once been. But now, thanks to Clint, she knew Mark had been trailing Susan. And her.

"Do you have any idea why your ex-husband would send Bolling here?"

"Mark was abusive, verbally and physically. When he became violent, I left. He fought the divorce, then he did everything possible to destroy me without dirtying his own hands. He almost succeeded. To escape his reach, I legally changed my name and Dr. Langford helped me do it. But Mark doesn't like to lose. Anything.

"I thought that period of my life was over, but earlier today, I had visitors. Mark's current wife and her attorney were somehow able to find me. She's desperate for a divorce, but he's holding their three-year-old girl, Melissa, as hostage. I don't think I can let him do that."

She looked at Clint's face. His jaw was set, his dark eyes glittering with something she couldn't read.

"What *did* he do to you?" Tony asked gently.

"First of all, Mark is a well-connected and respected banker in Boston. He comes from a very old and respected Boston family, donates to political campaigns and is a friend of the mayor and police officials. He is a sponsor of the symphony and supports other charities. He is absolutely charming. He can do no wrong in the eyes of most people. I thought so, too, until several months after I married him, Dr. Jekyll turned into Mr. Hyde."

She then told them everything she'd told David Matthews and Susan.

"Son of a bitch," Tony said when she finished.

Clint hadn't said a word. He'd kept the ice pack pressed against his eye, but his body was rigid. He looked nothing like the easygoing charmer now. The heat of his anger practically touched her.

Did he understand? Believe her? She shouldn't care, but she did.

She cared more than she ever thought she could.

The phone rang. Tony answered. "Doc is ready for Clint." Stephanie looked at her watch. Nearly two hours had passed.

Clint didn't move. "You obviously think he could come after you now."

She nodded. "I've had several anonymous calls from the Boston area. I haven't been ready to answer them. I do know that if he thinks I'm helping Susan…"

She stopped when she looked at him. She'd wondered more than once how the easygoing, friendly Clint Morgan could have been a chopper pilot at war. Seeing him now, she understood. His eyes squinted, had darkened into bottomless onyx. His lips were compressed into a tight frown. His body tensed like a coiled spring.

Tony hung up the phone. "Doc said Bolling has a broken leg, but it's a clean break, and he put a cast on it. The nose isn't broken, but it's going to hurt like hell. He doesn't see a need for a hospital, which is very good indeed. I'll go back and find out what Mr. Bolling has to say." He pointed to Clint. "You go get checked out by Doc. He's waiting for you, and it's past his bedtime. That makes him grouchy as hell."

"I don't think Stephanie should be left alone," Clint said.

"Stephanie makes her own decisions," Stephanie

said. "Believe me, I can take care of myself now. And Sherry and Stryker may look harmless, but they're very protective." She gave Clint a wan smile. "Now you, you look a little worse for wear. I don't think Covenant Falls is doing much for your health." She couldn't resist adding, "From foot to head."

Tony grinned. "Believe her," he said. "I've been target-shooting with her. She's as good as I am. I'm thinking this Townsend will be sorry if he takes her on again."

"Except *I'm* going to take *him* on this time," she said. "Tony, I want to turn the tables. Can you tap my office phone? Record calls?"

"Yeah. The former police chief salvaged all kinds of equipment. What are you thinking?"

"I know how to push his buttons. If he calls, maybe I can…"

"You know it wouldn't be legal in court," Tony said.

"Maybe not, but it's ammunition."

"I'll do it, but only if you promise to call me immediately if he contacts you."

"I will."

"I'll do it tonight."

Tony's cell rang again. "Doc says if you don't get over there, he's going to bed."

"I don't need…"

"I'll go with you," Stephanie said. "Tony can go talk to Bolling, then to Susan and David. They're still at the B and B, but plan to leave early in the morning. I'll call and tell them he'll be calling."

Tony left, and Stephanie was alone with Clint. "Thank you for stopping that PI. Now that I'm alerted, I'll be careful. How did you happen to see him?"

"Restless, I guess. I started walking and just kept going." He shrugged. "To tell the truth, I missed Bart."

The words hit her like a ten-ton truck. Eve had said they'd bonded, but she hadn't realized how much. Nor had she realized how lonely he must be in a strange town, unable to drive, unable to do the one thing he'd apparently excelled at. He'd made an effort to make friends, had tutored some of the oldest and most difficult residents and had made them smile.

He'd given up Bart because he didn't want to hurt a boy.

He was as different from Mark as any two men could be.

She touched his cheek. "I'm sorry," she said.

"I'm not. It felt damned good punching that guy. An outlet for my frustration, a psychologist might say."

"And you're frustrated?"

"On many fronts," he said with the smile that became more attractive day by day.

"Mrs. Aubry thinks you're very good-looking."

He laughed. "Is she your client, too?"

"Yes. She has a cat.'"

"I'm flattered. Dare I hope you agree?"

"Maybe if you didn't have a black eye, swollen cheek and a foot kicked by a heifer."

"Minor flaws."

He kissed her then, and she wasn't going to pretend she didn't like it, didn't want it, didn't need it.

The events of today had shaken her. They had brought back the pain, insecurity and helplessness she'd once felt. But they were receding now as Clint's arms wrapped around her and she burrowed herself in the warmth and gentleness that had once so frightened her. She hadn't trusted it then.

Maybe she still didn't trust it completely. But she was getting there.

His lips touched hers, and her world exploded. Need boiled between him, hers as great as his. It was the tenderness mixed with passion that inflamed every sense in her body, the way his fingers so lightly caressed the back of her neck.

She closed her eyes and leaned against him, feeling an oddly comforting protection. The kiss deepened and she was as much a participant as he. She wanted him as much as she sensed he wanted her. She moved closer and his body tensed. She heard the quick intake of breath and sensed it was from pain, not passion, though the latter was certainly present.

She stepped back. "Take off your shirt," she said.

"Yes, ma'am."

His well-toned chest and left shoulder were covered with large bruises. His cheek had become even more multicolored. His eye was red and the area under it already purplish blue. "We're going to Doc's," she said in a voice strange to her. She wasn't ready for the deluge of emotions rushing through her. She'd fought against them so long.

"You can trust me," he said, low, gentle. And she realized he knew exactly what she was thinking. "I'll never do anything you don't want to do."

It was as if he read her mind. As if he understood and was telling her he wanted her enough not to push.

She swallowed hard. Maybe she wanted him to push...

The phone rang. They both stood for a moment, unwilling to break the emotional spell binding them together. Then she forced herself to break away. "That will be Doc."

She picked up the phone. "Where in the devil are you?" Dr. Bradley said.

"We're on our way," she replied and hung up. She handed him his shirt. "I think we'll probably have an audience out there."

"You're coming with me?"

"Can't have you fainting on Main Street."

"Is that the only reason?"

"No," she said quietly and felt his hand take hers. She suddenly realized he had never once mentioned family or friends or a past beyond the army. More of her last existing resistance slipped away.

His black eye was, after all, her fault. His attacker had been sent because of her. Going with him was the least she could do.

"Stryker, Sherry, stay here. Take care of Lulu. Now we should hurry, or Doc Bradley will probably raid us."

CLINT AGREED TO GO because it meant spending more time with Stephanie.

He was fine. Better than fine. He felt positively giddy. His eye hurt, his cheek was sore and other parts of his body ached, but that was more than compensated by the knowledge that Stephanie wanted him as much as he wanted her.

And now he understood her reluctance to get involved despite the fact that from the day they had met there'd been something explosive between them. From what she had said about her marriage, she was understandably suspicious of the opposite sex.

She had dropped that guard, at least for tonight and let him inside her life, in the entrance only, but that was a beginning.

Doc Bradley waited at his front door. "About time," he said. "You know where the exam room is. Stephanie, you can wait out here."

He followed Clint into the examination room. He checked Clint's eye. "Have you seen it yet?" he asked.

"No. Just felt it."

"You were lucky. Doesn't look like any actual

damage to the eye, but it's red and the area around it is going to be swollen and discolored for a time." He removed the bandage, swabbed the cut and applied a new one. "I understand you were on the ground," he said when he finished. "Any blows to the head?"

"No."

"You sure about that?"

"Yeah."

"You realize you have to be careful to avoid any more concussions? There's an accumulative effect on your brain."

"I didn't choose that fight."

"Doesn't matter. You need to go out of your way to avoid them." He sat back. "Any more headaches?"

"One a few days ago."

"Less frequent?"

"I think so. There's not been a blackout since I left the hospital."

Dr. Bradley frowned. "All the more reason to be careful. Are you okay on pain medicine?"

"Yes. Haven't used much of it."

"And your foot is better?"

"Completely healed."

"Try to stay out of trouble, young man."

"That's my intention."

The doctor sighed. "My practice has increased since you came here."

Clint grinned. "I'll try to do something about that."

"Please do, young man." He let Clint go out into the main office where Stephanie waited.

"He's all yours," Doc Bradley said. "Please take better care of him. I'm getting too old for late nights."

"He's not mine," Stephanie protested.

"You're the one who keeps bringing him in," the doctor said briskly, but there was a hint of amusement in his voice.

They left the office. "I don't think he approves of me," Clint said.

"He only grouses at people he likes. It's all a big pretense."

They were silent as they walked back to her office. He wanted to go back upstairs and explore the opening she'd given him, but he feared pushing her too hard now. She was vulnerable. He knew that from her stilted, brittle voice when she had talked about her ex-husband. If Mark Townsend had been nearby, Clint thought there was a good chance he would have killed the man.

When they arrived at her building, she turned to him. "I'll drive you home."

It wasn't what he wanted, but it would do for the time being. He nodded.

He followed her to the back where she'd parked the van. It reminded him of the first day when she and the van had screeched up to the bus stop.

"It's not locked," Stephanie said opening her door.

Clint smiled. Very little was locked in this town.

Crime was rare, which is probably why the fight to-night would be all over town by breakfast.

The drive to his cabin was short, silent. He didn't know what to say, how to prolong those moments of intimacy in her apartment. She had exposed a painful part of her life to him and Tony, and he knew how difficult that was. When they reached the cabin, he knew she wasn't going to come inside with him. He touched her hand. "If you need anything…"

The wrong thing to say. He knew it the minute the words left his mouth.

She'd made an art of not needing people. He realized that now. He knew it because he had done the same thing.

But she surprised him. She slowly relaxed. "Thank you," she said. "I wouldn't have known about Bolling and Mark if you hadn't noticed something wrong." She shook her head and gently touched his cheek. "Doc was right. I seem to be your Jonah."

"A black eye does not a Jonah-class disaster make," he noted mildly.

She smiled at that. "Maybe not, but…"

"And it added a little zest to life," he said. "I think I needed that."

"It's not been easy, has it?" she asked. "I know from Josh how difficult it is to leave the army when you intended to make it your career. I can't imagine the kind of bond you guys have out there."

He smiled. "I have to say that Covenant Falls is a lot more interesting than I thought it would be."

She frowned. "You mean hazardous, don't you?"

"It's getting up there," he agreed.

"Sorry about that."

"Don't be. I would be bored silly if not for you."

"I don't know about that. Right now, you seem to be the most popular man in Covenant Falls, particularly among the seniors, and it had nothing to do with me."

"Yes, it did," he said, suddenly serious. "I was determined to impress you."

"Maybe, but you can't fake liking them. Nor the patience in working with them. Nor all the time you're taking. I'm sure it was originally supposed to be a few hours a week. From what I hear, it's turned into a full-time unpaid job."

"I like them," he said simply.

"I like *you*." She'd blurted it out, and it shocked him. Her, too, by the look of surprise on her face.

He leaned over and kissed her. Lightly. His lips barely touching hers. Demanding nothing. Asking nothing.

He wanted more. So much more. But he knew she was still hurting from the story she told. Mark Townsend had really done a number on her.

"I shouldn't leave you alone," he said. "Maybe someone should stay with you."

Wrong thing again. "The dogs are protective. I'll lock the doors and the police are right across the street. I'm sure Tony will make sure they keep an eye on my place. I don't need…"

He touched her cheek. "I know. You don't need anyone. Just be careful."

"That's an advantage of living across the street from city hall and the police station. I'm sure they'll keep an eye on me," she said. "Good night." He stepped out of the van before he lingered any longer.

She was tired, and he didn't want to take advantage of that.

She simply nodded.

The gravel scattered as she backed up, then wheeled out of the driveway with her usual speed. He watched until she was out of sight. He had broken through some of her barriers, but then what did he have to offer her? Not very much.

And Townsend was a phantom out there. In her mind and out.

Clint decided he was going to find out a hell of a lot more about one Mark Townsend.

CHAPTER NINETEEN

I LIKE YOU.

Why had she just blurted it out? Stephanie pulled out of his driveway agonizing over that question. She really didn't know him well. Two weeks? Not even.

But she *had* liked him the minute they'd met. Suspicious, yes. Wary? Certainly. She hadn't wanted to like him. But there'd been a genuineness about him that had attracted her. Reluctantly.

His humor enticed her. He found something amusing in almost every situation. He'd never once complained about his injury, and he'd pitched in at the community center with affable charm. He hadn't wanted a gift of anything. He wanted to earn everything.

Still, she'd been suspicious.

Tonight changed that. She had carefully watched his face as she told the police chief about her ex-husband. There was no mistaking the growing outrage in Clint's eyes. He'd not only been angered on her behalf but that of Susan's.

It really made no difference, though. She didn't

want to be dependent on anyone again and she didn't want anyone to be dependent on her.

Hard lessons learned well.

Clint Morgan was a danger to that.

She *liked* him. She couldn't let it go further than that. Still, she couldn't drive his image from her head. Clint with his black eye and torn shirt and indignation. She didn't believe in heroes, but...

She was wildly greeted by the dogs when she arrived home. She let them out in the backyard and poured herself a glass of wine. She'd never needed a glass more.

Tony called. "I saw your light go on. I can bug your phone now if you still want it."

She did.

When he finished, she glanced at the clock. It was nearly midnight and she had early-morning appointments. News of last night's altercation was, no doubt, going to keep phones busy, including her own. She owed it to Eve to call her first thing in the morning.

Her cell phone rang. Anonymous. She didn't answer. Then the other phone rang, the office phone that had an extension upstairs. "Anonymous" again. This time she answered it.

"Stephanie." She immediately recognized her ex-husband's's mocking voice. "I hear you finally finagled a two-bit practice in a nowhere town."

"How astute of you to discover that after five years," she shot back. "You're slipping." She wasn't afraid of him now, and she wanted him to know it.

"I wasn't interested until lately," he said. "I just wanted to give you friendly advice. Stay out of my business."

"Oh, do you mean your current divorce? Funny how you can't keep wives. Maybe Boston's finally figuring out why." He was silent. "Or," she added, "is it about the detective who is in our jail? I thought you hired better help."

There was a silence, then "Bitch." She'd heard it before. Too many times. It no longer fazed her.

"I'm bored, Mark. Good night." She cut off the phone and silenced the ring. He could call as many times as he wanted. She would have a record of them, though, and might well pursue stalking charges against him.

She knew him, inside and out. He wouldn't leave it there. He wouldn't let her have the last word. He would call again and she would have a proposition for him.

She'd promised Tony she would call him if Mark made contact. She would. She just wouldn't tell him what else she had planned. Not yet.

She made the call, finished the wine and went into her bedroom. Was Mark's detective after Susan or her? And what could he do to her that he hadn't already done? She'd really enjoyed Mark's moment of silence. She only wished she could have seen his face.

The detective would be in a puddle of trouble. Her ex-husband did not tolerate incompetence. Not only had the detective apparently trailed Susan, and most likely tapped her phone, he could also be charged with stalking Mark's ex-wife. She wondered if Mark had known his detective was in jail before she'd mentioned it. It would be even more interesting to see whether some crony of Mark's appeared to bail out the PI or whether he would be left to fend for himself. Loyalty was not one of Mark's virtues.

She thought about calling Susan and her attorney, and tell them about the call, but it was late. Tony had probably already talked to them anyway. Instead, she checked all the locks on her building and went to bed. Sherry immediately jumped up and Stryker took his position as watchdog on the carpet. Lulu, on a practice run outside the kennel, curled up next to him.

Stephanie was exhausted, mentally, physically and emotionally. She could erase Mark from her mind—temporarily—but she had a harder time doing that with Clint. She pictured him tackling a man many pounds over his own weight. Over and over again. Drat, the man wouldn't leave her head.

As EXPECTED, the next morning the town talked about nothing but the arrest of a Boston private detective. Because Stephanie lived immediately across from the episode, everyone assumed she would know what happened. She hated to lie, or misinform, but the Boston part of her life was over, and she didn't want to resurrect it. Tony, bless him, had limited his public comments and said only that the suspect seemed to be staking out Main Street businesses for some reason and had attacked the town's newest resident when questioned.

The immediate assumption was that the man was casing the small bank branch at the end of Main Street, or maybe the drug store. Then there was Maude's. Her café had been robbed six months earlier.

With the exception of a few fights, a couple of DUIs and one domestic fight, there had been little crime in town since a police officer had been charged with kidnapping Eve's son. This new news electrified the citizens of Covenant Falls, especially when they heard the veteran in Josh's cabin had apprehended the man. Or rather, stopped him until the police had arrived.

He was the hero of the hour, according to her callers. And he had been badly injured, according to the rumor mill. By 10:00 a.m., he was near death's door. A caravan of women planned to take food to him until Eve discouraged them. He needed a day to recuperate, then, she told those who had asked, he would be back at the community center. *Poor Clint.* Now every woman in Covenant Falls would want computer lessons.

Beth wanted to know every detail, and Stephanie told her only what she'd told everyone else.

Eve called to ask if she wanted to have lunch together at Maude's, and she agreed. Eve might know the latest from Tony and whether Bolling had said anything beyond what Stephanie already knew.

She told Beth she would be at Maude's if needed and walked to the café. As she thought would happen, several people stopped her on the street to ask questions. Fortunately, she had condensed her version to about fifty words, then she met Eve inside. The dining room was packed. They decided to get sandwiches to go and walked to the park.

When they reached a picnic table, they sat and Eve said, "Now tell me what really happened."

"Didn't Tony tell you?"

"He was holding something back. I think you know what it was."

"He probably did," Stephanie said, then told her about Mark Townsend and his wife's visit. "The private investigator has refused to say who he works for, but the fact he's from Boston and I had calls from his wife's attorney makes it almost sure Bolling is here on Mark's behalf." Then she told Eve about Mark's call and what she'd said.

Eve laughed. "You told him you were bored. I love it."

"I think Clint's weird sense of humor is rubbing off on me."

"You could do worse. He really is a good guy, Stephanie."

"I know. I realized that last night, although I think I knew it all along. I just didn't want it to be true. Maybe I still don't."

"Why?"

"Lots of reasons."

"Most of them named Mark Townsend?"

"Most." Time to change the subject. "How is Braveheart doing?"

"Not well. He's not eating. He's moping about and sits at the door as if expecting someone who is not already in the house."

"How does Nick feel about it?"

"He's coming to the realization that Braveheart wants to be with Clint. It's really hard on him. He wants to do the right thing. He likes Clint, but he's given his heart to protecting Braveheart." She sighed. "It doesn't help that he knows Clint may not be around long."

"Don't forget I have a pup that needs a home and the kind of love Nick offers. Her name is Lulu and she gets along well with my dogs."

"I know." Eve's eyes sparkled. "Nick loves eating at Maude's. Maybe I'll pick him up at school and tell him Josh won't be home until late so we'll have dinner at Maude's. Then it's only natural that we walk over and see you. And Lulu. He'll be very curious about what happened last night, too."

"How will Josh feel about that?"

"He's been worried about Nick, too. He and Nate can go to their favorite watering hole for burgers. I might suggest they take Clint, as well."

"Good idea. I think he's feeling rather alone.

That's why he was so conveniently where he was last night. He was restless, he said. Out for a walk."

"He seems a lot more sociable than Josh ever was. Or will be," Eve said thoughtfully. "Josh is a lot better than he used to be, but he's had to work at it. It seems very natural with Clint."

Stephanie didn't agree completely, but she didn't say anything. Clint had said nothing about his family. There were subjects he avoided. And while he was friendly with everyone, she'd sensed he was withholding part of himself.

She really didn't want to hear any more praise for Clint today. She'd stayed awake most of the night thinking about his kiss, how it made her body hum. More than hum. It had been raw and vital and yet so impossibly tender.

"I have to get back to the office," Eve said. "I have a council meeting tonight. We're still looking for a police chief. We won't be able to keep Tony much longer. He's too qualified for us, and he has his career to think about. I'm thinking we should look closer to home, maybe one of our veterans. Someone who knows the town and the people. They have weapons experience, and we can send them to law enforcement courses to get whatever else they need. Common sense is the biggest requirement."

Stephanie's antenna went up when she saw the gleam in Eve's eyes. "You aren't thinking of Clint? Don't forget why he's here. His injuries..."

"I hadn't, until last night. He handled himself

well. He wouldn't need to drive unless there's an incident. Then someone could drive him…"

Stephanie could tell Eve was thinking out loud.

"We really don't know much about him."

Why was she fighting this so hard?

"True, but he's meeting people in record numbers. He's all anyone talks about, and all the unattached ladies—with the exception of you—are figuring out ways of meeting him. Poor Bill Evans can't keep up with the demand for computer instruction."

Stephanie silently blessed the fact that Eve didn't know about that kiss last night. *Or did she?*

"What about Cody?" she asked.

"He's only twenty-three. Not enough maturity or diplomacy to handle some of our problems. And he's the best of our officers."

"How do you know Clint would be interested?"

"I don't. It's just an idea. He probably wouldn't even entertain it. I imagine it pays far less than what he made in the army." Stephanie could see the idea boiling in Eve's mind. It might have started out as a joke, or to provoke her, but now her friend had caught interest in the idea. "One of the main requirements," she said, "is to get along with people while being respected. He seems to do that naturally. And then there's his computer skills."

Stephanie needed to put the brakes on this. Eve always had provocative ideas, some good, some bad. Most, Stephanie had to admit, were good. She had single-handedly transformed a vacant building into a community center by sheer persistence. "I don't think it's a good idea."

"Why?"

"He has no training in law enforcement and you really don't know much about him. He's been here a very short time."

"Sometimes it doesn't take long to see a person's qualities, but, no, I am not going to do anything rash. As I said, it's just an idea. I haven't had any luck talking to other agencies or placing ads. The candidates are all too young or too old or have a bad record, or want more pay. I'd definitely run a more extensive background check. Josh basically relied on military records and the psychologist's recommendation in bringing Clint here."

"What about Josh? He would be perfect."

"Nepotism, my friend. We just went through that earlier this year. Don't forget Deputy Sam Clark and his uncle on the city council. Sam thought he could get away with anything, including framing Josh and kidnapping Nick. Never again, not while I'm mayor. But even if he wasn't my husband, Josh is dead set on rehabbing the motel and growing this town." She smiled. "You know that. And when Josh gets set on something, nothing deters him. He also does not accept fools gladly, and sometimes tact is required. As much as I love him, tact is not one of his attributes."

Stephanie had to agree with her there. "What about Nate? He's army."

"Same problem as Josh. He wants to be back in building and contracting."

"Clint doesn't even plan to stay here."

"Maybe because there was no reason to stay. Tony is impressed with him. Clint could work with Tony for a few months, take courses in criminal justice online. Cody's good on backup." Eve shrugged. "As I said, he probably wouldn't be interested anyway. Still…"

Stephanie wanted to say something else, but she feared she had already protested too much. "I have to get back. I have appointments this afternoon. But I'll see you and Nick around five thirty, and he can meet Lulu. He'll fall in love with her."

"I don't know," Eve said. "He usually likes the untouchables. He wouldn't know what to do with a perfectly normal pup." She hesitated, then added, "She *is* normal?"

"Perfectly. She's smart and affectionate and cute as a button. Looks like a female Benji."

They bundled up the paper box, cups and plates and threw them into the trash can. Stephanie glanced at the community center. Several people were going inside. Was *he* there now? Or was he hurting from the fight last night?

The rest of the afternoon flew by quickly. Nearly everyone had a comment about last night's events. The legend of Clint Morgan was growing by the hour. Her last appointment concluded at five. Beth left for the day and twenty minutes later, Eve and Nick came in through the open door.

"You should lock it when someone isn't here," Eve said.

"I'm not going to live in fear, and I knew you were coming. One of the things I like about Covenant Falls is I don't have to lock doors."

"Maybe now you should. Until we know more about this detective and your ex."

"I will," Stephanie promised.

Nick was oblivious to the conversation. He was looking around. "Mom said you had a new dog. A puppy."

"She's up in my apartment. Come on."

Nick followed her, and Eve behind him.

Stephanie opened the door. She fetched Lulu from the kennel and set her down in front of Nick. Lulu held out her paw, just as Stryker and Sherry did.

Nick took the dog in his arms, and Lulu licked his face. Nick giggled. Yep, done deal.

"How old is she?" Nick asked.

"I estimate four months give or take a week," Stephanie said. "I named her Lulu, but that's subject to change. She's had all her shots and I'll spay her next week."

"I really like her, Mom."

Eve looked at Nick. "We can't have six dogs."

"I know," he said sadly. "But Braveheart really does want to go to Mr. Morgan, doesn't he?"

"I think he does. That doesn't mean, though, that

Mr. Morgan will want that responsibility. You'll have to ask him."

"Why don't you do it?" Nick said in a small voice.

"Because he won't take Braveheart unless he's convinced it's what *you* want."

"I don't want it, but I think it's best for Braveheart."

"I am really, really proud of you," Eve said.

Stephanie watched and felt a tear in the back of her eye. Nick loved Braveheart. He had been the boy's favorite, although he tried not to show it. He wasn't trading one dog for another. He'd already made up his mind. She knew that after her earlier conversation with Eve.

"And you want Lulu?"

He nodded.

"Why don't you come over and play with her after school for the next few days, and after I spay her, you can take her home. Okay?"

"Thank you," he said. She noticed, however, the tears shining in his eyes. If Clint Morgan didn't take care of that dog, and treat him well, she would do bodily harm far worse than the detective had last night.

CHAPTER TWENTY

Clint spent most of Thursday nursing his injuries. He'd postponed his computer appointments until Friday. He was sore all over, and his face looked like it had been pulverized by a hammer. But all of it was worth it for the few intimate moments last night with Stephanie.

She liked him. Stephanie's declaration was the equivalent of someone else saying they loved him. She was still fighting it, but despite the bruises, he was happier than he'd been in a long time. He had something to live for now, something to fight for. The listlessness, the sense of failure, the loss he'd felt at losing the camaraderie of his unit, of chopper pilots in general, was receding. He missed it. He missed it all. He missed the sound of choppers lifting into the sky, the toasts the pilots made after a successful mission, knowing they had saved lives. Clint had tried to put it all behind him, look forward to a different life, but it was a very large shadow that taunted him. Last night had helped. So had the past few days of helping seniors. He'd enjoyed it far more than he had ever imagined. They were so hungry to learn and yet so hesitant about admitting it.

He had hoped to hear from Stephanie today, but then she would be busy at the practice. She might well be having second thoughts about their kiss and her admission that she liked him. He wouldn't blame her after hearing about her nightmare of a marriage.

At 4:00 p.m., Josh called and asked if he would like to go with him and Nate to the The Rusty Nail for burgers and beer. Eve and Nick planned to have supper at Maude's, "a mom-and-son thing," he said, obviously a bit miffed. "They're involved in some conspiracy. Only God knows what."

Clint readily accepted. Every bone in his body ached, his eye and cheek hurt, but it would do the same in the cabin, and he felt like a caged tiger. He needed out. He wanted to know what was going on. He wanted to make sure Stephanie was protected.

Josh picked him up in his Jeep. He said Nate would meet them at The Rusty Nail.

Clint liked Maude's. In fact, he was growing addicted to Maude's, but there was something about The Rusty Nail's greasy hamburger with cheese and onions that met a deep-seated culinary need in him. They were burgers at The Rusty Nail. Hamburgers at Maude's. There *was* a difference. And a beer sounded particularly good.

Nate was already there and had ordered the burgers and ice-cold beers. "You look awful," he said cheerily. "Hear you whacked the hell out of a bad guy."

"I think whether he is a bad guy is still to be determined."

"Anyone skulking around our fair town is a bad guy," Nate retorted. "You have any idea about the reason?"

"He's not talking," Josh said.

Clint held up his hands. "Don't look at me. I've been nursing this face all day."

"Hate to tell you, it didn't work."

"Thanks," Clint said with a pained smile.

Josh changed the subject to the dock. "Calvin said he'll have five helpers on Saturday. His son will take care of the store."

"I thought the idea was for me to do it," Clint said.

"It was. Then Calvin got involved. But what the hell, you're mentoring half the town on computers. You're busy." He took a sip of beer. "Eve is a very happy mayor, by the way. It's a beautiful thing to watch the way her mind works. She did the same thing to me. Before long, I was repairing someone's roof."

"He won't tell you," Nate said. "But he was quite happy about it as soon as he discovered he would be working at Eve's side."

"Eve was roofing a house?"

"A woman of limitless interests," Josh replied. "I keep being surprised by her."

Their food came, and conversation stopped. When they finished eating, Clint asked, "How is the motel renovation coming?"

"We start next week. We can use another hand," Nate said.

"I have some more computer appointments," Clint said. "And Josh's dock, too, but then I would like to give it a try."

He realized suddenly that he was thinking about staying longer than the couple of weeks he'd anticipated. He turned to Josh. "I don't know when you need the cabin back."

"You can stay as long as you want it."

"I can't stay there forever."

"You'll know when it's time. In the meantime, there's no hurry."

"This is the damnedest town," Clint observed.

"That's what I thought, too," Josh admitted. "But Nate says it's not all that different from other small towns. Are you a big-city boy?"

"I was born in Chicago."

"Grow up there?"

Normal questions, but they opened a box of pain. "Mostly in boarding schools," he said in a tone that cut off more questions on the subject.

Music suddenly blared from an old-fashioned jukebox, and it was too loud to talk. They savored another beer and then Josh stood. "I'd better get home. Eve and Nick should be there now. I promised I would throw a football to Nick."

They each threw in money for the bill and a substantial tip and left.

As Josh drove him home, Clint's head began to throb. Great. The beginning of a headache. It struck with full force just as he reached his front door. He'd barely made it to the sofa before everything went dark.

He was disoriented when he regained consciousness some time later. He made it into the bedroom, but his head continued to pound until late in the night, even with some pills.

THERE WAS STILL a residue of the headache when he woke. It was morning. Must be Friday. He felt washed out but he had appointments. He wanted to see Stephanie. Check on her without her knowing he was doing it. Dammit, he'd lost half a day yesterday. What had happened in that time?

He took a hot shower that soothed some of the bruises and sore spots on his body. He stepped out of the shower and looked in the mirror.

He shouldn't have done that.

The right side of his face was varying shades of purple and red and other ugly colors he couldn't identify. His eyes were bloodshot. A Band-Aid covered the cut on his cheek.

He knew, unfortunately from experience, that black eyes looked worse the second, third and fourth days than immediately after the event. He had that to look forward to.

But his bruises were temporary. What truly depressed him was the blackout. It had been a month since the last one, although he'd had headaches. He'd hoped the blackouts were gone for good. It was devastating they were not.

He groaned. A crowd would arrive at the cabin on Saturday to help build the dock. He better not get a headache then. He had meant to build the dock himself, but it seemed to have become a community event. Calvin Wilson had called last night and said not to worry about food or drink Saturday. Wives would bring that.

So much for paying back. But to insist on doing it himself would be like turning back the tide. He had learned that when Covenant Fall folks decided to do something, neither God nor man could stop them.

And then there was Stephanie. He had never before experienced the kind of emotion he felt for her; Wednesday night had only intensified it. He wouldn't call it love. It was too soon. But he was drawn to her as he'd never been to another woman. In a brief time, he had seen many sides of her. Gentle with the animals. Playful at times with him until she caught herself. Dedicated to rescue, which, he thought, might be attributed to her own need to be rescued years ago. Defensive and protective of her independence.

She was gutsy and determined and probably

always had been, which made Townsend's betrayal and retribution particularly damaging to her. He'd heard the reluctance in her voice as she told her story, the hint of the helplessness she had felt. He realized full well now why she had been so reluctant to open herself up to another man.

He wanted to do substantial damage to Mark Townsend.

Clint needed to get moving. He had appointments at the community center later this morning, and one of them was Cody's granny. He couldn't let her down.

He went into the kitchen and made coffee and waited until it was ready. Boy, did he ever need it this morning. He took a cup out to the porch. He hadn't locked the porch door and he was amazed to find a new assortment of culinary efforts, including cinnamon rolls and blueberry muffins.

At this rate, he was going to be double his weight in no time at all. What was it about this town that everyone thought food was the answer to everything? After one taste of the cinnamon rolls, he thought maybe it was.

He ate a second one, then went back to the bathroom and very carefully shaved. Then he dressed in jeans and a pullover shirt. He looked at his watch. He had an hour before his 10:00 a.m. appointment at the community center.

He wanted to call Stephanie, to see whether she had any more information, then decided to call Tony instead. But before he could punch in the number, the phone rang.

"Hi, this is Eve. I hope I'm not disturbing you."

"Not at all."

"Two things. I've talked to Stephanie and Tony, and I want to thank you for what you did Wednesday night."

"No need for thanks. He threw the first punch. I just responded."

"But if you hadn't stopped him, we never would have known Stephanie could be at risk."

"Have you heard whether Bolling said who hired him?"

"He hasn't said anything yet, and there's a fancy Denver attorney calling Tony about him and demanding he be released. He won't say who hired him, either."

"Anything from the man's camera?"

"Photos of Stephanie alone and with Townsend's wife and her lawyer. I'm not sure how he got those. Pictures of other stores in and around her building and pictures of the building itself. I don't like it. Tony called the Boston police to get information on Townsend. He was stonewalled, which didn't make him happy."

"How long can he keep Bolling?"

"Maybe a couple of days. The local magistrate has taken a sudden fishing trip."

"I do like the way you operate your city," he said.

"Just following procedure," Eve answered. "The

second thing…are you up to coming over for supper tonight? Spaghetti and salad."

He hesitated. He would be seeing Bart again. He wasn't sure that was a good idea.

"Nick would really appreciate it," she said.

He wasn't sure it was the best thing for Nick, Bart or himself. "I look like something out of a horror show."

"Come," she said. "Nick likes you. He's gone from wanting to be a policeman to wanting to be a chopper pilot. That is the word, isn't it? *Chopper* rather than *helicopter*?"

"It is among the pilots." He gave in. "Thanks, I would like that."

"About six, then? Josh will pick you up."

"Sounds good." He hung up, already regretting his decision. But maybe he would find Nick and Bart doing just fine together. It would be good. He was in no position to have a dog. And maybe, just maybe, Eve would invite Stephanie. Or have news of her.

Just then there was a honk outside. He went out and saw a truck loaded with timber. "Where do you want this?" the driver asked.

"I'll show you," he said.

"That's some shiner you have." The driver studied it with interest.

"I've noticed," Clint said dryly. He walked down the drive and across the road,

The water was about fifty feet from the road. Clint showed him where he wanted the lumber dropped, and signed the delivery papers. He looked at his watch. He had thirty minutes before his first appointment at the community center.

He helped the driver unload the treated timber, then thanked him.

"Hey, how about some cinnamon rolls? And can I catch a ride to the main road?"

"Sure thing," the driver said.

Clint hurried up to the cabin, cut out two rolls for himself and left the others in the disposable aluminum pan. He took the pan out with him, stepped into the cab of the truck and handed the rolls to the driver. "I can vouch for them," he said.

"Thanks, man."

Clint arrived at the community center fifteen minutes before his first appointment. However, a woman already waited for him in the computer room. She was tall, thin and regal with her white hair pulled into a French twist. She stood when he approached. "Mr. Morgan," she said. "Cody said he'd met you." She studied his face. "Are you well enough to do this? I can come another time."

"I'm fine. I just look bad," he said. He held out a chair at a computer station. "Call me Clint. What can I do for you? Why do you want to learn more about a computer?"

"I've always been a homemaker. Proud of it. I had four children, three of them moved away because there weren't many opportunities here. Cody's father stayed and worked for the bank, but I lost both my husband and son—Cody's father —on a fishing trip. All I have here now is Cody. He stays because he loves the mountains." She was talking nervously.

Clint listened intently. "I'm sorry," he said.

"I'm not telling you for sympathy. Just to explain. I've always liked books. Cody will tell you I have a room full of them. But they're hard to find here in town, and my eyes are going bad, and I thought one of those new reader things might help. Cody said he would help but I sometimes get confused…" Her voice trailed off. "I don't want him to know that."

"Do you have a reader?"

"My daughter-in-law in St. Louis sent one to me, but I don't know how to use it. She pulled a box out of a very large knit bag she had beside her and handed it to him.

"Have you tried it?" he asked.

"There's no instructions."

"I know," he said. "You can get them on the computer."

"But if you don't know how…" Frustration colored her words.

He walked her through the steps, helped her register a password and open an account with an online book store. Then he showed her how to search for books by category or author and make purchases. They waited as the books downloaded, then he demonstrated how to enlarge the size of print. The delight and surprise in her face was all the thanks he needed.

"That was so easy," she declared.

"You know Cody would have been really happy to help you."

"I was afraid."

"You shouldn't be. You're a smart lady. You know what your grandson said? 'She can do lots of things I can't.' He would like to share knowledge with you."

She sat taller and beamed.

He stayed with her and showed her how to use the desk computer, as well. Then he introduced her to Google. After a few minutes, she was lost in information.

She was smiling when they finished.

"You can come here anytime you want to use a computer," he said. "Maybe you'll want one of those, too."

"Cody told me you were a nice man," she said. "That I could trust you. Thank you." She pulled out a tissue-covered package. "I know you won't take money, but I hope you will accept this." He unwrapped it and found a soft wool blue-and-gray scarf.

"I made it," she said. "I know it's too early to use it, but our winters are cold, and I thought…" Her voice was uncertain and trailed off.

"It's one of the best presents I've ever received," he said. "Thank you. It's very handsome." He wasn't lying. It was second only to the guitar. Not that he hadn't received gifts, but not ones handmade like the scarf and not one as meaningful as the guitar.

He handed her a file card with his name and number on it. "You call me if you have any problems."

"I certainly hope you stay in Covenant Falls, young man," she said, then clutching her knit bag with her reader in it, she left.

He looked at the scarf again. It really was very, very nice.

"One of Mrs. Terrell's famous scarves," came a voice from behind him. "You really do rate."

He turned at the sound of the voice, and couldn't stop a grin from spreading across his face.

"I thought I would check and see if that eye was as bad as it was yesterday," Stephanie said. "It's worse."

"You have a lot of experience with black eyes?"

"Enough," she said. "I saw Cody this morning at Maude's. He said you were seeing his grandmother this morning."

"I like her."

"I could tell she likes you. She doesn't give those scarves to everyone. They're considered a badge of honor. She sends most of them to a gift store in Denver. You are fast becoming the most talked about man in Covenant Falls."

"Probably because I keep getting wounded."

"Consensus is they like you. You've made a hit with your computer assistance."

He shrugged. "Hell, it's not difficult to help a few people for an hour or so in return for using the cabin. It certainly doesn't make me a saint."

"No, it doesn't," she agreed, "but it's the way you do it."

"What do you mean?"

"I was watching for a few minutes. I ducked out when Mrs. Terrell left. They're frightened, you know. They are scared of being old and left behind and most of all being a burden on their children. You were very good with her."

He didn't know what to say. He was too astounded. Her blue eyes were softer than he'd ever seen.

"You weren't acting," she added.

It wasn't exactly a question. But she seemed to be waiting for an answer.

"No," he finally said.

"You really like helping them."

"I didn't know my grandparents. I like to think they would have been like Mrs. Terrell or Mr. Stiles or Mrs. Aubry, and I hope someone would help them."

She tipped her head. "You keep surprising me."

"Why?"

"I don't know too many guys who have the patience to work with our older citizens and enjoy doing it."

"And you didn't believe I did it because I wanted to?"

"Did you?"

He grinned. "No. I didn't think I would be any good at it, but I felt I owed Josh and Eve. I didn't know that many senior citizens, not up close and personal. I surprised myself at how much I enjoy them and how much they want people to respect them for what they do know."

She sighed. "I'm not very trusting."

"I got that. I also understand why." He wasn't going to say anything about the blackout.

Her gaze held his, then she nodded. "I have to get back. A client canceled an appointment, and I knew you were going to be here. I did want to thank you and, well, apologize."

"Why?"

"I haven't been exactly welcoming."

"I haven't noticed," he said, not trying to keep a grin from his face.

"Anyway, thanks for tackling that PI and being understanding about everything."

"Why shouldn't I be?"

"Because I was incredibly stupid with Mark. To marry him. To stay with him."

"I was married once, too," he said. "To this day, I don't understand why except I probably got too drunk one night and maybe I thought I wanted a home to return to. First deployment after the marriage, she bedded a number of other chopper pilots, all of which got back to me. Problem was I really didn't feel that bad about it. Indignant, yes. My pride was wounded, but my heart wasn't that unhappy. We divorced when I returned. We both knew it was a mistake. No contest. No alimony. No child. I was lucky. It could just as well have been a personal disaster for both us."

She nodded and bit her lip.

He really wanted to hit the hell out of that slime in Boston. She was still so damned vulnerable for what he'd done. He touched her cheek. "You are one of the strongest women I've ever met. Don't let someone like Mark make you doubt that. You left him. You succeeded. You defeated him by doing that. He's the loser, not you."

The outside door opened and she moved away from him. "I have to get back to the office."

"I'm going to Josh's tonight for dinner. Maybe tomorrow you can come over to the cabin and I'll cook for you."

"You cook?"

"Omelets. I was famous for them on base."

"I like omelets," she replied.

"Good. Around six."

She nodded and left. Stunned that she had actually accepted, Clint watched her go, her back straight and determined, her stride long and swift. There was the slightest lingering floral scent.

Grinning like a fool, he sat and waited for his next client.

CHAPTER TWENTY-ONE

STEPHANIE DASHED OUT of the community center with his touch still burning a brand on her cheek and her emotions in turmoil.

Why had she agreed to have dinner with him Saturday night? Because when she was with him, she lost all reason. She didn't want to like him as much as she did. She didn't want him to stir emotions she thought under control. She didn't want to be vulnerable again.

But, dammit, her heart thundered when he was near. Her breath came shorter. She experienced a longing so strong she could barely contain it. And she couldn't stay away.

Which was why this morning she found herself stopping by the community center. She'd made up an excuse to justify it. She was going to thank him for his actions Wednesday night. In truth, she was appalled at her behavior with Eve yesterday. She had said way too much in protesting any idea that would keep Clint Morgan in town. She was reminded of the Shakespeare quote. Something like "The lady doth protest too much."

She knew she'd been transparent with Eve, but Stephanie was terrified of falling in love again. Not just scared. Not just afraid. Terrified. No matter how nice or kind or terrific or good-looking Clint might be, she would be giving up a part of herself again. She wasn't willing to do that again, not for anyone.

She'd decided after the divorce she was meant to be single and she was happily so.

She reached her office just in time for her next appointment: a dog with an ear infection. Once finished, she headed out of town to vaccinate eight horses at a ranch thirty miles away. She liked driving. Nothing soothed her more than the plains framed by the mountains. A visual pleasure.

She drummed the steering wheel. What was Mark plotting with his phone calls and photos? His call had been a warning not to interfere. She knew things about him, about his relationships and methods. She was sure he was hiding money overseas, but he'd kept all his papers at the office. She just didn't know if another voice—Susan's—was sufficient to break through the legal wall he had built around himself.

Maybe Susan knew more than she thought she knew. Maybe she should have urged David and Susan to spend more time delving into Mark's business affairs. He donated lavishly to political campaigns and other causes, but he didn't make *that* much with the bank. True, he was a senior vice president, but still...

He always said the contributions brought him

bank business, but it also bought him prestige and friendships that might be important someday. She hadn't wanted to step in the mire years ago. All she wanted was out, but maybe it was time...

She would call Susan's attorney later tonight.

Maybe she could get some satisfaction that she hadn't had after the divorce. Lack of closure had hobbled her life. She had always been protective of herself, the residue of an abusive childhood. She'd always heard that abused daughters often married abusive husbands. She often questioned if somewhere deep inside, she believed she didn't deserve more, and whether that was the reason she had let Mark's abuse go on for as long as she did.

It was also why she was distrustful of all men. It wasn't the men she feared as much as herself. That she unconsciously picked bad guys because that was who she deserved, that was what her father had always told her.

And now there was Clint who, on the surface, seemed to be one of the world's good guys, and she was running away because she didn't believe in good guys. At least not for her.

She arrived at the ranch and greeted the owner. He had just purchased the new horses.

"Hey, Steph," he said. "I have some beauts."

She grabbed the bag from the van and grinned. She loved horses, and keeping them healthy was her favorite part of her job.

Maybe she would ride Shadow this afternoon and clear her head.

Sounded like the best idea all week.

THE REST OF the day went rapidly for Clint. After his last appointment, or lesson, he headed back home. To the cabin. He had to keep reminding himself it wasn't his home, although it was beginning to feel like it.

He was going to Josh's tonight. He worried about taking too much of his host's time, but spaghetti sounded mighty good and he would see Bart.

He hoped the pit bull was happy to be back in his home. Clint showered and pulled on the polo shirt he'd washed in the sink. He seriously needed new clothes. The general store carried a limited amount of items: jeans, work shirts, T-shirts and some pullovers. There was also some Western-style shirts and pants, but he hadn't gone the cowboy route yet. Basically, the selection was limited. Maybe he would go online and see what he could find.

He sat down and turned on his laptop. In thirty minutes, he'd ordered three casual long-sleeve shirts, a sweater and a pair of slacks along with more jeans since that was what most of the people in town wore. When he checked out, he realized he was buying clothes for Covenant Falls.

He reminded himself he was here temporarily, and yet, he had quickly fallen into the fabric of the town. He had debated whether he wanted to live near an army base, but that, he realized, would be too painful. Getting his degree had been an option, the most sensible course, but he kept putting off doing anything about it. Admit it, he told himself. Leaving Covenant Falls, and Stephanie, was more than depressing. He liked the weather. He liked the view. He liked the people. He liked the relaxed mood. But how could he make a living here? He saw no raging need for a chopper pilot with blackouts.

He looked at his watch. Josh would arrive soon.

He grabbed his guitar and went out on the porch to wait. He played with chords, then a melody emerged. Intrigued, he developed it to see where it went. He was lost in the music when a knock on the screen door startled him. He hadn't noticed Josh's approach.

"I like that," Josh said when Clint gestured for him to come inside. "What is it?"

"Just something I'm playing with."

Josh looked surprised. "You composed it? It's damn good. You didn't tell us you played."

"I play at it. It's relaxing."

"Thought about doing it professionally?"

"I'm nowhere near that good. You haven't heard my voice." He stood and placed the guitar inside, then locked the door. He followed Josh out to the Jeep. Amos sat proudly in the backseat.

"You didn't have the guitar when you first came here," Josh said as they stepped into the Jeep. "I remember you had damned little."

"Some guys at the base sent it to me. Mine was destroyed in the car crash."

"You miss driving, don't you?"

"Every day. I don't let myself think about it. I learned a long time ago that what is done is done, and you'll drive yourself crazy with what-ifs."

"Smart man. It took me a lot longer to figure it out."

"How is it for you?" Clint asked. "Small town. Family. Herd of dogs. You were a lifer like me."

"After I recovered from a severe case of cultural shock, fine. As I said the other night, sometimes I have to go up in the mountains. You might like to go fishing with me up there. Terrific trout streams, and a quiet and peace that puts everything in perspective."

"Are all small towns like Covenant Falls?"

"In what way?"

"Everyone knows everyone's business. Friendly. Accepting. The police department's actually helpful."

Josh chuckled. "Evidently, you know some that are not."

Clint grinned. "A few."

"Back to your question, I don't know. I was never around small towns before. But I do know that what's happening here now is due in much part to Eve and Stephanie. They spearheaded raising funds for the community center, and it's really brought the town together. Lots of activities, learning experiences. Damn, I sound just like my wife."

Clint didn't have time to answer as they reached the Mannings' ranch house. He heard the barking inside. Nick barreled out followed by the strange assortment of dogs. Déjà vu. Bart was last until he saw Clint step out of the Jeep, then his stub of a tail wagged madly. He raced toward Clint and put his front paws on his legs, trying to reach his face.

Clint bent down and he knew he must have a ridiculous grin on his face. He'd never before been greeted with such undiluted joy. His arms circled the dog and he rubbed his hands in Bart's fur as the animal frantically licked his face.

"He's Clint's dog, all right," Josh said from the side.

Clint straightened. Bart *wasn't* his dog. He was Nick's, and maybe this greeting wasn't the best thing.

"Nick has something to tell you," Eve said.

Clint looked at Nick who had a sad expression on his face. Sad but determined.

"Braveheart...Bart...wants to be your dog," he said. "He's barely eaten since he came back and he doesn't take his eyes from the window. He's been waiting for you to come and get him."

"But he's yours."

"No, and it's okay." Nick swallowed. "Stephanie has another dog for me, one that needs us. Bart needs *you*."

Clint didn't know what to say. It was too sudden. What would he do with a dog? But Bart stretched up and delivered a big wet, sloppy kiss, and Clint knew he would do whatever it took to keep him. "Thank you," he said. "I received a present today, a really nice scarf from a really nice lady. I thought it was one of the best presents ever because she made it, but nothing can top the one you just gave me." He reached out his hand, and Nick took it, giving him a strong handshake.

"I think it's time to go inside," Eve said, and Clint spotted tears hovering in her eyes. "Dinner is ready."

"Mom makes great spaghetti," Nick said, his glance going back to Bart. "I can come and see him?"

"You betcha. Any time you want. I think he's going to miss you."

Nick smiled. "Josh says some dogs are like that. They pick their person. Amos is Josh's dog. And he says Amos was his friend's dog before that. He really grieved when his first person died. Others like Fancy and Miss Marple and Captain Hook, they're happy with everyone who feeds them and loves them."

"You are going to have to tell me more about canine likes and dislikes," Clint said gently. "You'll have to tell me all about Bart and what he likes and doesn't like. Will you do that?"

"Yes. I would like to."

Eve ushered them inside and she introduced him to a large, older man who sat in the living room with a beer in his hand. "This is Tom McGuire. He was the police chief here for nine years. Before that, he was with the state police and sheriff's department over in Pueblo. He was my father's best friend and he's like an uncle to Nick."

Eve headed to the kitchen and the man stood and shook Clint's hand. It was a hardy shake. "Heard a lot about you. Okay if I call you Clint?"

"Everyone does," he said. "Good to meet you, sir."

"Heard you did a damn good job in taking down that suspect the other night."

Clint touched his face. "It was close. If your patrolman hadn't been alert…"

"According to him, you were hanging on for dear life. Not about ready to let him go."

"I didn't like his attitude."

McGuire laughed. "My guys didn't, either. He's not having a happy time in jail. The food sorta depends on attitude. Maude's if you behave yourself, and beans and tasteless oatmeal if you don't."

Clint laughed. "I'll have to remember that if I ever inhabit it."

"You don't look like a fella that would."

"I've had my moments."

Eve poked her head into the living room and announced supper was ready. They followed her into the dining room. A bottle of red wine and a big salad sat on the table. In another minute, Eve served a steaming plate of spaghetti and a bowl of red sauce with meatballs. The spicy aroma filled the air.

Josh poured the wine and Eve passed the spaghetti, then the red sauce. "This recipe comes from Josh's grandmother," she said. "I make a big batch, then freeze portions so I can just throw it into a pot."

"Don't let her lowball it, Clint," McGuire said. "I always covet an invitation on spaghetti night." He accepted a glass of wine from Josh. "I heard you're volunteering at the community center."

"Just a few hours and really simple things."

"They're not simple to the folks you've helped."

"It's not very much in return for the cabin."

"Maybe not to you." McGuire heaped spaghetti on his plate and covered it with sauce and meatballs. Everyone fell to eating, Clint relishing every bite and every taste of a good wine. Conversation was scarce. He liked that, but then he liked everything about Josh and his wife and son. He envied them their easy and affectionate manner with each other, and the way Nick was brought into every conversation.

It hadn't been like that when he was Nick's age. At boarding school, meals were strictly regimented.

When he was almost finished, McGuire asked, "Do you know yet what you want to do?"

"To tell the truth, sir, no. I had been thinking about finishing a degree in computer engineering, but I'm not so sure now."

"How many years do you have?"

"A little more than two, plus I can claim credit for some military courses and experience. It would probably take a year."

Eve and Josh had been mostly silent. Eve and Nick took the plates to the kitchen and returned with a plate of chocolate cookies. Josh hadn't yet figured out why everyone in Covenant Falls wasn't at least a hundred pounds overweight.

McGuire stood. "I have to get home, but thank you, Eve. It was a pleasure as always." Then he turned his attention to Clint. "Good to meet you, son." He peered down at Bart who hadn't moved more than an inch from Clint. "Seems you have a way with dogs like you do with our seniors. Again, real good to meet you."

"And you, sir," Clint said.

"Hope you hang around for a while."

After he left, the four of them went outside, the dogs following.

Eve brought out coffee.

"Josh, have you heard any more about the guy in jail?" Clint asked.

"Only that his attorney is going nuts, talking about violation of civil rights and on and on," Josh said.

"But he's still there?"

"If Tony has anything to do with it, he'll be there for the next six months. He's really annoyed now. All kinds of pressure is being applied from different sources, and he's been delaying arraignment. But the guy isn't saying anything."

"Has he learned anything about Stephanie's ex-husband?"

"Nope, but Tony has been checking," Josh said.

"He's apparently really bad at marriage. Susan is the third. Stephanie didn't know about that. Apparently, the first marriage happened when he was in college. It didn't last long."

"Stephanie said he stole the money from the sale of her practice. It might be interesting to see if his other wives had money that disappeared."

"Tony said he got nothing from the Boston police," Eve said. "No record. Not even a parking ticket."

"Boston, and no parking tickets?" Clint said. "That has to be a record."

"You know Boston?"

"Visited there a couple of times with a buddy."

"Do you like big cities?"

"Can't say I do."

He saw looks pass between Eve and Josh and wondered what in the hell was going on.

He looked at his watch. It was nine. Not late, but he had people coming over early in the morning to help with the dock. And tomorrow night, dinner with Stephanie. He'd stopped by the grocery on his way home earlier. He only hoped the dock construction wouldn't extend past 6:00 p.m. Josh obviously noticed the gesture and stood. "I think it's time to drive Clint home. He's working on the new dock tomorrow."

"Thanks for doing it," Eve said. "Josh has been wanting that dock for months. He'll probably start camping on your yard."

Clint laughed. "I'm not doing much. The town's taken over the project. Calvin says he's got a good group of men coming."

"I know," Eve said. "My husband is one of them."

"I don't know if that's allowed," Clint said with a grin.

"Try to keep me away," Josh said. "By the way, Eve, Clint plays one hell of a guitar."

Eve's eyes lit up. "You do?"

"A little. Just for friends and myself."

"Next time you come, bring it," Eve said. "I love guitar music."

Clint thought he saw another glint in her eyes. He feared he would be volunteered again. Eve seemed to be very, very good at volunteering people.

"Nick," she called. Nick, who had been throwing a ball to Miss Marple, Fancy and Captain Hook, came running to the table. "Clint is leaving," Eve said. "Please give him Bart's bowl, bed and toys."

Clint felt like a dognapper as Nick nodded his head. The boy leaned down and gave Bart a huge hug first. Bart licked him, but didn't move from Clint's side. Five minutes later, he was loaded down with dog stuff and a dish full of spaghetti.

"Thank you, Nick. That was incredibly generous of you, and you can visit any time. Eve, thank you for supper. It was terrific."

Then they were in Josh's Jeep, Amos and Bart in the backseat.

CHAPTER TWENTY-TWO

DRENCHED AND COVERED with dirt and mud, Clint thanked and said goodbye to the men who had helped frame the dock and push PVC pipes three feet beneath the lake's bottom.

Calvin had been right. He had needed help. Water had to be pumped from the pipes before the treated posts and cement could be placed inside. Now they would have to wait until the concrete dried. In the meantime, they marked each post to choose the height of the dock.

Conversation ranged from the unusual heat to last week's altercation with the Boston detective. Everyone wondered why he was photographing buildings in town, especially at night, and even more why he'd attacked Clint.

Clint feigned ignorance. Then talk turned to two new forest fires in northern Colorado. There were some, as well, in New Mexico and Arizona. Heavily forested areas throughout the West were at risk. The volunteer firefighter units were on alert. Three of the crew today were members.

So was Stephanie. A shiver of fear ran down Clint's spine.

They had lunch, brought by several wives, then left at three. Nothing more could be done until the concrete dried. Several said they would return Sunday after church to frame the dock. The cement would be dry then.

Bart had not left his side since they'd arrived home. He had crawled up in bed with him and frantically waved his backside when Clint asked him if he wanted to take a walk at dawn. Then he'd stayed with him all morning, ignoring the other humans who attempted to say hello. The dog obviously was trying to strike a happy medium between fear that Clint might disappear again and his fear of strangers. Clint had won, and he felt that was a huge victory for both him and the dog.

When the last pickup left his driveway, he went inside with Bart and threw his muddy clothes on the floor. He jumped in the shower, washed his hair and stepped out. Bart sat happily on Clint's muddy clothes, mud all over his face.

"We're having company tonight," he said with a grin. "Now you need a bath, too."

He put the clothes into the sink, then pushed and shoved Bart into the shower and closed the curtain. He turned the shower back on and Bart panicked, jumping out and shaking himself, spreading water all over the floor. As Clint tried to catch him, Bart ran and jumped onto the bed, drying himself on the clean sheets Clint had optimistically put on the bed.

Owning a dog did have its challenges.

He spent an hour cleaning up the bathroom floor and changing a wet bed, which was damp down to the mattress. Bart licked him when he bent down to scold him, then he forgot about it. Clearly, Bart just did what dogs do.

Clint turned his attention to himself. He shaved with great care since his face was tender from the fight. He noted that his face still sported any number of colors. Then he dressed in clean clothes. He half expected Stephanie to call and cancel any minute, and his heart jumped when the phone rang. It did, several times. A reporter from the weekly paper wanted to interview him about the altercation at the courthouse. Someone who said he couldn't come today to help with the dock wanted to know when he could help. Someone who *had* helped had left gloves behind.

At five he made a salad for two and checked items he needed for an omelet. He had picked up some spices and other ingredients at the local grocery. All he needed was wine, but he hadn't been able to find any at the grocery.

At six, he and Bart went out to the porch. He'd never felt this kind of expectation before. Or wishful thinking. She was definitely guy-shy, with good reason. He didn't see a victim, though. He saw a fighter. A capable, compassionate woman who was damn attractive.

What if she had second thoughts?

Through the pines he saw the boards stacked on

the side of the lake and poles sticking out of the water. He planned to do most of the dock work himself Sunday and Monday. Once the cement settled, it shouldn't take long to fill in the frame.

Stephanie drove up at six thirty and exited the van with a package in her arms and Sherry at her side. Bart stood and wagged his tail. Apparently Stephanie and Sherry were on Bart's approved list of visitors.

Clint stood and opened the door to the porch and took the bag from her.

"I thought an omelet might need some wine," she said. "I didn't know whether you had time to get any. It isn't easy around here."

"I didn't. I didn't see any in the grocery store."

"You won't. Colorado laws are pretty weird. You have to buy wine and beer in a licensed liquor store. Nearest one is ten miles away in the middle of nowhere. My guess is the owner has friends in high places. I keep some wine in stock."

Stephanie wore brown slacks and a brown-and-white-checked blouse. Her hair was pulled back by a brown ribbon. Sherry said hello to Bart by touching his nose. They sniffed each other.

"I didn't think you would come," he said.

"My curiosity won out. I had to see whether you could cook an omelet as good as you claimed."

"It's my culinary skills that drew you here?"

"What else?" she asked. "Maude does many

things well, but an omelet? Not so good. She's more the scrambled-eggs-and-steak cook."

"I hope you don't have great expectations."

"I do, after you bragged about it at the center." She leaned down and stroked Bart. "I hear you're the new proud owner of Braveheart."

"Bart. It's official now."

"You went to court?"

"Nick's court. He approved."

"He's a neat kid."

"He is that, and more. *I* hear you're giving him a new puppy. Is it Lulu?"

"You remembered in all that confusion."

"I remember everything about you." He longed to lean over and kiss her, but reined himself in. She was the usual cool veterinarian now, not the vulnerable woman he'd seen after the attack.

He opened the door to the living room and she went in first.

She looked around. "You haven't changed anything."

He shrugged. "I'm only a temporary resident."

"I see the dock is underway."

"A community effort this morning." He took the bottle of wine. "Thank you." He paused. "I was afraid you would reconsider."

"I almost did."

"What stopped you?"

"Seeing you yesterday with Mrs. Terrell. You were so easy and patient with her. You can't pretend that. And Braveheart—oops, Bart. He's gone through bad times with bad people. There's no way he would make such an attachment to you if there was the slightest doubt you were a good guy."

"I'll have to bribe him again with an extra piece of cheese tonight."

"I don't think he can be bribed," she said. "And I'm hungry."

"Good. I couldn't find everything I wanted at the grocery here, but enough."

"You said you were famous for your omelets. Among whom?"

"Doubting my word, are you?"

"Just gathering all the facts. That's what a vet does."

"Fellow chopper pilots. Four of us shared a house off base and others often crashed with us. We took turns cooking when we were together. Our schedules weren't always normal, and omelets were good at any time of the day."

"Am I supposed to be impressed because a bunch of guys are impressed?" She grinned.

"Of course not. I intend to present proof. In the next few minutes, if you will kindly leave the kitchen."

"Can't I watch?"

"And reveal my secret? Most definitely not. But you can open the wine and set the table."

She gave him a searching look, but her wariness was gone. For now, anyway.

STEPHANIE GATHERED THE WINE, wine opener and two glasses from the cupboard and carried them into the dining room. She placed the glasses on the table and opened the bottle easily. Then she looked around the room. It was familiar, and yet it wasn't without Josh and Amos. There were subtle changes. Her eyes spied a guitar resting against the easy chair and some paper scattered around a lamp table. She walked over for a look. He had written music on plain white paper. She didn't know music well enough to hum the notes.

Another aspect of Clint Morgan she hadn't known existed. He was full of surprises. She had liked him the moment she'd met him, although she'd fought that liking tooth and nail. Then she'd done everything she could to avoid him, but he wouldn't be avoided. It was as if they were being drawn together in some big scheme of things.

There was so much she didn't know about him: why did he never mention family? Where was he from? She didn't even know how he had been wounded. Then she mentally listed everything she did know: chopper pilot, teacher, dog whisperer, fighter, dock builder, cook and now musician. What else was packed inside that very nicely formed body?

Her body warmed thinking about it, and she found herself smiling at his wry one-sided smile. It got to her every time. Of course, he could be a terrible cook, but she doubted that. Whatever he did, he seemed to do well. It was unfair. Fate was playing with her.

Even if he planned to stay, she wanted no long-term involvement. She didn't want her life overtaken by someone else's. She wanted to go where she wanted to go and when she wanted to go without worrying about someone else.

She touched the guitar. He hadn't had one when she picked him up in Pueblo, and no one sold guitars in Covenant Falls. Someone must have sent it to him or maybe he had bought it online. It did look well used, though.

"Ready," Clint called, standing in the doorway to the kitchen. He was holding a platter as if it were pure gold. "You can get the salad on the counter of the kitchen."

She hadn't known omelets could smell so good, but this one did. She suddenly realized she hadn't eaten since breakfast. She hastened to get the salad.

Then she sat down as he held a chair out for her, resting his warm hand on her shoulder for a moment. Mark had also held a chair out for her in the beginning, and she was surprised she didn't resent Clint for doing the same. Maybe it was the warmth of his hand, the gentleness of it, the way he left it on her shoulder as if he didn't want to break that fragile contact.

Clint poured the wine before sitting down. He divided a huge big fluffy omelet that smelled heavenly, and put half on her plate. She took a bite, and was blown away. There was ham and cheese, some onion and finely chopped pepper, but it was the lightness and spices that made it great.

"Okay, I'm convinced," she said. "The salad's great, too. Maybe you should open a restaurant."

"And compete with Maude? I don't think so. Besides, all I can do is omelets. I'm a one-trick pony."

"I seriously doubt that," she replied. "What have you been thinking about doing?"

"Ah, that's the million-dollar question. I'm a damned good chopper pilot. But as long as I have blackouts, I'm grounded. I'm definitely out of the service for good. A few years ago, I could have returned if the headaches and blackouts magically disappeared, which, according to the docs, they could. There's no reason for them except what my doc called a bruise to the brain which may, or may not, heal by itself. But now the army's downsizing and they have more pilots than they need."

"I'm sorry," she said.

He shrugged. "Thanks. But I was lucky. I got to do what I loved doing for more than seventeen years."

"You always wanted to fly?"

"Always. I even tried to fly off the roof of my house when I was seven."

"What happened?"

"Nothing good," he said, not elaborating. Because of the sudden cloud in his face, she didn't push. "I'm also a good chopper mechanic. I used to haunt the shop when I wasn't flying. Problem there is I don't know if I could be around them and not fly."

A shadow appeared in his eyes. Regret? Or maybe an emptiness he hadn't revealed before.

"Enough about me," he said. "Did *you* always want to be a veterinarian?"

"I've always loved animals," she said. "As a teenager, I worked at a vet's office. He taught me lot, mentored me, helped me get into college, then vet school."

"Your family?"

"Best forgotten," she said shortly.

"I'm sorry. I didn't mean to pry."

"Why not? I have."

He laughed. "The first thing that attracted me to you—other than how pretty you are—is that unwavering honesty."

Mark had hated it. So she learned to be dishonest with him.

"You're thinking of him again," Clint said softly. "Your ex."

"He creeps into my head. He does it all too often."

He simply nodded. He understood.

"Thank you," she said.

"For the meal? It really wasn't that big a deal."

"No, for not giving up on me."

"As if I could," he replied.

"You play the guitar," she said, changing the subject.

"A little."

"Would you play for me?"

"If there's not great expectations."

She smiled. "I have none."

He picked up the guitar and sat on one of the dining chairs. He played a few chords, then a haunting melody she'd never heard before. He was good. More than good. But she should have expected that. He was good at everything, drat it.

But then she was lost in the melody as it went through various moods. Wistful, then lighter, somber and finally a jig. She wouldn't forget it.

"I've never heard that before. What is it?"

He dipped his head. "Just something I've been playing with."

"You wrote it?"

"It kinda wrote itself."

He put the guitar down and offered her his hand. She stood, looking up at him, the warmth in his hand spreading up her arms and through her body like honey. His eyes were darker now. Intense. The attraction between them, always there but held under control, simmered, boiled over.

He kissed her. Their lips met with a fierceness and need that rocked her to the core. Her mouth opened and her tongue met his naturally, and she knew she was seducing him as much as he was her. His fingers kneaded the back of her neck, and electricity flashed between them, sparking and sizzling.

The kiss deepened. She hadn't known him long, and yet she knew him well. In the deepest, most important way, she knew him. He had revealed more to her tonight than he knew. Like her, he hurt inside, but he'd become quite good at hiding it just as she had. She leaned against him and his arms tightened around her until she felt as if they were one.

Then he took a step back, his fingers touching her face, exploring the curves, hesitating at her mouth. "Damn, but you're pretty," he said.

She didn't think she was. Her hair was too unruly, her body too lean, her cheekbones too angular. But she knew he believed it, and she felt an unanticipated pleasure in the words.

"And you have a beautiful smile. It's not there enough," he added. It wasn't a critical observation, she knew. There was a regret in his voice that such a thing was true and at the reasons behind it, even if he didn't know *all* the reasons.

But at the moment, it didn't matter because his lips found hers again and touched them with a barely restrained hunger that fueled her own. She opened her mouth to his and their tongues met and teased each other until all her senses were inflamed.

She had never felt so alive, so completely enveloped in waves of sensation as their bodies pressed together with a need as elemental as a sudden and violent summer storm. She hadn't known she could feel like this, that she could want someone like this. Want with all the fiber in her body.

"Stephanie?"

She knew what he was asking. She was scared.

Terrified. But there was a deeper pull, a need that came not only from her body, but from the heart she'd walled up.

"Yes," she said simply.

"Sure?"

She looked up at him. "Are you trying to wriggle out?"

He burst out laughing. "Never."

He took her by her hand and led her into the bedroom, closing the door before the two dogs could enter. "Some things are meant to be private," he told them through the door, causing Stephanie to giggle.

He took off his shirt, and she saw scars. She didn't know whether they were from battle or not, but it didn't matter. He'd been hurt. She touched them with her fingers then stared up at his face. Handsome but with character. Strong lines. Laugh lines. Lines from pain. "I like your face," she said. "I really tried to dislike you when I first met you because I liked your face."

"That's convoluted," he said.

"Not if you're me," she replied, biting on his lip.

"Well, *I* liked you because you took such an immediate dislike to me."

"Now that *is* convoluted."

"Not if you're me," he retorted and unbuttoned her shirt.

"I think we might be in trouble," she said. "Two convoluted souls."

"Exactly what does convoluted mean?" he said

between kisses and stepping out of his jeans and helping her out of her slacks.

"Something like twisted," she said and giggled again. She was appalled. She never giggled. His quirky sense of humor was contagious.

"My doctor at the hospital would have lots of fun with that one," he replied as he finished undressing her. They fell on the bed and he kissed her again, long and hard while his hands caressed her body, each touch sending waves of sensation cascading through her. He went slow, stopping to kiss her again with so much tenderness it hurt. It was as if he knew it had been a long time for her, and he was taking his time in awakening her body.

His lips found her breasts, first one and then the other, and spasms of pleasure swept through her even as she throbbed with need for more. He stopped as if to ask whether he should go on.

To her surprise, she had no reservations after having had so many. The last forty-eight hours had changed a lot, and both physically and emotionally she wanted him. She looked at him and nodded in answer to his unspoken question. His hands moved down her body leaving trails of fire behind them, leaving her skin alive with feeling, with wanting. Nerve endings erupted. The sheer strength of the need frightened her, but there was no stopping now. The fire was too strong.

Her hands went to the back of his neck and her fingers tangled in his dark hair as he gave her a smile she would always remember. Tender and sweet and sexy. And real. No guile. No holding back.

She knew in that moment that she did trust him. She could always trust him. "Yes," she said. He turned around for a second and she realized he'd picked up the little foil package on the table next to the bed.

Then he turned back to her, and ran his fingers along her body. The heat grew, a soul-deep heat that melted any lingering resistance.

He kissed her, a kiss so tender her heart melted even as her body reacted with a fierce need. His hands slid down to the triangle of hair, his fingers gently exploring, soothing and inciting all at one time. Her skin burned where he touched.

She wanted him. She wanted the tenderness and the barely contained passion he was trying so hard to control. Tremors ran through her.

Her legs gripped around him, pulling him even closer to her. Waves of sensation rocked her body as he entered her. Slowly. Deliberately. She relished the feel of him as he thrust deeper. She moved with him, the crescendo building, their bodies rocking in tandem until a final explosion sent billows of fulfillment racing through her.

They lay together, Clint still warm within her as aftershocks of pleasure continued. Was he as awed as she? Never, ever had she thought anything could be as grand as this. She hadn't imagined sex—or was it love?—could be anything like this.

Clint enclosed her in his arms. "Wow," he said.
"Double wow," she replied and snuggled deeper
nto their embrace.

CHAPTER TWENTY-THREE

AFTER SEVERAL MINUTES of silence, a mellow and contented piece of time when words weren't necessary, a sated Clint lifted his head and studied her "You are so darn irresistible," he said.

She started to protest. He could tell. He stopped i by kissing her for a very long moment, long enough to feel his body heat again. "You're strong and kind and smart and...well, you make splendid love."

"Splendid?" Stephanie said with a grin.

"No other word came to me because that's what i was." He paused touching her hair. "I've never fel this way before. From the moment I met you, I've wanted to make you smile, make you laugh, be with me. It's not just sex, although that was, well, terrific Hell, I don't know, but it's so much more than that.'

In her blue eyes was a softness he hadn't seen before. And then she sighed. "I surrender," she said with the frankness that always intrigued him. "I feel that way, too. I didn't want to. I knew you were dangerous to my equilibrium. I've made mistakes. Really bad ones, and I don't want to make another one.'

He took her hand. "I *could* be one. God knows my

'uture is uncertain. I don't know if the headaches or blackouts will ever go away, and I have damn little training for anything useful except flying, certainly nothing here in Covenant Falls."

Her fingers tightened around his. She knew how he felt. Exactly how he felt. She'd been there after he divorce.

"You have a lot more talents than you think you do," she said. "People like you. *Really* like you. You have a knack that I don't have. I tend to be..."

"Cautious," he said. "You've been hurt by people you trusted. So it's easier not to trust. It's natural."

"Maybe," she said. "I've had sex before, I've never made love. I never knew it could be like this. Or maybe I did. I watch Eve and Josh together, the way they touch each other. Their connection is so obvious, even when he just puts an arm around her shoulders. It's like no one else is there. I just didn't think..."

"What didn't you think?" he asked softly.

She averted her eyes for a second. "That anyone would feel that way about me. Or I would feel that way about them."

He grinned. "I've had similar thoughts."

"Mark wasn't my first marriage," she said, nesting her head in his arm. "You should know everything before this gets deeper than it already is."

"Well," he said, "it's pretty damn deep now. I would say Challenger Deep."

"Challenger Deep?" she asked.

"It's the deepest part of the ocean. The Challenger Deep is in the Mariana Trench. One of those odds and ends a pilot learns. Your eyes make me think about that. They are so damned blue."

"I like that, the Challenger Deep," she said. "Where is it?"

"The western Pacific Ocean near the Mariana Islands."

"I'll remember that for crossword puzzles. I like crossword puzzles. Do you?"

"You're changing the subject," he said.

"Yes," Stephanie said, frowning. "I don't know if I'm ready for this. It's too fast. Too powerful, maybe even world-shattering. My world, anyway."

He touched her face. "I know. The timing sucks. I'm in limbo now. I don't know whether I can ever fly again. I don't know how I'll earn a living. I don't know if the blackouts will last another week or for years. I have damn little to offer any woman. But I can't seem to stay away from you."

A smile played across her face. "And me, you. I gravitate toward you, no matter how hard I fight it. And God knows, I've fought it."

"I noticed. I've never cared for anyone like I care about you. I know it's fast, probably too fast, but I lost my heart the first time I saw you in that dirt-splotched shirt." He stroked her cheek. "I never believed in that stuff—the idea of love at first sight, or that lightning strikes. But lightning did strike me." He paused. "I won't push. I won't ever consciously hurt you."

SHE LIKED HIM even more for that. He understood her at a gut level. It was scary, but it also warmed her. And she believed him. He had never pushed. He'd just been there when needed. His honesty deserved her own. "That same lightning? Well, I felt it, too." She bit her lip. "You know about Mark, what a disaster it was for me. You should know all of it."

His fingers went around hers, reassuring.

"I was married when I turned seventeen," she said, her voice strained. "My father was physically and verbally abusive. Not sexually, but he liked to bat me around if he disapproved of anything I said and did, and almost everything fit that description."

"Your mother?"

"He did the same to her. I begged her to leave him, to take me with her, but she didn't think she could survive without him. How would she take care of me?"

"What did you do?"

"I solved the problem by marrying Rick. He was the high school's bad boy, and he'd just graduated. He had movie-star looks. I never really understood why he was interested in me. I was a reader, an A student. One of the nerds. I was going to go to college one way or another, even if I had to sell my soul. I was not going to be like my mom and father.

"But Rick persisted in chasing me. I think now

it was the challenge. I was the only girl who *didn't* jump in bed with him. I was a virgin and intended to stay that way until I was married. My father forbade me from seeing him which, of course, made me do the opposite. After a vicious beating, I left the house and called Rick. He took me to his home."

"My god," Clint murmured.

She took a deep breath. "Rick was my knight who saved me from my father's increasing violence. His family seemed normal. Nice. When he asked me to marry him, I agreed. His father supported our decision and said we could live in the garage apartment behind their home. I was too young, of course, but his father got mine to sign a form giving his approval. To this day, I don't know how or why he convinced him, but I have my suspicions.

"To make a long story short, I thought Rick worked with his father in a trucking business. He did. In a way. He also shipped illegal drugs. Four months after we married, Rick was killed in a shootout with an undercover agent. I was questioned for weeks, but I didn't know anything and was eventually cleared. Rick's father was arrested and his mother lost everything."

Stephanie took a breath before continuing.

"I couldn't go home. My father had disowned me when I married Rick, and my mother wouldn't argue with him. I was desperate to finish school. Then I saw a help-wanted sign in a veterinarian practice near the school. I always liked animals, although my father wouldn't let me have one, and I was the first to apply. For eight months, I washed cages and took care of the animals after school. I slept on buses at night."

She was aware of his arm tightening around her. His dark eyes were even darker as he listened.

"When the vet—Dr. Colin Drake—found out, he let me sleep in the clinic. We became friends. He was in his sixties and had lost his wife. They didn't have children and he took me under his wing. He helped me obtain a scholarship for college, then he helped me get into veterinarian school. I continued working for him as a vet tech. After getting my degree, I went to work for him as a partner because he wanted to slow down.

"He died of a heart attack two years later and left the practice to me. I was twenty-eight. Two years later, I met Mark who was attending a conference in Pittsburgh. I'd had a few dates, but not many. Mark seemed to be everything Rick wasn't. Respected. Honest. Had a lot of friends and people who admired him. He wined and dined me, sent flowers every few days. When he asked me to marry him, he said he would take care of selling the practice and I would use the proceeds to start one in Boston. He would help."

"That jerk," Clint seethed.

"I thought I loved him, but later I realized I wanted to fall in love. It had been twelve years since I had had a serious relationship. I was lonely. I missed my friend, the former vet. The practice was in a poor part of town, and I worked twelve hours a day, six days a week and often on Sunday. I loved it, but I needed something more." She touched his hair.

"What happened next?"

"You know the rest. It didn't take me long to learn I'd made another mistake. I have a terrible track record with the opposite sex, which is why I tried to stay away from you."

He kissed her. "I can tell you I have never sold drugs and I have never harmed a woman, at least knowingly. It sounds like Rick cared about you."

"I think he did. He wanted us to have a baby. I couldn't do that..."

"No wonder you ran like hell when that particular streak of lightning struck us." He kissed her. Slowly, tenderly. "I would have done the same."

"Do you have any hard feelings about your marriage?"

"Oh, I had some, particularly at first. No guy wants to be known as the butt of jokes. But I learned long ago not to worry about things I can't change. Just change directions."

"And that's what you're doing now?"

"I'm trying. There's not much call for a damaged chopper pilot. But I'll find something else to be passionate about." He grinned. "In fact I already have."

She smiled and snuggled against him. "You could build docks," she said.

"I've already dismissed that idea. You should have

seen me earlier. I was covered with mud. Head to toe. I looked in a mirror and a creature from a horror movie looked back at me. I have to find a cleaner occupation."

She grabbed at the lighter subject. "I wish I could have seen that."

"No, you don't. I even scared the hell out of Bart."

"You have a way with dogs," she suggested.

"One dog," he corrected.

"Sherry and Stryker like you, too, the traitors."

"Because they didn't bite me? Maybe I'm just not tasty."

"Can't be that. You're very tasty."

"Why thank you, ma'am. I think that's the nicest thing you've said to me."

"Back to a future," she said. "You seem to have a knack for computers and teaching."

"Nearly anyone can teach someone to turn on a computer," he said.

"Not so they *want* to open a computer. Of course, teaching seniors in a community center doesn't pay much."

"I understand it doesn't pay at all," he joked. "But then if I cared about money, I wouldn't have joined the army."

"There is that," she said. Why was it she felt so comfortable with him?

She had told him more than she'd told anyone else. Why did she instinctively trust him?

"What do you care about?" she asked.

"You. And I'm becoming rather fond of Covenant Falls, too. It has a unique personality."

"Where are you from?"

"I was born in Chicago."

"And raised there?"

"Kinda. I attended boarding schools."

She looked at him, sensing there was much more behind those words. Would he tell her? A few seconds passed.

"Okay," she said simply.

Clint's eyes found hers and he touched her cheek then he sighed. She knew her acceptance had shattered his defenses.

"My mother died of cancer when I was seven," he said in a low, intense voice. "My father owned an investment firm in Chicago and was on the board of a half dozen companies. He was never home, and when he was, he didn't want to be bothered with children, meaning me.

"On the other hand, my mother was great, and she tried to make up for his absence. When she died he hired a nanny for me and was gone even more."

Stephanie snuggled in his arms. "I'm so sorry," she said.

"Four months after my mother died, my father married a client who I'm pretty sure had been having an affair with my father *before* Mom died. Even at eight, I knew that something was off, and I wasn't very welcoming to say the least. She disliked me immediately and intensely, probably because of my own attitude, but I was a grieving eight-year-old," he said. "She quickly became pregnant, had a son and saw me as a threat to her own child. Not physically, but as a competitor for my father's wealth. I was the firstborn, after all."

Stephanie kissed him. "I hurt for that eight-year-old boy."

Clint shrugged. "He grew up. Nora, my stepmother, convinced my father to send me to a boarding school where I would learn some 'discipline.' I was thrown out of there before landing in the last one. It was a military school, and I had a great instructor who got me interested me in flying. When I was sixteen, I joined the Civil Air Patrol and learned to fly, but what I really loved was helicopters. The instructor, a former pilot himself, told me about a special army program that accepted qualified high school graduates for helicopter training. I knew I had to have really good grades to qualify. I worked my ass off and graduated near the top of my class."

"Did you go home summers while at school?"

"I never went home again, although my father visited several times a year. Stilted, duty calls. I stayed at the school during the holidays and summer vacations while my father and his new family went on skiing vacations and saw the world. After the first four years, I no longer cared, or told myself I didn't. Like you, I decided to make my own way. When I graduated high school, my father offered a college education if I majored in business. I said no.

I didn't want anything from him then and I haven't seen him since."

"And when you were injured?"

"I asked that he not be notified. I doubt he would give a damn anyway."

"And your brother?"

"Half brother," he corrected.

"Your half brother then?"

He shook his head. "I haven't seen him since I joined the army. We barely knew each other." He tensed. "And I wasn't wounded in battle. At least not the injury that put me out of the service." He played with her hand that was still in his, rubbing his thumb against her skin. "I was on leave. I'd restored a Corvette and wanted to try it out before leaving on a new deployment. A buddy told me about a long empty stretch of road between two ghost towns, or almost ghost towns. Never any traffic, he said. I was reaching ninety miles an hour when an old truck turned out of a dirt road. I swerved to miss it and my car turned over. The bar probably saved me, kept me from being thrown out, but my head slammed against the side of the window.

"I woke up about two weeks later. I'd been in an induced coma because of swelling on my brain. I had other injuries, but they were all relatively minor. My problem was continuing headaches and blackouts. I learned then the brain is still a mystery. The doctors couldn't find the cause. Could be a brain bruise. Another said it was an insult to the brain. Could go away tomorrow or six months or six years. I was medically discharged because of it."

"And you miss flying?"

"Every day. I wake up and I'm not where I'm supposed to be. I'm not there to help out my buddies or the soldiers that rely on us. I felt, still feel, like I let them down. I was the 'old man' in the group, the most experienced." He ran his fingers through her hair, then continued, "It's always hard to explain to nonmilitary people. It's not that we want to go to war. Or like it. But the camaraderie built in places like Iraq and Afghanistan is strong. It's an incredibly close bond. You live, eat, play and fight together. We've shared fear, even terror, and saved each other's bacon more than once."

"You lost two families," she said. "Three if you count the marriage."

"I don't," he said.

"You can have a new one in Covenant Falls. You already do. Bart. Josh. Eve. Nate and the other veterans."

"But no job. I can't keep living off Josh."

"I think he believes you're earning your keep."

"Hell, everyone and his brother is helping with the dock."

"But not helping people with computers. That was one of Eve's pet projects, one of the reasons for the community center."

"There has to be others who can do better. Surely there are teachers at the school…"

"Eve tried. But there's a shortage of qualified volunteers. The biggest obstacle had been a reluctance among our seniors to learn from someone they knew well. For some odd reason, they connect with you. They like you. You don't make them feel stupid because they haven't learned on their own."

"No one learns on their own."

"They don't know that. To them, everyone knows how but them. It makes them feel lacking." She tickled his bare chest. "Are you ticklish?" she said.

He chuckled. "No."

She licked his chest.

"Well, maybe," he admitted.

She traced the scars on his chest. "Were these from the accident?"

"No, my chopper was hit by gunfire. We crashed."

"Then what happened?"

"Another chopper picked me up."

"Any other injuries?

He winked. "Just a cow stomp."

"It's not nice to remind me."

"It was worth it. It broke the ice. Kinda."

"I did feel bad about it."

"I couldn't tell."

"I didn't mean for you to. I knew you were dangerous to my world the minute I saw you."

He played with one of her curls. "Do you still feel that way?"

"Oh, yes. Definitely. Quite assuredly."

"Do you have to be so indecisive?" he asked before he leaned over and kissed her.

SHE TASTED SO damn good. She felt even better. Her eyes sparkled with life. They had always been breathtakingly blue, but they'd been cautious. Tonight there was no caution.

Her fingers touched his face, exploring its planes and he caught her hand. He brought it to his mouth and kissed it. He liked her hands. Long, strong and callous, but he also knew how gentle they could be.

He stroked her face, then her neck as their bodies came together again, his body fitting her long lean one as if she was made for him. Then he kissed her with a fierceness that was equaled by hers. His mouth touched her breast, teasing and inciting and her body trembled beneath his.

He rose above her, his body teasing hers until she arched upward to meet him. She was ready this time. Ready and eager and ever so responsive. Her arms went around him, pulling him closer, her need clearly as great as his own. He entered slowly, tantalizingly slow, although it took every bit of his willpower. She cried out and wrapped her legs around him, drawing him in deeper.

Her body moved in concert with his in a sensuous dance that gave him a pleasure he'd never experienced before. His tempo increased and then there was an explosion of sensations. He fell on her and they rolled over to lie side by side. Neither said anything, but he took her hand in his and clutched it tightly.

He wanted to say something, but he had no words. He could make no promises. He knew she didn't want any. He could only let her know that this had been extraordinary. He'd never felt like this before. He thought he never would again...with another woman.

The timing was all wrong. He had barely anything to offer. But at this moment, it didn't matter. Nothing mattered except the warm intimacy that wrapped around them.

"Come take a shower with me," he said.

She nodded. She took his hand and stood.

He opened the door and Sherry and Bart looked at them with reproach.

"I think they disapprove," she said.

"Only because they weren't invited inside," he replied and led her to the shower.

CHAPTER TWENTY-FOUR

THERE WERE TWO calls on her office phone when Stephanie reached home. She was mellow. Sated and happy. Really happy. She took Lulu and Stryker outside. This would be Lulu's final night with her. She'd had the last of her shots and tests and she would be going home to Eve and Nick tomorrow.

It was late—nearly midnight—when she checked the messages. One was from the number Mark had used to call her. The second wasn't familiar. She listened to that one first.

"Hi, it's David Matthews. I'm calling on a private cell outside the office. Sorry to bother you on Saturday night, but call me when you can. Townsend is on a rampage. He stormed into my office and demanded to know why we were in contact with you. He called you every name in the book. Happily my voice recorder was on. Maybe some people won't think he's a saint once they hear it. But I have to warn you. I think he's dangerous."

That was the end of the message. She would call him first thing in the morning. Then, bracing herself, she listened to the other message. "It's not a good idea to get involved in something that's not your business." Then an abrupt hang up. The tone was icy cold, and she knew it well. Although not a direct threat, she knew him well enough to know it was a real one. She saved both messages.

She poured a glass of wine. She'd just gone from the sublime to the pits. She didn't want to deal with Mark again, but she wasn't going to sit back and let him do to Susan what he had done to her. Tomorrow—no, today—was Sunday. No appointments.

She had a few questions she wanted to ask David. And a few suggestions, too. After their call, she would ride Shadow. Riding always cleared her head, and her head really needed a good clearing right now.

Clint said he would like to ride.

Tempting. Everything about him was tempting. His smile. His humor. His gentleness. More important, he understood her. Not many people did. Eve, yes. Josh, yes. A few others. And it was her fault. She'd allowed only a few people to get close to her. She'd been wary. Part of it was her distrust of people, another part was what she considered her own bad judgment.

Her father had limited her friends when she had been young. After her marriage to Rick, she did nothing but study and work for more than nine years, then she worked long hours at her practice. In her final stupidity, she had married Mark who had done everything he could to limit her relationships. Other than a few friends in vet school, she'd never had time to develop friendships or circles of friends. She'd always trusted animals more.

In the past five years, Eve had pushed her kicking and screaming all the way into the community life, challenging her into the search-and-rescue program. The volunteer fire fighting had been her own idea. But she suspected Eve had a lot to do with pushing Clint in her direction.

"Okay, dogs," she said. "Time for bed." Sherry and Stryker dashed for the bedroom, Lulu following behind. Stephanie slipped into a large T-shirt and climbed into bed. Sherry jumped up beside her. Stryker was happy in his dog bed. Right now, Lulu was sharing it.

She closed her eyes, hoping her sleep would be filled with Clint and not with Mark.

CLINT ROSE EARLY Sunday morning. He took coffee up the mountain path and watched the sunrise. Bart was at his side.

It was a glorious morning in more ways than one. No headache, and he felt hopeful and alive for the first time since the accident. He and Stephanie had not exchanged promises. It was far too early. They both were wary of commitments, Stephanie far more than he.

But he could wait. Take it slowly. It meant finding a job in town. No easy task, from what he understood. Nate had mentioned what a problem he'd had to make a living in Covenant Falls before he and Josh decided to partner. Even then, it had been Josh who had the starting capital.

But nothing could dim this morning. They might not have talked of love, but he knew he *was* in love, and she was reluctantly leaning in that direction. She'd looked beautiful last night with her face flushed and her eyes sparkling with lovemaking.

Would he see her today? He knew Eve, Josh and Nick went to church, but he didn't know about Stephanie. Should he call her? He was like a schoolboy hungering after the prettiest girl in class. Just as uncertain as to how to proceed.

He looked down at the town below him. A pretty town. Four church steeples punctuated the neat streets and rows of houses. He thought most of them would be filled today. Covenant Falls was a churchgoing town. How would he fit in? He'd been a warrior.

But there were other warriors here. Brothers. And he loved the mountains behind him. He would like to spend time in them.

Clint started the trek down the mountain. He would grab something to eat and start work on the dock. The cement should be hard enough to lay the framing timber. It would keep his mind off Stephanie. Or not.

He was making more coffee and frying a couple of eggs when the phone rang. He recognized the number and his heart cartwheeled. He clicked the answer button. "Hi," he said for lack of a better reply.

"Hi," Stephanie replied. "I received two phone calls. One from the attorney who was here with Mark's wife, and the other from Mark. I would like you to listen to them."

"I'll be right over."

"And Clint, I'm going riding today. You said you would like to learn. Want to go with me?"

Hell, yes, even if I fall off the horse. "Sure," he said instead. "Sounds good." *I hope.* "I can walk over there." *The dock could wait.*

"I have some eggs if you'll fix another omelet."

"I'll be delighted."

"Wear a long-sleeve shirt, the heaviest pair of jeans you have and sturdy shoes. There might be branches."

"Yes, ma'am."

A pause, then she said, "Did I sound that authoritative?"

"In a very sexy way," he said.

A silence. "Is that good?"

"Everything about you is good."

"I'll expect you in, what, twenty minutes?"

"That sounds reasonable. Can I bring Bart?"

"Of course. He's always been my favorite of Eve's dogs. She found him on a road half-dead. Someone just dumped him. Probably dogfight organizers. He wasn't any use to them anymore."

"I guessed at something like that because of the scars."

"I'm glad you have him," Stephanie said. "He needed more attention than he could get with all the other animals at Eve's. Nick understood that, too. I'll have coffee ready." The phone clicked off.

He gathered a few spices. "Come on, Bart," he said. "We're going to see Stephanie." The dog wagged his rear end. Clint leaned down and rubbed his ears. Sadness flooded him as he thought of how the dog had suffered, and yet had so much love to give. "I'm going to take very good care of you," he promised. "No one is going to hurt you again. Ever."

He and Bart reached Stephanie's office eighteen minutes later. He tried the door. It was open. He went to the counter and rang the bell.

She came out wearing riding clothes: the same worn riding pants she had on the night of their first kiss, boots and a long-sleeve blue plaid shirt. Her hair was pulled back in a long braid, but curls escaped and framed her face.

He held out his arms and she came into them. He held her for a minute. She felt so incredibly good there, as if she belonged next to him.

She broke away first. "I want you to hear the messages."

She reached for a phone on the counter, picked it up and clicked the message button.

He took the phone, listened to the attorney's voice. Then she clicked it again. Clint could barely keep his anger under control at the sound of her ex-husband's voice.

"I think you should tell Tony about this," he said. "I don't like the rage in his voice."

"I don't, either. But it makes me more determined to help Susan. I can't let him keep a child."

"What can you do?"

"Breakfast first," she said.

She led the way upstairs and showed him into the kitchen. She had eggs out, and milk, cheese and tomatoes.

"Got bacon or ham?"

She did, and it took him only a few minutes to make the omelet. "I don't use milk," he said, "just a touch of olive oil." She watched as he whipped up the eggs to a frothy mixture, then carefully poured it into a hot frying pan. When the eggs had firmed on one side, he added the other ingredients and neatly folded the mixture over and flipped it. In another two minutes it was ready.

She inserted bread in the toaster and placed honey and jam on the small table in the kitchen. She poured coffee and orange juice.

They both ate in comfortable silence, which was more satisfying than words. They weren't necessary. He would look at her, and she would smile, and that made his heart soar.

When they finished, they took the dishes to the sink, rinsed them, then put them in the dishwasher.

She refilled the coffee cups, then led the way into the living room.

"Remember, I told you how he stole the $50,000 I had from selling the practice in Pittsburgh?"

"You didn't say how much."

"It wasn't a lot for a practice as prices go, but my mentor—who was also my best friend—gave away a lot of services, and I did, too. We weren't in a wealthy part of town. People loved their pets, but they didn't have enough money for spaying and shots. We did a lot of stuff free or at below cost, and he also donated services to an animal shelter. The building was leased so basically all I sold was equipment and a client base, but I thought it was enough to buy into a practice in Boston. I didn't want to depend financially on Mark."

"But he made you dependent," Clint guessed.

"Yes, except I didn't see it right away." Her voice was matter of fact, but he saw the strain in her face.

"What are you thinking?" he asked. He knew it was something, which was probably why she asked him to come over.

"Mark was a vice president in the investment arm of the bank. He knew everyone who was anyone in Boston. I think he steered investments to a friend of his, Michael Donnell, who supposedly invested in gas and oil wells with huge dividends for the investors. Without my approval, Mark put my money into the fund. Two years later when we were divorced, I discovered my balance was about ten dollars. The gas wells that I supposedly invested in did not pan out. However, others were doing well. Too bad for me."

Clint's eyes narrowed. "I think I would like to meet this guy." It wouldn't be a pleasant meeting.

"I know. Mark convinced the judge he'd warned me it was a risk, but that I had insisted on it. Somehow my name was on the transaction. I never signed it. When I protested, he paid some men to say they had sex with me. By the time he was through, he was the poor abused husband and I was an unfaithful gold digger.

"The point is," she continued, "I didn't ask Susan and David whether she'd had any money going into the marriage, and whether she'd ever heard of Garrett Investments. Now fifty thousand isn't a lot of money to Mark. He spent money like it was candy after Halloween, but I don't think his salary was large enough to cover all the donations and contributions he made. I know from comments that the family money was almost gone."

Clint took her hand.

"I'm ashamed now I didn't fight harder, but by then, I simply wanted to get out, and I didn't have money for a good attorney or the financial experts I would need."

He listened intently. "Have you looked up Garrett Investments?"

"I tried to then. It's a private entity."

"Why don't you call David and see whether he

knows if Susan's family has ever invested in them?" Clint sat back and looked at her.

"Good idea. I'll call David now."

DAVID ANSWERED IMMEDIATELY. He'd obviously been waiting.

"Stephanie," he said.

"Hello, David."

He got right to the point. "Townsend called Susan and went ballistic, said she would never see her daughter again. I sent Susan to stay in a cottage owned by my cousin. But there's a preliminary hearing on custody next week."

"Maybe you should call me at a different number," she said.

There was a long silence. Then, "What number should I call?"

She gave him Tony's cell number and asked him to wait for fifteen minutes. She figured Tony's was the safest number. It had occurred to her that maybe the guy who was taking photographs might also have been able to tap into her phone. She was probably paranoid but better safe than sorry.

She hung up and told Clint about the conversation. "If Bolling was able to tap into the system and tries to locate the owner of that number, he'll discover it's the police chief. That should give him something to think about."

She punched Tony's number and told him she

needed to see him immediately. "Clint will make you an omelet," she added.

"I'll be there. Tell Clint to start the grub. I want to hear everything, especially the phone call from your ex."

"What about the guy you have in jail?"

"He's still there. The magistrate is still fishing. I told him not to rush back. In the meantime, I'm getting lots of phone calls from Boston attorneys who think they can push a small-town police chief around. I'm rather enjoying it."

"Good," she said.

"I'm on my way over to you."

When she hung up, Clint looked amused. "I heard you offering my culinary excellence."

"As far as omelets go." She grinned. "I haven't tasted anything else."

"Is that a challenge?"

"Just an observation."

He stood and kissed her long and hard. "How's that for heating something up?"

"Mmm," she murmured. "I like that. I'm not so sure that Tony would, though. Better get cooking."

"No reason until he arrives." He ran his hand down her cheek.

The doorbell rang.

"Damn," he said. "Faster, or hungrier, than I thought."

"I'll open the door. You can start the omelet."

"I hope this won't turn into a habit. Cooking for all your friends. I mean. Not kissing."

The bell rang again.

Clint grumbled, but he went into the kitchen as she ran down to open the door.

CHAPTER TWENTY-FIVE

IT WASN'T TONY.

By the time she got downstairs to unlock the door, she saw a delivery truck disappearing down the street and a package leaning against the door.

She picked it up and took it inside her office. She cut the wrapping and looked inside. Roses. Yellow roses. There was no card. But they were what Mark had always given her after an argument. She had come to hate them, and he knew it.

Chills ran down her arm. He was telling her he knew where she lived, that he could reach her.

There was a national florist's name on the box. She would give it to Tony.

Just then, she heard knocking on her door. Tony.

He noticed the flowers on the counter. "An admirer?"

"No card, but I'm sure they came from Mark Townsend. One of my last comments to him was that I hated yellow roses. He always sent them after an argument. He's telling me he not only knows my number but where I live."

"He has to know we have his private investigator."

"Another warning," she said. "But neither the flowers nor the phone call are overt enough to cause him legal problems."

"Bastard," Tony said.

"Wait until you hear his telephone call. But have breakfast first. Clint's omelet should be ready and you don't want it to get cold." She led the way up the stairs, and into the kitchen. The plate was on the table with napkin, knife and fork. Clint had poured cups of coffee. Everyone took a seat.

Tony didn't speak until he had finished eating. "You ought to open an omelet shop or something."

"Nope. Just make them for friends."

"I'm damn happy I'm a friend, then." Tony pushed back his chair. "I want to hear the call."

Stephanie gave him the phone, and Tony listened. His mouth grew grimmer.

He looked at Stephanie. "He sounds like he's spiraling out of control."

"Susan's attorney is calling me shortly on your number. I want to know if she made any investments on his advice and if so, what happened. I also want to know more about that fund."

Tony listened, then said, "I talked to Tom Mc-Guire and asked him to make some queries for me. He knows people I don't, and he knows people who know people."

"I met him at Josh's," Clint said.

"Then you know he was police chief until I took over temporarily two months ago. He was also with the state police and was with the sheriff's office of this county. He has contacts in nearly every law enforcement agency. I asked him to check with friends on our guest in jail. Bolling's an ex-cop with the Boston Police Department. He was 'retired' because of several charges of brutality."

Stephanie's mouth dropped. "How did he get a private investigator license?"

"He was never convicted of anything. It was handled internally."

Tony's phone rang. It was David Matthews.

Tony turned it on speaker and handed it to Stephanie who answered. "David, you're on speaker. With me are police chief Tony Keller and a friend, Clint Morgan. They heard your message this morning, and Mark's. We have some questions. Okay?"

"Go ahead," David said.

"I received a call warning me not to interfere and this morning received a bouquet of roses from him. I don't think there's much doubt he intended it as a threat. And now I'm all in with you. I'll do anything you need. But I have a question. Did Susan have any money coming into the marriage, money that disappeared in an investment fund?"

"She had a trust fund that came to her when she married. A hundred thousand dollars from her grandfather. I've made queries. Mark said it's gone. A bad investment."

She couldn't believe Mark would be so reckless as to do the same thing again. Except it had been years since she disappeared, and since it worked once, maybe it would work twice. Or was it only once or twice? How many investors had been cheated in the same way?

"Have you checked on the investment company?" she asked.

"Haven't had time. He just sprang that on us when we asked for assets. That's when we heard that she was an unfit mother and he was filing for sole custody. He obviously wants to use Melissa as a bargaining chip."

Tony looked at Stephanie. "How far do you think he might go?"

"I don't know, but I do know he's a pathological liar."

"Family?"

"Old money at one time, but I think most of it is gone now. Father died of a heart attack when Mark was a teenager. That was one reason I was drawn to him. His mother dotes on him. She's very respected, and she didn't exactly approve of me. I was an outsider and, God forbid, I worked with my hands. She was icily polite."

"She was all kindness to Susan," David said.

"Susan is from Boston and didn't work with her hands. And Mrs. Townsend did want grandchildren."

"Well," David said. "She has one."

"What can we do for you?" she asked.

"Testify at a hearing about Mark hitting you."

"There's no proof. I didn't go to the hospital."

"Still, I'm hoping to find some others. There's umors he patronized a gentleman's club."

"Why am I not surprised?"

"I'll see what I can discover about Susan's 'in-estment.'"

"And we'll see what we can do to nudge authori-es to look into it," Tony said.

They hung up then. "I'm calling a council of war," ony said. "I think we should include Tom, Eve and osh."

"How much longer can you keep Bolling in jail?"

"He's been charged so we can keep him until rraignment, but I would rather not be forced into etting him go. Maybe two more days at most."

"He's not saying anything?"

"Oh, he's saying a lot, just not about Townsend. Ie's going to sue us for not taking him to the hos-ital."

"How in the hell has someone like Townsend con-nued to be a hero in Boston?" Clint asked.

"Same reason I looked up to him for a while," tephanie said. "He's dynamic, successful and very ood with people who can help him. He comes from respected family, which means a lot in Boston, and e has great manners. Problem is that under all the nining tin is a sociopath. We can't let him get cus-ody of Susan's daughter."

"Tom will have some ideas," Tony said, then urned to Clint. "I do know that Stephanie shouldn't e alone."

"It will be a hardship, but I'll stay with her," Clint said with a straight face.

"I have Sherry and Stryker. I don't need anyone.

"Do you have a gun?"

"Yes," she said.

"Clint?" Tony asked.

"No. Left all that back in Afghanistan."

"But I take it you know how to use one."

He nodded.

"I'll loan you one. I don't suppose you have carry permit?"

"No."

"I'll make you a temporary deputy then, if that okay with you."

Clint raised an eyebrow, then nodded. "I'll do any thing I can."

"I'll call Tom and Eve and see whether we can get together later this afternoon."

"I…" she began. "Clint and I were planning t go riding this afternoon out at Eve's so any time i good for me."

Tony nodded. "I'll call you when I get Ev They're probably at church now."

He left and Stephanie looked at Clint. He too her in his arms and held her. "I'm sorry," they bot said at the same time. That wry lopsided smile sh straight into her heart. She couldn't believe she wa already giving at least half of that organ to him. N after she'd sworn never to do that again.

But then she'd never met anyone like Clint befor

There was no pretense about him. It had taken her while to understand that what she saw was what he got. Smart, but unimpressed by it. And she loved the way he laughed at himself.

He was the total opposite of Mark who always had to be the center of attention, who wouldn't dream of going out of the house without wearing a tie and who took himself very seriously.

She looked at her watch. As Tony had said, Eve and Nick, and maybe Josh, were probably still in church. It amused her at how quickly Josh, the iconic loner, had fallen so easily into the role of family man.

"Let's go for that ride," she said. "I need some fresh air."

"What about the dogs?"

"We can take them with us. I need to take Lulu to Nick anyway. Bart can see his friends. Sherry and Stryker can run along with us."

"Run? We're going to run? Like we were going to roll a cow?"

She was enchanted by him. No one made her laugh like he did. "Well, maybe a slow run," she conceded.

They cleaned up the kitchen together, then climbed into her van with the dogs.

They passed families walking home from church or going by the Dairy Queen or walking to Maude's for sandwiches in the park. She knew every single one of them, and she hated the idea of possibly

bringing violence to town. It would be her fault. He
very faulty decision eight years earlier.

"This is by far the most peaceful place I've eve
lived," he said, and she realized he was thinkin
the same thing.

They reached the house, and saw both the Jee
and Eve's pickup.

The dogs started barking inside and Stryker di
the same. Sherry was too mannerly and Bart to
fearful to reply. But once they were at the door, Nic
came out to meet them.

Stephanie held Lulu and put her in Nick's arm:
His face lit up as he hugged her. "She's beautiful.
he said.

"Are you going to rename her?"

"Naw, I like Lulu." He put her down and hugge
Bart. "I'll always love you, too," he said, and Ba
gave him a big sloppy kiss, then returned to his plac
beside Clint.

Eve smiled and nodded to Stephanie. All wa
good. They went inside.

"I thought you would be in church," Stephani
said.

"We decided to be lazy today," Eve said. "Jos
and Nick went up to a stream at daybreak and caugh
some trout. We're going to have them for dinne
There's plenty for you guys, too. Josh is in back
cleaning them."

"Have you heard from Tony this morning?"
Stephanie asked, moving out of Nick's hearing.

"No. Is there a problem?"

Stephanie nodded. "He wants to meet with you, Josh and Tom McGuire this afternoon. My ex-husband is apparently stalking me, or else trying to frighten me into crawling away."

"Does this have to do with your visitors and the man in jail?"

"I think so."

"Then why don't we make this a fish fry and invite Tony and Tom over," Eve said.

"Thanks. I thought I would try to teach Clint to ride. We need to get some air. Okay if he takes Beauty?"

"Sure. You know they're available to you any time. Maybe Nick…"

Then she looked at them closely. First Stephanie, then Clint. A long searching glance, then she grinned. "Or maybe not. We'll see you later. I'll time dinner in two hours."

Stephanie led the way through the gate and the three horses cantered up from the pasture to say hello. She led them into the stable and reached inside a closed box to extract three carrots. She gave one to Clint for Beauty and she fed Shadow and Beast.

When the horses finished eating, she showed Clint how to saddle a horse. He watched carefully, and then saddled Beauty as she supervised. "Nicely done," she said as he finished.

"A compliment?" He raised an eyebrow.

"I'm beginning to suspect you're not such a ten derfoot, after all."

"I swear I have never been on a horse before," h said. "A camel, maybe," he said with a twinkle. " fell off."

Dear heaven, but he was disarming. "Okay, I sup pose you know you get up on the left side."

"I do watch movies."

"How can a grown man not have ridden a horse?"

"Us city slickers are just plain backward."

The tension slid away from her, which was, sh knew, his intent.

He mounted easily and settled into the saddle, bu then she knew he'd told the truth. He had not th slightest idea of what to do with the reins. He wa a fast learner, though, and a natural rider. A wee ago, she would have been annoyed at that. Now sh enjoyed watching him. After they walked around th pasture several times, she leaned over and opene the gate. She waited as he rode out, then she leane down and fastened it.

They walked for a while, passing the smal ranches as they headed toward the mountain.

"Want to try a trot?"

He did, and why was she not surprised?

They reached a path winding upward.

"We're going up a little way," she said. "There' a small waterfall ahead and a little pool." They rod another fifteen minutes, then they saw it. It wasn' a high, straight waterfall, but rather a lot of littl umbling cascading falls ending in a pool. Sadly, he water had thinned to a trickle because of the drought. She slid from her horse and he did the same.

It was quiet, peaceful and very private. She leaned against him, and he put his arms around her, drawing her close to his body. "This is my favorite place," he said softly. "I like it better than the big falls. Eve told me she used to ride over here when she was young."

"I can see why," Clint murmured.

"One of my favorite books as a child was *The Secret Garden,* and oh, how I wanted one. But we lived in a poor neighborhood in Pittsburgh with few gardens, much less secret ones."

"So this became your secret garden," he said, his hand stroking her back.

She turned around and faced him. "I like you, Clint Morgan. I like you very much."

"Ditto." He kissed her hard. "Double ditto."

"That's good. Let's take it slow. Not because I want to. I feel I'm on a speeding train when I'm with you."

"I know. And I'll take it as slow as you want, but right now..."

Right now they didn't take it slow at all.

THEY WERE ALL THERE, gathered outside around a grill. A plate of trout was on a portable table next to it.

Waiting for them to return were the former po-

lice chief Tom McGuire, Tony, Josh and Eve. Nic
was taking care of the dogs, although Bart made
beeline to Clint as soon as he arrived.

McGuire shook his head. "Never would have ex
pected that of Braveheart."

"Bart," three people corrected at once.

"That's gonna take some getting used to," Mc
Guire grumbled.

Clint grinned. "Bart has a mind of his own."

"I see that," McGuire said.

Clint was only too aware that other eyes were o
them, moving from his face to Stephanie's flushe
one.

"How did it go? You said you didn't ride," Ev
asked.

"I managed to stay aboard," he said. "Barely."

"Don't believe him," Stephanie said. "He's a nat
ural rider, although he did confide that he fell of
a camel."

"*Confide* is the word," he said, pretending to loo
betrayed. "Meaning *confidential*."

Eve grinned. "I'm glad to see you two gettin
along."

Josh laughed. "There's something in the air i
Covenant Falls."

He placed the trout on the grill and closed the to
to let them smoke.

"Drink?" Eve asked. "We have beer and wine."

"A beer would be great," he said. "Can I get it?'

"Sure. Top of the fridge."

He went inside. Bart followed. Clint worried that Nick would feel abandoned. But then he saw Nick, who seemed totally absorbed in teaching Lulu to retrieve a ball.

He found a beer and returned to the yard. Smoke spiraled up from the grill. It was only a matter of minutes before Josh took the trout off the grill.

"Everything else is ready inside," Eve said.

They made their way to the dining room table. It was already set. Eve brought in coleslaw and potato salad. Josh trailed with the platter of fish. The other guys got beers, as well, while Eve and Stephanie shared a bottle of wine.

After the meal, they headed back outside while Nick stayed to put the dishes in the dishwasher and stay with the dogs.

Kids were beginning to look pretty good to Clint.

"Down to business," Tony said. He brought the others up to speed on what had happened in the past few days, particularly what could be a possible threat to Stephanie. He turned to Tom. "You know anyone in the Security Exchange Commission that could look into the investment firm?"

"I might have a contact. I'm not sure how strong it is or how long it might take. If I mention it could involve political figures he could make a quick check to see if there's been any complaints or investigations. I can check on whether it's registered and/or connected with any financial institution. If it's completely private, it could be difficult."

"Make sure the request comes from Washington not from Colorado," Tony said. "I don't want to pu Stephanie in danger."

Tom nodded.

Tony turned to the others. "I didn't like the ton of the phone call, nor the flowers, nor someone tak ing photos of Stephanie's building. I also don't lik the fact that Bolling isn't talking. He's either afraid which is truly worrying, or he doesn't think there ar consequences. He's probably rethinking that now I intend to keep him in Colorado. I'm also wor ried that this Townsend has a pattern of abuse an feels free to hire people to lie about his spouses. H clearly feels untouchable. People like that can b dangerous."

Clint gripped Stephanie's hand.

"I don't think Stephanie should go away from town alone, particularly driving out in the country, Tony continued. "When she's in town, I think w should all be alert for any strangers asking question or just looking out of place. Let it be known to var ious people like Maude and others who live clos to Stephanie to be alert. And let me know if there' anything that doesn't seem normal."

"I don't need babysitters," Stephanie said.

"Not babysitters," Clint said. "People who car about you. And I'm one of them. I'm free most o the time. I volunteer to keep an eye out."

Stephanie frowned. "What about the dock?"

"To hell with the dock," Josh said. "That can wai

volunteer, too. Both Clint and I have had weapons training."

Tony spoke up. "Eve, I want to deputize Clint if
that's okay with you. I've run all the checks."

Eve nodded. "What can I do?"

"Keep in touch so she's not alone."

Stephanie grimaced.

Clint knew exactly what she was thinking. She
prized her independence above all else. What she
dreaded most was losing it.

"We might all be wrong," she said in a low voice.
"He might just be making trouble, trying to scare
me."

"Maybe. Maybe not," Eve said. "But we underes-
timated Sam and I could have lost Nick."

Clint raised an eyebrow. "What happened?"

Tom answered this time. "Sam was one of my
deputies who wanted my job. He saw Josh as an opportunity to show what a great lawman he was, tried
to set him up for a series of burglaries and ended
up kidnapping Nick when the boy saw him planting
evidence. He's awaiting trial now."

Tom looked at his watch. "I have to get home. I'll
make those calls first thing in the morning."

"And I have paperwork to do," Stephanie said.
"Thank you all."

Clint and Stephanie left first with her two dogs
and Bart.

When they reached her building, he went in with

her. All the doors were still locked, and the dogs gave no cause for alarm. No suspicious sniffing.

When Clint finished checking everything, Stephanie touched his arm. "I really do have to work," she said. "And I'll be safe here. Stryker and Sherry are very protective. I'm sure Tony's officers will be checking every few minutes."

"If Townsend calls again or you have any feeling that things are not right, call me," he said. "And please don't leave town without me."

"I won't," she said. "I swear."

"Okay." He kissed her lightly. Slow, like they'd agreed.

Slow.

He left, worrying and aching and yet knowing that to push now would not be appreciated. Tony had it under control.

But he and Bart would be watching.

CHAPTER TWENTY-SIX

STEPHANIE'S LANDLINE WOKE her up first thing Monday. Light was beginning to creep through the windows. She looked at her clock. Seven thirty.

She should have been up by now. She needed to take the dogs for a walk before the office opened at 8:00 a.m.

She looked at the caller ID. "Anonymous."

She picked it up.

"How's my little redhead?"

"Not yours any longer, Mark."

"I don't think you paid any attention to me the other day," he said. "I hear someone from Colorado is making inquiries."

"Why should I pay attention?"

"Because I'm looking out for your best interests. David Matthews isn't."

"And what are my best interests?"

"Tell your friends to release Mr. Bolling."

"Again, why should I?"

"There could be a rather large lawsuit against the town."

"Why don't you tell them yourself?"

A silence.

"Why exactly was Mr. Bolling here?" she asked. "Why was he taking photos?"

"I'm still looking out for you," he said in that charming voice. "I was told some of the buildings there were old. I know you don't have much money. Maybe a contractor could help improve the fire standards."

She went cold. She knew exactly what he was insinuating. But he was being very careful with his words. She knew it was a threat because she knew him. But for someone else, someone who didn't know him, it could be construed as helpful.

"Maybe if you gave me my money back, I can do it myself."

"Is that what you want, Stephanie? Money?"

"Just what you owe me."

"Let's meet and talk about it."

"Are you here?"

"Close enough."

She was silent. He was desperate. She sensed it now. He couldn't afford more bad publicity. Two stories, much the same, and missing money.

"Where do you want to meet?"

"There's a closed motel outside of town," he said.

"Someplace public," she insisted.

"You name it."

"The park at the lake."

"I've missed you, Stephanie. That spark. Your fire. I never should have let you go."

"You didn't let me go. I ran."

"We can forget all that." This was old Mark, thinking his charm still worked. Even after the warning he'd made on the phone.

She didn't answer.

"When?" he asked.

"Noon."

"Noon, it is."

"Bring my money," she said, "and I'll try to get your man released."

She hung up and immediately called Tony to tell him about the conversation. He was at her office in minutes and listened to the recorded call. "Pleasant chap on the phone," he said.

"Too pleasant," she said. "He's afraid of something. Maybe he's worried about queries into the investment firm or what Bolling might say. Maybe he thinks paying me off will shut down any more investigation."

"Why would he meet in a public place?"

"Because I wouldn't meet anywhere else and he still sees me as the helpless person I was years ago. He really doesn't like women. He doesn't give them any credit for brains. I think he actually believes he can give me some money and I'll go away along with any bad publicity."

"And if you're wrong?"

"I'll be in a public park, and I suspect he'll know you or other officers may be there. It's our best chance to get him to say something we can use."

"Clint won't like it. Neither will Josh, but you might be right. As you said, he won't try anything in public. I'll wire you and I'll have officers in the park." He rubbed his chin. "Sure you want to do this?"

"Something has rattled him since two days ago. He's always been able to charm himself out of trouble. I guess he figures he can do it again."

"I'll be here at eleven thirty with the wire. Just go along with him. Find out what he wants."

She nodded, but she had no intention of doing that. None at all.

She was going to push every one of his buttons. She wanted assault charges. She wanted him on tape and camera.

She somehow got through her morning appointments and cancelled the others. At eleven, she rushed upstairs and changed into a pair of slacks and a silk blouse. She brushed her hair and pulled it back with a silver clip. Then she carefully put on makeup. She knew she should call Clint, but Tony had probably already done that.

She was right. He came in the door with Tony at exactly 11:30 a.m.

"I don't think you should—"

She shook her head. "It's the only way to help Susan and her little girl. I have to goad him into saying something that can be used in court. Any other way is too slow. Please don't argue with me."

"I'm going to be there. With Bart."

"Good. I'm taking Stryker, as well. Sherry's too gentle."

Tony looked at his watch. "It's time."

The two men headed out back. Stephanie put a leash on Stryker and Sherry barked at being left out.

"Sorry, girl. Not this time."

Stephanie and Stryker exited the office. She took her time, strolling the distance. She wanted to be a little late. That would annoy Mark. Her heart pounded. He'd caused her so much grief.

She finally reached the park and saw him standing next to the monument. She glanced around. Tony was in workman's clothes fixing a swing. Clint was sitting at a picnic table with Bart and one of the woman dispatchers at the police department. Stephanie didn't see Cody, but knew he must be nearby.

She calmed her nerves as she approached Mark. It had been five years since she'd seen him, and he looked a little heavier, his hair a bit thinner, but he was still a handsome man. He smiled when he saw her, but his eyes didn't.

"You look beautiful," he said and reached out to take her hand. She took a foot backward to avoid it.

He ignored the slight. "You always were a striking woman."

"You weren't as nice on the phone the other night."

"I'm sorry about that. I was just…"

"Worried that I would help your wife dig up dirt?

What dirt is there to dig up?" She tilted her head. "An investment company, maybe?"

"I'm sorry you lost money," he said carefully. "I'm willing to give you what you lost. I have a check."

"I want twice as much," she said, "after what you did to me, the jobs you made sure I didn't get."

His mouth tightened. She knew then that she had been right. He *was* worried about the investment company. Word must have leaked that someone from Colorado was asking questions. He'd thought a few words, a smile and some money would buy her off. Of course, he'd spent his life doing exactly that to people.

"I don't have it all now," he said. "I can give you a check for twenty thousand, the rest later this month."

"A check from you? I don't think so. You're a bully and a liar and a cheat, and soon everyone in Boston will know it." She had just gone off script.

Mark's face flushed. She knew the signs. An explosion was coming.

"Tell me about the investment company," she continued. "How many of your friends have invested in it, and how many wells does it really own?"

"You silly bitch," he said, his voice rising. "You really think you can touch me."

She saw Clint standing.

"Not only do I think," she said. "I can. You think you're untouchable, but you're not. Other authorities are looking into your donations. I took some papers you carelessly left in your office one day. I wasn't

quite the quiet little mouse you tried to make me."
It was lies. All lies. But he didn't know it.

He exploded then. Just like she knew he would.
He struck her in the chest with his fist, a blow that
knocked her to the ground. He leaned over to strike
again. Stryker lunged at him, caught his wrist and
held on.

Mark tried to throw the dog to the ground. Her
ex-husband was too furious to see Clint and Tony
behind him.

She could hardly breathe. She barely managed
to call Stryker off. The dog reluctantly obeyed, and
Tony and Clint grabbed Mark as blood dripped down
his arm.

The pain came, but every second of it was worth
it. Mark was being trundled off in handcuffs.

Clint kneeled beside her, his hands running over
her body. "You could have a cracked rib."

"Good," she said with satisfaction, although she
winced as she said the word. "But I don't think so.
I...think he just...knocked the breath out of me."

Open-mouthed, he stared at her. Then he said,
"That was the dumbest, most idiotic, foolhardy
thing..."

"It was...the only way to get him," she said. "I
hope that...Marilyn got a good photo."

Clint turned around. Marilyn was a neighbor of
his, as well as a reporter for the local weekly and
a cousin of Bill Evans. She stood fifteen feet away
still snapping photos.

"I…called her and told her something interesting might happen at the park," Stephanie said. She tried to sit up and pet Stryker, but the pain was growing by the second.

"Dammit, be still," Clint ordered. "And remind me never to make you mad," he added.

Two officers from the police department arrived with a rolling stretcher and eased her onto it.

"Poor…Dr. Bradley," she said, then she looked up at Clint. "Can you take Stryker home? Give him a reward?"

He nodded. "I'll give him two. Maybe five. I'll meet you at the doctor's office."

Then he leaned down, and in front of a growing crowd, kissed her.

THE PHOTO OF Mark striking her was on the front page of the local paper and was picked up by the Denver paper. Marilyn then sold it to the Boston papers. One displayed it on the front of the local news page along with the story, via David Matthews, of Mark's divorce problems and missing money. It was considered news because of his political contributions to a number of prominent politicians.

Susan emailed Stephanie the story and then snail-mailed a copy of the paper.

Her ribs had not been cracked or broken. The breath had been knocked out of her and she had a huge bruise—and some pain—but it was worth it.

Tony had been mad as hell, as had been Josh, that she hadn't told them what she had planned to do.

After his initial outrage, Clint understood. He got her.

He realized it was something she had to do for herself before she could leave the past behind her.

A week after the incident, Mark had been moved to the county seat where he was charged with criminal assault. In the initial hearing, he was denied bond because he wasn't a resident of Colorado and could be a flight risk.

Stephanie knew the next few weeks would be nasty, but a lot of Mark's influence vanished with his arrest. Politicians were giving his contributions back and he was kicked off several boards. The Boston papers were all over it now, going back over coverage of his divorces.

Despite the lingering pain of a bruised rib, Stephanie's week was much better when Susan called. She'd won temporary custody of her daughter, and David was convinced it would be permanent. Mark was in jail, denied bail since he was from out of state. Stephanie had finally defeated him. She was falling in love, and now she no longer feared it. Clint had given her a precious gift. He'd known her well enough not to interfere. He'd realized she had to fight her own battle to free herself.

CHAPTER TWENTY-SEVEN

WILDFIRE!

Stephanie received the call at 6:00 a.m. Tuesday morning, one week after her encounter with Mark. Her volunteer firefighter unit was called up.

The fire was just twenty-five miles northwest of Covenant Falls. Their unit was the closest one, although other teams were being flown in.

No one knew the exact cause of the fire, although there had been heat lightning during the night and a second wildfire flared up fifty miles north.

Stephanie called Dr. Langford and asked him to cover the clinic for the day, possibly for several days depending on the fire. Having once been a member of the unit himself, he readily agreed. Then she called Beth and told her that Dr. Langford would be taking over.

She also called Clint since they'd planned to have dinner that night. He answered immediately. She should have known. He never seemed to sleep.

He was already aware, having heard news of the fire via the Covenant Falls grapevine.

"Are you well enough?" he asked.

"No pain for the last two days," she said. She neglected to tell him, though, that there were still sore places. "I have to go," she said and hung up. She dressed quickly in her uniform and pulled on the heavy boots that were always within reach of her bed. She then grabbed the rest of her gear: fire-retardant coat, protective helmet, gloves, radio harness, wildland pack, hydration bottle, her tools. Reggie, the mechanic at the local garage, called and offered to pick her up. He was also picking up Calvin Wilson, who was also a volunteer.

Five minutes later, they were at the park. Two helicopters, one a Black Hawk, the other a Chinook, sat in the cleared parking lot. Most of the members of the team were already there. Several cars screeched into the parking lot. She noticed Nate approaching.

And saw Clint. He stood next to the Black Hawk, a wistful expression on his face as he talked to the pilot. When he saw her, he hurried over. "Damn, but you look good in all that paraphernalia."

She couldn't help but smile. He always made her smile. "No, I don't," she said. "I look like a creature from outer space."

"Buy me a ticket, then," he said. Then the smile disappeared. "Be careful."

She was glad he didn't ask her not to go. Of course he wouldn't. He knew her too well. She could tell, though, that the fact he couldn't go was slowly killing him.

"We're really well trained," she said. "Josh would be here, but he hasn't finished training yet."

"You know I'm falling in love with you." The angst in his voice reminded her of the dangers in going to a fire line. The change of wind, a flying spark, so many things could go wrong. She'd been at several funerals of firefighters killed in wildfires.

"Me, too," she admitted as the one paid member of the Covenant Falls Volunteer Fire Department, Sandy Kiper, cleared his throat to get everyone's attention.

"We have twenty members here," he said. "I don't have to tell you to be careful and look out for each other. You know the procedures. If I give the sign to go, you run like hell, but stay together as much as possible. Keep your radios on.

"Now gather around." He showed them the map and the area that was their responsibility. "Other units will be joining us soon. We'll be digging a fire line and telling the choppers where to drop water. Down the hill is a stream. If there's any trouble, head for it. Other units will join us.

"We'll be flying in the Black Hawk. The Chinook will be using the Bambi buckets to dump water on the area where we will be working and will make continuous runs. The Black Hawk will join him after delivering us so we should have good coverage."

She could barely hear as the helicopters started their engines. Dust flew everywhere. She started for

he chopper when Clint held up his hand to stop her
nd climbed into the cockpit.

"What the hell?" said Sandy, running over to con-
er with the pilot and Clint.

He returned to the team. "Mr. Morgan heard
omething in the engine that shouldn't be there. The
ilot, after listening, agreed. The tank will have to
e refueled, but we're going in with the Chinook.
'll drop the water, then deliver us. We'll have to
appel down because of the bucket."

Had Clint raised a false alarm to keep her from
oing in? She dismissed the thought nearly as fast as
t had developed. The one quality that had won her
ver was his acceptance of her, and who she was.

She climbed into the chopper with the others and
hey took off, leaving the Black Hawk behind. She
eaned back, keeping her thoughts and fears at bay.
ire did frighten her. It was one of the few things
hat did. It was possible to stop people like her ex-
usband. It was damned hard to stop a fire hell-bent
n burning an entire forest.

She pulled on a face mask and fire hood as they
pproached the fire. The air was filled with smoke.
he dreaded having to rappel with all the equipment
he was carrying. There was also a large bag to get
own with them. Shovels, picks, other tools.

"Listen, all," Sandy said. "The pilot will land us
t our anchor point. The anchor point is a rock slide.
t's pretty much barren, so we don't have to worry
bout a fire outflanking us. Our job is to clear as

much brush as we can between the fire and anchor to starve it."

They stayed belted in their seats as the chopper delivered the water over the encroaching fire, then hovered near the ground as the firefighters rappelled down. The bag of equipment came next, and the chopper lifted back into the air. "Okay, we're going to move as quickly as we can to this spot," Sandy said, pointing to a spot about a fourth of a mile from the rock slide.

CLINT SAT WITH the Black Hawk pilot as the fuel lines were cleansed and the chopper refueled.

When the pilot had started the engine earlier, Clint recognized a barely noticeable skipping sound. When he had mentioned it to the pilot, he had asked about the earlier refueling. The pilot said it had not come from the normal refueling station. Apparently there wasn't an adequate mixture of the gasoline with the oil. It could be harmless. Or not. It could certainly damage the engine.

The pilot swore, but he had called in, and it had been decided the chopper's fuel tank would need to be emptied, cleaned and refueled. He would have to fly to a refueling station. They were lucky one was close.

"How in the hell did you catch that?" the pilot asked.

"I'm an old chopper hand. Army. God knows how

many engines we ruined by flying with bad fuel. I learned real fast how to detect it."

"How many years?"

"Seventeen."

The pilot was quiet after that, and Clint kept looking at his watch. He'd delayed aid coming to Stephanie, but a choked engine wouldn't help, either.

It was two hours before the copter was refueled and they returned to the staging area at the lake.

Tony was there. "What's happening?" Clint asked anxiously.

"The fire has intensified and is moving toward the trench," Tony said. "The Black Hawk arrived just in time. We need more water out there."

Clint watched as the Bambi bucket was attached to the chopper. The pilot scooped it full of water and took off. The Chinook was on its way back for refueling.

The sun had turned downward and smoke, with its astringent odor, drifted over Covenant Falls. Then came the steady voice of the leader of Stephanie's unit. "We have to pull out of here," he said. "The fire's skipping over the trench. We're heading for the rock slide. Now!"

Tony contacted the Black Hawk, which was still in sight. "Return to base to drop the bucket. We must evacuate the team. Repeat. Return as quickly as possible."

"They might need help," Clint said. "I want to go

back with the chopper." He'd already decided he wa
going, permission or not.

Tony nodded. "With all the smoke, the pilot wi
probably need his copilot in front with him. If it'
good with him, it's good with me."

As the Black Hawk landed, ground members ra
to help release the bucket. Tony signaled the pilc
to land. Both he and Clint ran over to the cockpit.

"Okay if Clint Morgan goes with you?" Tony saic

"Sure, jump in," The pilot lifted off as Clint bal
anced himself behind the pilot's seat. "You help th
crew chief," the pilot said. "I've seen that terrair
They'll have to come up the rope, one at a time usin
the winch and rescue basket."

Clint's heart beat faster. It wasn't just Stephanie
the heart of the town was down there. People wh
weren't paid to put their lives at risk. He thought c
Calvin Wilson who had left his store to help buil
the dock, and two of the veterans he'd met at th
community center, and Nate.

After what seemed like hours, the pilot said, "W
should be there in two minutes."

Clint felt the heat on his face. He could barel
breathe for the smoke. He searched down below an
saw the huddled group. They had drawn a circle an
were protecting themselves with the fire shield a
flames whipped toward them, feeding on the sma
pieces of growth. It was the wind that was the prob
lem, and the wind was affecting the helicopter, to

The pilot was right. No place to land. The copilot and a third crew member hooked the basket to the rope and lowered it. The first person came up. He had burns on his arms from flying embers, but he brushed them aside. "Get the others."

Each time Clint prayed, and he didn't do that often, that the next person would be Stephanie. But the injured came up first, then the most exhausted, then there was an argument when there were only two below. The flames were almost to them. He and the crew chief were lifting the basket as fast as they could, but he knew, and the pilot knew, the flames were too close. If they reached the chopper it would explode.

Then Stephanie came, having lost the battle to the team leader, and she was up. He wanted to hug her, to kiss her, to never let her do any goddamn stupid thing again.

"Hey, he's not getting into the basket," the pilot said, "and we gotta get the hell out of here."

"I'll get him," Clint said, and before anyone could stop him, he slid down the rope, heedless of the burns on his fingers. The man had lost consciousness. Clint piled him in the basket and signaled the copilot to take it up.

He felt the heat from the fire, the first burn on his leg, then the basket was back and he was hanging on to it as the helicopter lifted from the flames. He was pulled up to the chopper by helping hands from every direction.

BOTH HE AND SANDY were admitted to the hospi
tal in Pueblo, having been flown there. Stephani
had escaped the more serious burns and was treate
by Doc Bradley, but she had immediately driven t
Pueblo and taken up residence in Clint's room. H
had more serious burns on his legs.

The nurses allowed Bart into the room in the sec
ond week, after Stephanie lied and said he was
certified service dog. Cody's grandmother had eve
made a coat for him saying as much.

Stephanie's arm still hurt from the burns, but he
heart hurt even more so as she saw the joy in Bar
when he spied Clint in bed. He seemed reassure
just to see Clint and sensed he couldn't touch hir
after a word from Stephanie. "Maybe tomorrow,
she said, "but only while the nurse is gone."

"I heard that," the nurse said as she entered to re
fill Clint's IV. "But I'll pretend I didn't. I have tw
little guys myself. But don't let the head nurse se
him, or you and the dog will be out of here."

Stephanie nodded. "Understood."

The nurse left.

Bart took the opportunity to sneak a big swipe o
Clint's hand. His eyes opened. Slow at first. The
jerked wide open when he saw her a few feet awa
and Bart eagerly trying to kiss him again.

"Now, that's plain pitiful," he said. "I woke t
what I thought was a kiss from a beautiful lady
and what do I get?" But his hand went down an

ondled Bart's ears. The dog made a low moaning noise of ecstasy.

"Now, *that* is disgusting," she said.

He held out his hand and she took it. Both legs were bandaged. She was sure there was a high level of morphine in the IV. His legs had burns worse than her superficial ones. But the doctor said that while there would be some scarring, no nerves or muscles had been involved. He'd been lucky.

And still he made light of it.

She wondered if he would always make her laugh. She had been worried sick about him. Him, apparently, not so much.

"By the way," she said, "you have a job offer."

"I do?"

"The pilot of that chopper apparently told his boss that he should grab you. That you heard something even he had not, and how efficiently you handled the rescue effort. The owner wants to offer you a job as a crew chief."

"Where?"

"Denver." She paused, then continued, "And you have another offer."

"I'm speechless."

"You're going to be even more speechless. Eve, Tony and Tom want you as police chief. Tony has to leave, and you would work with Tom for several months as chief deputy, take some courses, but then if it all works out, the job would be yours. Money wouldn't be as good as the other job. In fact, it's

downright insulting, but costs are cheap in Covenan
Falls, and the job includes free vet care."

"What more can anyone ask?" he said, but sh
knew the morphine or whatever was in the IV wa
working. He was fighting to keep his eyes open.

She leaned over and kissed him. "Thank you,
she whispered. "Thank you for me and for Sand
and for Bart."

"I love you," he replied sleepily and closed hi
eyes.

STEPHANIE DROVE CLINT back to the cabin ten day
later. He rode in her van with Bart at his feet.

He recalled his first ride from Pueblo more than
month ago. A lifetime ago. Aeons ago. And he sti
liked looking at Stephanie. She wore a clean shir
today, and clean jeans. He missed the cow stains.

They had not talked of love again. Or the futur
He sensed she didn't want to push him and he didn
want to push her. They might go this way until ete
nity. Someone would have to take a stand.

When he arrived at the cabin, he was shocked t
see the entire street filled with cars. "What's goin
on?" he asked.

"Mrs. Davies down the street is having a birth
day."

He nodded. "I'll have to go over, maybe…"

"Make her an omelet," she finished. They wer
doing that a lot lately.

"You don't think she would think I was court-
g her?"

She laughed. "No, you're much too young for her."

She stopped the van and got out. He did the same,
though his legs were still bandaged and hurt like
ll. At least he hadn't had a headache since the fire.

The cabin looked welcoming. Cozy. It was home
w. He hadn't realized how much until this mo-
ent.

As they reached the porch and he started to un-
ck the door, he found it already unlocked. Bart
owled beside him. "It's okay," he said soothingly.
he first thing he saw as he opened the door was a
ge sign spread all the way across the room: Wel-
me Home, Clint.

Then the room came alive with people. So many
couldn't count them.

Josh stepped forward. "We're not going to stay
ng," he said. "We know the only thing you prob-
ly want to do now is go to bed. But everyone
anted to thank you. We didn't want to do it at the
spital. You saved lives the other day. The town
ill always be grateful, and everyone wanted to
ow their appreciation. A lot of people sent a small
ft, not expensive, but something meaningful to
em." He gestured to a table laden with packages.
nd I imagine you will be drowning in bakery
odies for the next year or so if you choose to stay.
e hope so."

Then they left, each one shaking his hand. Thank ing him. Hoping he would stay.

When the last visitor left, he turned to Stephani "You knew about this," he accused.

"I did," she admitted, kissing his lips. "I hop that's better than Bart's," she added after a long m ment.

"Poor Bart. He sinks to second in the kissir competition, unless maybe we should try a secor round."

"I should probably go, too, and let you rest."

"Come sit with me," he said. Tears pricked th backs of his eyes. He hadn't cried since he was eig years old and knew, beyond any doubt, that no or wanted him.

Now an entire town did. *Wow.*

Someday he would tell Stephanie the story be hind the gift he'd just been handed. Not now. H was much too contented with her hand in his, h head leaning against his heart. He knew he love her. He also knew now that she loved him. It was i her eyes, and her smile and her laughter.

The rest would come.

THE MORNING AFTER the party, he and Stephani walked up the mountain trail at the edge of the cabi and looked over the town. His town. Holding he tightly, he knew he had found something more im portant than choppers and fast cars: a fascinatin woman, a community that welcomed him with ope

ms and now a job. Today, he would accept Eve's
fer as police chief in training.

Stephanie looked at him and her smile lit his
eart. It would always light his heart.

Bart barked. Sherry looked concerned. Stryker
nored them.

Clint and Stephanie stooped down to soothe Bart.
heir heads bumped.

They looked at each other, and their laughter
emed to echo down into the valley.

* * * * *

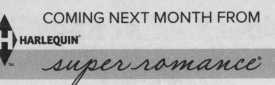
#1976 THE COMEBACK OF ROY WALKER
The Bakers of Baseball
by Stephanie Doyle

When Roy Walker left his professional pitching career, he was on top...and had the ego to prove it. Now, with a much smaller ego, he needs to make a comeback—something he can't do without the help of physiotherapist Lane Baker. But first, he must make amends for their past!

#1977 FALLING FOR THE NEW GUY
by Nicole Helm

Strong and silent Marc Santino is new to the Bluff City Police Department. His field training officer, Tess Camden, is much too chatty—and sexy—for comfort. When they give in to the building attraction, the arrangement is just what they need. But, for the sake of their careers, can they let it turn into something more?

#1978 A RECIPE FOR REUNION
by Vicki Essex

Stephanie Stephens is tired of people not believing in her. So when Aaron Caruthers comes back to town telling her how to run his grandmother's bakery, she's determined to prove herself. Unfortunately, he's a lot cuter than she remembers him being...and she definitely doesn't need her heart distracting her now!

#1979 MOTHER BY FATE
Where Secrets are Safe
by Tara Taylor Quinn

When a client disappears from her shelter, Sara Havens teams up with Michael Eddison to find the missing woman. The strong attraction between them complicates things. Michael's strength is appealing, but his young daughter makes Sara vulnerable in a way she swore she'd never be again.

LARGER-PRINT BOOKS!

HARLEQUIN *Presents*

PASSION
GUARANTEED
SEDUCTION

GET 2 FREE LARGER-PRINT NOVELS PLUS 2 FREE GIFTS!

YES! Please send me 2 FREE LARGER-PRINT Harlequin Presents® novels and my 2 FREE gifts (gifts are worth about $10). After receiving them, if I don't wish to receive any more books, I can return the shipping statement marked "cancel." If I don't cancel, I will receive 6 brand-new novels every month and be billed just $5.05 per book in the U.S. or $5.49 per book in Canada. That's a saving of at least 16% off the cover price! It's quite a bargain! Shipping and handling is just 50¢ per book in the U.S. and 75¢ per book in Canada.* I understand that accepting the 2 free books and gifts places me under no obligation to buy anything. I can always return a shipment and cancel at any time. Even if I never buy another book, the two free books and gifts are mine to keep forever.

176/376 HDN F43N

Name	(PLEASE PRINT)

Address		Apt. #

City	State/Prov.	Zip/Postal Code

Signature (if under 18, a parent or guardian must sign)

Mail to the **Harlequin® Reader Service:**
IN U.S.A.: P.O. Box 1867, Buffalo, NY 14240-1867
IN CANADA: P.O. Box 609, Fort Erie, Ontario L2A 5X3

Are you a subscriber to Harlequin Presents books and want to receive the larger-print edition?
Call 1-800-873-8635 today or visit us at www.ReaderService.com.

* Terms and prices subject to change without notice. Prices do not include applicable taxes. Sales tax applicable in N.Y. Canadian residents will be charged applicable taxes. Offer not valid in Quebec. This offer is limited to one order per household. Not valid for current subscribers to Harlequin Presents Larger-Print books. All orders subject to credit approval. Credit or debit balances in a customer's account(s) may be offset by any other outstanding balance owed by or to the customer. Please allow 4 to 6 weeks for delivery. Offer available while quantities last.

Your Privacy—The Harlequin® Reader Service is committed to protecting your privacy. Our Privacy Policy is available online at www.ReaderService.com or upon request from the Harlequin Reader Service.

We make a portion of our mailing list available to reputable third parties that offer products we believe may interest you. If you prefer that we not exchange your name with third parties, or if you wish to clarify or modify your communication preferences, please visit us at www.ReaderService.com/consumerschoice or write to us at Harlequin Reader Service Preference Service, P.O. Box 9062, Buffalo, NY 14269. Include your complete name and address.

HPLP13R

ReaderService.com

Manage your account online!

- Review your order history
- Manage your payments
- Update your address

*We've designed
the Harlequin® Reader Service
website just for you.*

Enjoy all the features!

- Reader excerpts from any series
- Respond to mailings and
  special monthly offers
- Discover new series available to you
- Browse the Bonus Bucks catalog
- Share your feedback

Visit us at:
ReaderService.com